MW00950674

We're All Savages

By

Emmanuel Jean-Pierre

Special thanks

Yasmine for giving me great ideas for the real estate scenario
Lou and Naomie for being beta readers
Erik and Christina for that inspiring conversation
Heather and Cece for reading the first 5 pages on short notice
My wife Yolanda for helping me be patient and keeping me from publishing it before it was ready

To all my TikTok followers who requested this. You're the reason I was able to start, finish, and self-publish this in less than a year. If this book blows up, it's all because of you.

"We are all civilized people, which means that we are all savages at heart but observing a few amenities of behavior."

–Tennessee Williams

Chapter one:
"Welcome to the Black Parade"

"FOR PROM!!!"

The whole class exploded into chaos. Kids were throwing books across the room, smashing windows with their chairs, and flipping tables over. Some of them started fighting each other and some even attacked the teacher at the front of the room. I rushed out the door, dodging swinging elbows as I did, and discovered the entire school had descended into pandemonium. Students were brawling in the hall, spray painting profanities on the doors, some were urinating on the lockers, and one kid was setting his textbooks on fire. I sprinted around the corner, planning on making a run for the exit when something metal hit me across the face. When I looked down and saw what it was, my jaw dropped in panic.

You're probably wondering what in the world is going on here. For starters, I'm Nicholas Toussaint—seventeen-years old, son of Haitian immigrants, and the only black kid at Hamilton High, one of the most prestigious private schools in New Jersey. But if you wanna know how we went from pristine picturesque to absolute anarchy, let me take you back to the beginning...

***

The year was 2006. George W. Bush was president, Hannah Montanah had just come out, and Britney Spears was going through Hell. Popular shows included *Lost, Smallville*, and anything on Toonami. There were no iphones or androids, no apps or even instagram. Facebook had just gone public for anyone at least 13 years old with a valid email address, but was only available on your computer. I know—sounds like the Stone Age.

My story starts off on a crisp October afternoon right after school. My best friend Lance and I were behind the weight room building. I was staring up at the side of the building, a 15-foot brick wall with some padding on the roof, like it was begging me to do this.

"You got this," Lance egged me on as I wiped dust off the bottom of my sneakers.

Every day for the past week we'd come out here after final period and I'd try to run up and climb to the roof. Parkour wasn't a global phenomenon yet and wouldn't be until 2007. But I had been doing stuff like this since third grade because I grew up watching *Aladdin* and Jackie Chan movies. I'd already pulled off a whole bunch of other stunts around school. This was just my latest one.

I did a few practice runs to get myself warmed up and made it up three steps each time. The grip of my sneakers against the brick was perfect. I had a good feeling about this. Today was the day.

"You excited about the homecoming game?" Lance asked me out of the blue.

I shrugged.

"C'mon, it's your first one," he went on. "And your last one. This is the first and last time you get to see Hamilton High take on Jefferson High at homecoming."

I shrugged again then did another run up the wall. I had never been to a homecoming football game. I'd been to a few regular season games here and there, but even those were only because my sister Fabi hadn't been able to pick me up until after her afternoon class. I didn't have that much school spirit. Maybe it was because I didn't fit in. Or maybe it was because I got bullied. Or maybe it was just that the high and mighty, snotty rich kid atmosphere was too suffocating to sit through. Plus, we weren't even that good at sports. Football was the only thing we were fairly decent at. The only reason I was even going this year was because Lance had convinced me.

"You should try out for a team this year," Lance suggested.

"No way," I grimaced.

"C'mon," he insisted. "With all this natural athleticism, you'd definitely make the track team at least."

"Maybe," I said. I made one more practice run and took a deep breath when I landed. I could feel it. Today was the day. I was gonna make it.

"Well lookee here," a voice said and I groaned without even turning around. From the overwhelming onslaught of Axe body spray, I would've known who this was even if he hadn't spoken.

"Just keep moving, William," I said.

But Billy Richardson didn't keep moving. I turned and saw that he was with his two teammates, Gary and Dean. They were still in school uniform with their varsity jackets on, but they were all carrying their duffle bags over their shoulders with all their football gear in it. My guess was they were on their way to the locker room to change for the game, but they decided to make a pit stop when they saw me. The locker room was on the other side of campus. They'd gone out of their way to come here.

"Did you lose something up there, Tootsie?" Billy asked me. "Or do you just like vandalizing school property? Should we call Principal Hanes?"

"We're just minding our business, William," I said to him. "You should try it sometime."

Billy chuckled then glanced at his boys. His eyes flashed with mischief and he crossed his arms over his chest. With his blonde hair, blue eyes, and chiseled physique, he looked like Brad Pitt from *Troy*, but acted like Chris Evans in *Not Another Teen Movie*.

"Don't tell me you think you can run up to the roof," he snickered.

Lance and I glanced at each other.

Billy burst out laughing. "This kid thinks he's Spider Man. This I gotta see."

I sighed as Billy dropped his duffle bag at his feet. Now he wasn't gonna leave until I tried it. I looked at Lance again and he shrugged. See, my issue wasn't that I didn't think I could make it in front of Billy. Like I said, I had a good feeling that today was the day. But I couldn't be sure Bully wouldn't pull something like pants me when I came back down. So I took a deep breath then got into position.

"Let's see what you got, Peter Parker," Billy chuckled.

"Isn't Spider-Man white?" asked Gary.

"Shut up," Billy scolded him without looking. He was actually focused on me. He really wanted to see me do this. But still, I would be stupid to let my guard down.

I sprinted at the wall, ran up three steps, kicked off…

And I grabbed the roof.

My heart leapt as I heard Lance and the others go crazy beneath me. I pulled myself over the roof then turned and sat on the edge.

Billy, Gary, and Dean were actually cheering and Billy was even clapping.

"That's what I'm talking about!" Lance screamed, pumping his fist in the air.

My heart was racing as I grinned down at them. I'd done it. I'd climbed the roof. I felt like a boss. I dropped down and landed with a smooth roll at the bottom.

"I gotta admit, Tootise," Billy said, picking up his duffle bag. "I'm impressed."

"Thanks," I said, confused by the sudden lack of douchebaggery.

"You think you could do it in two steps?" he asked.

"No way!" Gary laughed. "Not even Spider-Man could do that!"

"I bet he could," Lance said, smacking me on the back.

"Two steps?" Gary went on. "No way. He barely made it in three."

And something stirred inside me. Now I had to do it. "Watch me."

So I walked back to get a good running start and took a deep breath. Then I blasted forward fully focused on the wall. And because I was so focused on timing my steps, I didn't notice Billy lower his duffle bag to his side. And I definitely didn't see it coming when he swing it into my face. My head exploded in pain like I was getting hit with a baseball bat, I went airborne, and I landed on my shoulder blades, legs flailing above me.

Billy and his boys hollered like hyenas and high fived each other.

"What a loser," he snickered.

"You guys are jerks!" Lance shouted.

But I didn't see if he did anything to them. My head was spinning and throbbing. Billy's helmet must have been in that bag. His cleats too. Because this hurt like nobody's business. But I couldn't say I was surprised. I should've seen that coming.

I didn't know how long I laid there, but eventually I sat up and rubbed my forehead. I could already feel a quarter-sized lump there and winced as I touched it.

"You gonna be okay?" Lance asked above me.

I looked around. Billy and the others were gone and it was just the two of us again.

"Yeah," I groaned.

"I hate those guys," Lance spat.

I shrugged. "At least I did it."

He smiled at that.

"Yeah, well if—" Before he could finish his cell phone rang and he picked it up. He frowned quickly and said, "Are you serious?! But...I completely forgot..."

I watched carefully, trying to focus on who Lance could be talking to as a way of distracting me from the throbbing pain in my head.

"Okay. I understand." Lance sighed heavily then hung up his phone.

"What happened?" I asked him.

"I forgot I promised my Dad I'd go see some houses he's gonna flip," Lance explained. "He wants to start showing me the ropes."

I squinted at him in frustration. "Are you kidding me?" Mr. Fairmount was a jerk. He was obsessed with money and getting more of it no matter what. So much so that he had missed Lance being born because he apparently had to wine and dine some client. He actually left Lance's mother at home when her water broke and made her get a taxi so he wouldn't miss the reservation. He hadn't even been to the last seven of Lance's birthday parties because of work. My parents missed some of my basketball games in middle school because of work, but they weren't CEO's with 500 employees who could cover for them. Maybe I didn't know how rich companies worked, but I knew how fatherhood worked and Mr. Fairmount was trash at it.

Lance waved me off like he didn't feel like explaining. "I didn't realize it was on homecoming. He's had this planned for weeks."

"So why don't you tell him you can't go?" I asked.

He shook his head. "I gave him my word, man."

I nodded. Lance was a by-the-books kid. Principles were everything to him. If he promised he would or wouldn't do something, he'd do whatever it took to keep that promise—even not going to homecoming with his best friend. But more importantly, despite how trash Mr. Fairmount was, Lance was loyal to him like a dog.

"He's already here to pick me up," he told me.

I groaned as he helped me to my feet.

"I'm sorry, Nick," he said.

This sucked. Lance was leaving, my head was pounding, my parents were at work, and my sister Fabi had taken an afternoon shift at her job because she'd already planned on picking me up after the game.

So it turned out I was going to homecoming by myself.

***

I hated every second of the game. By the fourth quarter we were down by seven and these stupid Moms behind me would not stop yapping about their pretty, prim, proper, porcelain doll, prissy daughters. Normally, I'd be able to just block out this kind of nonsense, but my head was still throbbing from Billy's duffle bag attack.

I rubbed my fingers into my temple and watched him screaming at his teammates during the huddle on the sideline. I wished he'd get sacked in the next play. I hated that he was our quarterback. It'd be so much easier to have school spirit if the face of our athletics wasn't such a certified douchebag. Can you imagine the inner turmoil I'm feeling right now? You can't. And neither could you imagine how irritating these mothers' voices sounded. And this was all because Lance had to be Mr. super-loyal son and leave me at this stupid game by myself.

"Shelly just got accepted into Harvard," one Mom was saying.

"Oh my God!" another squealed. "Good for her. Angie got into Yale."

"Stop it!"

I rolled my eyes. Why were they here? Their daughters weren't even cheerleaders. Shelly was the captain of the soccer team and Angie wasn't even an athlete.

"How's Sarah?" one mother asked.

There was a short pause and I guessed Sarah wasn't doing so well. There were dozens of Sarah's in school, but only about 6 were seniors. Half of those 6 were either in dance clubs or art clubs, 2 were getting full-rides on volleyball scholarships, and one had recently started to get in and out of detention. My guess was this Sarah was the latter one.

"She's doing well," the mother replied. "But uh...I'm a little worried about her boyfriend."

"Oh..." said Shelly's mom. Then she whispered, "It's Billy, right?"

"Yeah," Sarah's mom whispered back. "He seems like a good kid, but I just have this bad feeling about him. She's been acting differently ever since she started dating him. I don't think he's a good influence on her. But every time I talk to her about it, she doesn't wanna hear it. And I don't have any reason to not like him. It's just...it's just a feeling, you know? I wish there was a way for me to know for sure what he was like."

I couldn't help but grin as I listened. I probably wasn't gonna get my wish of watching Billy get the pants sacked off him. But at least I could get *some* satisfaction. Turns out these Moms weren't completely useless...

"Excuse me," I said, turning around to face them. "I couldn't help but overhear and I think I can help you with your problem."

The mothers looked down at me and blinked quickly, apparently surprised that someone could actually hear them.

"What do you mean?" asked Sarah's Mom.

I glanced left and right at the people nearest us then gestured for the mothers to lean in closer.

"I can tell you the dirt on Billy," I whispered.

Sarah's Mom put her hand on her chest. "Wait...are you serious? What do you...what do you know?"

I swung my legs all the way over the bleacher so I was facing her then cleared my throat. "He's a bonafide douchebag. If a girl on this campus has a vagina, chances are he's been in it or tried. I know for a fact that he's banging your daughter more than that drum on the marching band and when he gets tired of her, he'll just move on to a horny freshman."

The mothers' jaws dropped like they were about to puke all over me and I realized I probably should've censored that. But it wasn't every day I got a chance to give Billy Richardson what he had coming to him. Could you blame me for adding some salt to it?

"Well...thank you," Sarah's Mom said. Then she stared at the bleacher and I could tell a montage of memories was playing in her head. "That makes sense...I knew it! I knew it. I *knew* it!"

I turned in my seat to get back to the game, but she grabbed my shoulder and stopped me.

"What do I do?"

I looked at her hand then at her desperate face. "What do you mean, 'what do you do'?"

"I can't let this happen! If he's...if he's...doing what you said he's doing, then...they have to break up!"

I shrugged. "I guess...?"

"Don't listen to him," Shelly's Mom said, eyeing me. "Aren't you that Haitian kid?"

I braced myself for whatever flavor of ignorance was coming next. Voodoo priest. HBO--Haitian Body Odor. "How can you afford to be here?" But I wasn't ready for--

"Don't you have AIDS?"

I blinked. What did she just ask me? She scoffed as she tucked her hands under her armpits like she was trying to keep me from infecting them.

"You have to do something," Angie's Mom went on like nothing had even been said. "Your daughter's dignity is at stake. Should we call the principal?"

AIDS. I couldn't stop thinking about it. That was a new one.

"No," Sarah's Mom shook her head. "That'll make it worse. I learned that from experience when Sarah dated that Black kid in eighth grade."

On that note, I decided it was time to check out. I turned again, but she grabbed my shoulder again.

"I need your help," she said. "Make them break up."

"That's an easy one," I replied. "No."

"Please!" she said, grabbing both my shoulders now.

"Look, maam. Billy Richardson hates my guts. I'm not about to ruin his relationship. He'll *kill* me."

"But she can't be with him!" she pleaded. "He'll ruin her future! She has so much ahead of her. What if she gets an STD? What if she gets pregnant? Or worse...what if people find out?"

I gave up on trying to follow her logic and shook her hands off me. "Look, I told you what I know. I did my job. Now I've gotta go."

I turned and stood, ready to climb down far away from these Moms like I should've done a long time ago. But then she said three words that changed everything.

"I'll pay you."

I stopped in my tracks with my back to her. This woman was willing to pay me to make her daughter break up with her boyfriend? The boyfriend that had been a pain in my left buttcheek since freshman year? I could get revenge on the biggest jerk in school and get paid while doing it?

I slowly turned and faced the Moms again.

"Go on..."

Chapter two:
"Love Don't Cost a thing"

"I'll pay you $1,000," Sarah's mother said.

My jaw dropped. She was joking. She had to be joking. So I just laughed and waved it off.

"Even if you were serious," I said. "Billy would probably lynch me."

"Don't be ridiculous. He probably doesn't even know how to make a noose."

I felt that knot in my stomach I got whenever someone said something gut-wrenchingly awkward. It was an all-too familiar feeling at Hamilton High. "I don't know…"

"$1,500," she went on.

I squinted at her. Was she really serious?

"$2,000."

"Wait," I held my hand up to stop her. I almost expected her to pull out one of those auction paddles and keep bidding. Her eyes were wide and she hadn't blinked since she'd said $1,000. She *was* serious. "So lemme get this straight. You're willing to pay me $2,000 to make your daughter break up with her boyfriend?"

She nodded, still not blinking. Her friends looked back and forth from her to me and I could tell they were just as confused as I was.

"Don't be stupid, Nora," I heard Shelly's Mom whisper. "He'll probably just take it and run. You know how they are."

"Stop it, Karla!" the other one whispered back, slapping her shoulder.

Sarah's Mom was still staring at me without a blink.

"You really wanna do this?" I asked her.

"Absolutely," she nodded. "I will not stand to the side and watch some snot-nosed douchebag ruin my daughter's future. And my husband's a hedge fund manager so you know I'm good for it."

I couldn't argue with her there. Almost every kid at Hamilton had rich parents. But Sarah Gibson was one of the top tier kids. Always got dropped off and picked up in a Bentley, always wore her Louis Vuitton shoes, Gucci bags, and spent every winter break, spring break, and summer in a different European country. We all knew she was wealthy. So I knew her mother had the money. I was just still stunned that she'd actually use it to fund a break up.

I scratched the back of my neck as I thought about the offer. I could already hear all the bones that Billy would snap in my body. All the port-a-potties he'd lock me in and roll down the golf course. I shivered just imagining him recruiting the entire football team to hunt me down and hang me from the goal post. Everything in me was screaming to run the opposite direction. This was not a good idea.

"Don't waste your money on him," Mrs. Karla chimed in, not even bothering to whisper this time. "He should be minding his own business anyway."

$2,000.

I could buy like a hundred games with that. Probably a couple PS2's while I was at it. And Jordans. I could even pay for a class at NYU with that money. My parents would love that.

"Please," Mrs. Gibson said, snapping me out of my daydream. "Will you help me?"

I looked up at her and she was begging me with her eyes. I took a deep breath, looking from her pleading face to Mrs. Karla's disapproving one.

"I'll think about it," I finally said. But I wouldn't. I turned to leave again and Mrs. Gibson grabbed my arm for the third time.

"Take my number in case you change your mind."

I sighed as she started rummaging through her purse for a paper and pen. "Where is it...? Why can't I ever...? Okay...here we go..." She scribbled furiously then handed me a Starbucks napkin with her number on it.

I took it and turned it over to find a $100 bill on the other side.

"Think of it as a down payment," she winked at me.

This woman wasn't playing around. I slipped the bill and the napkin into my pocket as politely as I could then turned around and finally left. But like I said, this wasn't the end. Far from it.

Chapter three:
"Changes"

When Fabi picked me up from school, I didn't even tell her what happened. I was still processing it myself.

"What happened to your face?" she asked, poking the welt on the side of my head.

"Billy," I said, swatting her away.

"Again?" she sucked her teeth. "You need to fight that kid back. You can't just keep letting him do this stuff to you."

"I'm not *letting* him do anything, Fabi. Can we just go?"

"You want me to fight him for you? Cuz I will."

"Can we go please?" I insisted.

She drove off and instead of lecturing me, she blasted one of her Tupac CD's and we rapped along all the way to my parents' bakery to grab a quick bite before going home.

My parents had immigrated to America from Haiti with nothing. But through hard work, prayer, and a little luck, they had started Bethanie Bakery all on their own and had been running it for over twenty years. It wasn't a Fortune 500 company or anything, but it paid the bills and was the reason my parents could afford—barely afford—to send me to Hamilton.

Fabi parked halfway down the block and we ducked under some scaffolding on our way to the bakery. Part of the sidewalk was blocked off and I noticed one of the liquor stores was boarded up.

"Where'd all this construction come from?" I asked.

Fabi shrugged. "I dunno. I just hope they're building something good."

"Like an arcade," I added.

"Ooooh that'd be cool!" she agreed.

As far as I knew there weren't any arcades in our town. Orange wasn't that kind of area. We had parks and basketball courts, sneaker stores and liquor stores. But nothing fancy like arcades or malls. I used to not know that Orange was "hood" because I'd always compared us to places like Camden, Trenton or Newark. I didn't realize I was living in the hood until I started telling Lance "funny" stories like that time a kid brought a gun to the court. Or that time a kid chased me and my friends with a stun gun because our team beat his. Or that time a guy got stabbed because he beat another guy in one-on-one in front of the guy's girlfriend. I thought that kind of stuff happened everywhere. Apparently not.

We walked into the bakery and let me tell you, there's nothing like the smell of freshly baked Haitian bread. On top of that, the air was filled with the sweet scent of my parents' homemade cakes: carrot cake, upside-down pineapple cake, and cheesecake just to name a few. I took a deep breath as I stood in the doorway and inhaled it all. It smelled like home.

My parents had named the bakery Bethanie because in the Bible Bethany was one of Jesus' favorite towns to hang out in. Their dream was to have a bakery where everyone in town would not only enjoy quality food, but also quality time. And the whole time it had been open, it had done just that.

Kompa was playing from the speakers and two old men were playing dominoes in one corner and a grandmother was feeding some carrot cake to her granddaughter in another corner. On my left a family of four was dipping Haitian bread in their hot chocolate while swaying to the music and on my right a single mother was on the phone next to her little boy playing his PSP in between bites of a cookie. It was almost always busy and almost always filled with people chilling and snacking.

"*Sak pasé!*" my father said from behind the counter.

"*Nap brulé!*" Fabi replied as we walked up.

The door chimed as a round white man with a snowy beard walked in.

"Hey, Mr. Franklin," I greeted him and he gave me a hearty handshake. Mr. Franklin was the landlord. The bakery was on the first floor of this building, the second floor was a dance studio, and the third floor was where Mr. Franklin lived. He was probably the nicest old man I'd ever met and Fabi and I used to call him Santa growing up because he looked like him and because he always brought us presents on Christmas and our birthdays.

"How was the game?" he asked me.

"We lost," I shrugged.

"Ahhhh," my father sucked his teeth.

"You should play for them," Mr. Franklin encouraged me. "I've seen you run and do all that…that…Spider-Man stuff. Put that to good use on the field."

"Or at least play soccer," my Dad said. "Represent your people, man."

"I dunno," I shrugged. I honestly didn't care. Like you saw, my school spirit was in the negatives. What I did care about was getting myself a beef pattie. Jamaicans weren't the only ones who made awesome patties. There was nothing like those flaky layers packed over a mound of ground beef. Yeah, sometimes you ended up with 80% crust and 20% meat, but that was part of the experience.

The door chimed again and a woman dressed in all black with a wide brimmed church hat walked in. At the same time, my mother appeared from the back of the bakery carrying two white boxes of patties.

"Oh, sister Patrick!" the woman said, clutching her chest. "God bless you! Thank you so much!"

"Don't worry about it," my mother replied. "*C'est mon devoir.*"

The woman took the boxes and Mr. Franklin hurried over to hold the door for her.

My father crossed his arms as he cleared his throat at my mother. "Did she pay for that?"

"No, Patrick," my mother waved him off. "Sister Mardi has a funeral. It was a gift."

Fabi and I groaned at the same time that my father smacked his palm to his face.

"This is a business, Marie," he scolded her.

"It's a ministry," my mother replied back. "God blesses us so we can bless others."

"Blessings don't pay bills."

"Fine," my mother shrugged. "I'll pay for them. Relax."

Fabi and I rolled our eyes. My parents had very different ideas of how to run a business and it was always entertaining to see them go at it.

The door chimed again as Mr. Franklin returned, sifting through his wallet. "That homeless man is back, Patrick."

"Oh, Thomas?" my father said, eyebrows shooting up.

"Yeah," Mr. Franklin pulled out a bill. "Let me get a pattie for him."

My father already had a bag ready with three patties and a soda and handed them to Mr. Franklin. "It's on the house."

Mr. Franklin took the food and walked out and we all snickered at my father.

"I thought this was a business," Fabi said.

"And I thought you were leaving," my father sucked his teeth at her. Then he tossed a few patties in a brown paper bag and handed us two bottles of Kola Lakaye and shooed us out of the bakery.

"See you at home!" Fabi called as we left.

And with that, we walked back to the car eating our patties. It didn't matter that we were gonna see our parents in like half an hour back home. There was something about Bethanie that always reeled us in even if we didn't have to come. I guess my parents' dream for Bethanie was working on us too.

***

"*Mangé paré!*" my mother screamed from downstairs. Dinner was ready.

Within minutes, we were all sitting at the table enjoying yet another immaculately home-cooked Haitian feast. There was a bowl of white rice in the center next to a smaller bowl of *sauce pwa*--black bean sauce. Then there was a pot of stewed chicken swimming in a mouth-watering sauce and of course *banan peze* and *pikliz*--fried plantains and...um...I don't know how to translate *pikliz*. It's just a bunch of spices, pickled cabbage, and scotch bonnet peppers in white vinegar. I've heard it described as "Haitian kimchi". Either way, it's amazing and makes everything mind-blowingly hot and delicious.

"How was school today?" my mother asked as I wolfed down some rice.

"*Pran san-ou*, Nicholas," my father scolded me to slow down.

My parents usually spoke Kreyol at home with my sister and I usually responding in Kringlish. But to keep things simple I'll just translate everything as best I can here.

"Sorry," I replied as I swallowed. "Umm...school's still school...how was work?"

My parents exchanged a look and my Dad cleared his throat. "Fine. Work is fine."

I stopped chewing and squinted at him. What was that hesitation for? But before I could ask about it, my mother swung the subject back to me.

"Have you made any new friends this year?" she asked.

"Not really," I shrugged. "It's still just Lance."

"Has his father said anything yet?"

"Nope," I said bluntly.

"Wow," my Dad chuckled. "Some people go to class, but they don't have class."

My Mom and Fabi both nodded and "Mmmm"'d in agreement. Lance had gotten really sick one night this past summer. His Mom was away on a girls trip with her friends and it was one of the rare times his Dad was home with him. But Mr. Fairmount didn't know what to do so Lance called my Mom for help. She made him soup and drove out to drop it off. But when she got there, Lance was home alone because Mr. Fairmount had gone back to the office to deal with some work thing. So my Mom stayed and nursed Lance back to health. Lance called us the next day to thank us, but we never heard a word from Mr. Fairmount. Not a call, text, or email. Not even a "Lance, tell

Nick to thank his Mom for me, will ya?" Nothing. I didn't expect him to pay us or send a thank you card or anything. But to not even mention that someone had basically saved your son's life when you were too incompetent and too busy to do anything? The guy was a jerk. I was glad Lance wasn't anything like him.

"But Lance is still fine," I added. "But the school still sucks. I don't like it."

"Still? Why? *Cheri*, it's been three years."

"It's all the *moun blanc*," Fabi answered for me. "He's the only *zo* in the whole school."

Moun blanc were white people and *zo* was what Haitians called each other.

"Exactly," I agreed. "There's no other black kids--let alone Haitian ones. And everybody's mad racist too."

"*Everybody?*" my Dad looked at me doubtfully.

I rolled my eyes. "Well, not *everybody*. But you know what I mean. The majority of them are *mad* disrespectful. Like today, somebody's Mom asked me if I have AIDS. Like, what?"

My mother sucked her teeth in that way only Caribbean mothers could.

"That's real *frekan*," Fabi shook her head. "She said that to your face?"

"Yeah. What's that even about? That's so random."

"You were probably too young to remember, but in the 90's, people used to think Haitians brought AIDS to the U.S.," my Dad explained. "We weren't even allowed to donate blood because of it."

"What?" I shook my head. "See, that's what I'm talking about. That's the crap I have to deal with every day. Can I just transfer for my last year? I could go to Zenith. They're more diverse so I won't be the only black person there. I heard they even have Haitian kids."

"No," my father said. "We're not paying all that money just to send you to a number ten school. You're staying at number one so you can be number one."

"They're not ten anymore," I clarified. "They went up to number three. They're right behind Hamilton and Jefferson."

My Dad shook his head without even looking at me. "It is what it is, son. Just make the best of it and keep moving."

"*Non*, Patrick," my mother cut in. "They can't be saying stuff like that to my son. Uh-uh. Somebody's *mother* said that? *Non*. Mmmm-mmmm. We gotta call the school."

"For what?" my Dad pushed back. "So they can do nothing again? And you think there's not gonna be racist people at Zenith? Are you gonna call the principal every time somebody says something racist to him for the rest of his life?"

I lowered my head and slapped some *pikliz* on my plantains as they went back and forth. This was usually how conversations about racism at school went. My mother always wanted to call the principal and throw hands and my father always wanted to save face. But at the end of the day they usually settled on not dwelling on it too much. It was annoying. Sometimes I wished they were less like MLK and more like Jean-Jacques Dessalines, who would've rolled up with machetes swinging. But at the same time I couldn't argue with them. Like I said, they had come to the U.S. with literally nothing and had built their own business from the ground up. They weren't the Gibsons, but they were doing really well for themselves. And they'd done it all while going through more racism than I'd lived through. So in a sense, they were right--there was no point in sitting around and complaining about it.

"Let me tell you something," my Dad said to me, snatching me out of my thoughts. "You're Haitian. You're not allowed to give up. The slaves didn't give up when France, Britain, and Spain attacked them. We didn't give up when we came to the U.S. with no money. So you can't give up just because some kids call you names."

I sighed.

"Yeah, Nick," Fabi said. "Don't be a loser." She winked at me then swiped one of my plantains from off my plate.

"Hey!"

But she'd already popped it into her mouth.

"Listen, *cheri*," my mother said, reaching across the table to touch my hand. "I know it can be hard sometimes. But remember what we taught you. Haitians live by 3 L's. *Legliz. Lekol. Lakaye.* As long as you stay focused on your church, your school, and your home, you're gonna be successful, okay?"

I sighed again. I guess that sort of mentality had worked for them. But would it work for me at Hamilton? Or would I just end up dropping out?

Chapter four:
"A Friend Like Me"

The next day at school, I walked through the cafeteria on my way to my usual spot in the corner. And as usual, my path gave me the scenic route of every group at Hamilton High School. Like most teen movies in the 2000's, Hamilton had very clear cliques. Except our cliques were a little more…unique. We did have the standard ones like the jocks where Billy Richardson and his teammates were taking turns tossing cheese puffs into each other's mouths. And the cheer squad table where all the violently attractive girls were twirling their hair and gossiping about the less aggressively attractive girls. But then we had cliques like the Travel Agents, the kids who were always going to different countries every chance they got where Emily Reynolds was showing off pictures of Bali on her camera phone. And the Cartesians, kids whose parents were all grad school professors so all they talked about was philosophy and socioeconomics. There was the Chess Club table–pretty self-explanatory–where kids were always playing each other. And there were the Outcasts–they actually called themselves that—where the theater kids, poets, and A/V club members were apparently reenacting a scene from *The Princess Bride*. And last but not least there were the Muggles– the rest of us who didn't really fit in anywhere so we just kind of precipitated to random spots on the fringes of the room. Like me and Lance.

I dropped down across from him and he gave me an up nod as he took a bite of his meatball hero.

"About time, bro," he said with a mouthful.

"The line at the microwave was long," I explained, setting down my plate of rice and beans and plantains.

He clapped his hands as he jumped right into the topic of the day. "So…NBA finals. Who do you have this year? I say the Spurs are going all the way."

I sucked my teeth. "No way, man. The Cavs. LeBron's gonna smack Tony Parker."

"You're out of your mind, bro! The Cavs have never won a championship. Ever."

"Cuz they never had LeBron," I countered.

"They've had him for three years and he still hasn't gotten them a ring."

"And he keeps getting better and better. I'm telling you, this is gonna be our year."

"If the Cavs and the Spurs make it to the finals, Tony Parker and Manu Ginobli are wiping the floor with the Cavs. I'm calling it."

I was about to spit back some stats at him, but a boy with sandy brown hair walked up and placed a CD on the table. I looked up to see Kyle Johnson grinning down at me.

"You asked," he said. "I delivered."

Kyle was a nice kid, never bothered anybody, had a few friends, but wasn't crazy popular. He was a sophomore and for the most part was an all-around nice guy—one of the very few kids besides Lance at Hamilton that didn't radiate complete douchebaggery. He was part of the A/V club and a whiz with anything music related which was why he had just dropped off this CD he'd burned for me. Yeah, before Spotify, YouTube, or Soundcloud, we had to burn music onto CD's using very questionable pirating sites like Limewire. Everyone had horror stories of trying to download a pop song and getting a video of three girls having sex with a goat instead. Dark times. But people like Kyle could finesse their way around the murky music world and had turned it into a side hustle. So for $10, I could get my own custom playlist of 15 songs.

"You're the best, man," I said, sliding him the money.

"You know you should really get an iPod," he said. "All those songs are just a dollar on iTunes."

"Yeah," I said, carefully putting the CD into my backpack. I knew all about the iPod. But I also knew that the PS3 was coming out in November and my parents weren't gonna buy me both.

"What songs did you get this time?" Lance asked me as Kyle left.

Before I could answer, a girl with short red hair walked past and sat down at the table nearest us. She was wearing the same Hamliton girls uniform—a khaki skirt with a navy sweater over a white blouse—but I could always tell her apart no matter where I saw her. This was Laura Wood. President of the chess club, debate team member, and in my opinion, the prettiest, smartest, and all-around boss chick in all of Hamilton. Imagine all the spunk of Avril Lavigne and the smarts of Shuri wrapped into one person. That was Laura Wood.

The kids at the table leaned in to watch and that's when I realized there were three chess boards with three separate opponents sitting across from

Laura. She gave them all a casual salute then pressed play on her iPod and "A Friend Like Me" started playing from a speaker in the middle of the table. I'd seen her do this so many times and it never stopped being the most ridiculously attractive flex. I'd even seen her offer her opponents a little more baklava on beat too. She would play three kids at a time and only move her pieces whenever the chorus came on, dropping her pieces on beat to the words "friend like me." If you know the song, you know that line is only sung four times. Which means Laura planned to beat these three kids in four moves each.

"She's right there, man," Lance kicked me under the table as the game went on. "Just ask her out."

"Shut up," I kicked him back, half from wanting to watch and half from not wanting her to hear us. But the music was loud enough to hide us anyway.

Two minutes later, Laura dramatically made her final moves across all three boards in perfect sync with the song then laughed along with Genie on the speaker.

Four moves. That was it. First game of lunch and she'd beaten three people in four moves while timing them to a freaking Disney song. Why was that so insanely attractive to me?

"Just ask her," Lance whispered. "You've liked her since freshman year. This is your last chance. You know she can go to whatever school she wants, right? She could go to Harvard or Yale and you'd never see her again."

I looked away as three new kids sat down at the three boards.

"I already told you," I explained to Lance for the thousandth time. "Haitian kids don't date non-Haitian kids. My parents would probably disown me or something."

"Well, that's stupid."

"I didn't make the rules. I just follow them."

"Well, maybe you should break the rules sometimes."

I scoffed at him. "You're telling me to break the rules sometimes? You're the biggest rule follower in the whole school. You won't even sneak out of class without a hall pass."

"Because those rules make sense. I just think you should be allowed to date whoever you want."

I shrugged and took a bite of a plantain. "Speaking of ethics…hypothetical question for you."

"Hit me."

"Let's say someone said they would pay you $1,000 to do something you thought was wrong. Would you do it?"

"No."

"You're not even gonna think about it? $1500."

"Still no."

"$2,000."

"No! Final answer."

"Really?"

"I'd rather be poor with a clean conscience than rich with a ruined one."

I scoffed at him. "And you want me to break the rules. Wow, you're a rebel." I took a bite of rice and made a mental note that Lance was probably a snitch. I glanced over at Laura and noticed the games had already started. But she'd opted out of the song this time. I was about to scan the closest board to see how she was doing when suddenly three guys blocked my view and an overwhelming cloud of Axe body spray assaulted my nose. Billy chewed his gum with more force than a cow as he laughed down at me.

"What's up, Tootsie?" he sneered.

"It's Toussaint," I corrected him. "We've been through this before, William."

"I got a question for you," he went on. "Do you have HBO?"

His friends snickered next to him in anticipation. They literally did this every day. Why did they still think it was so hilarious?

"Haitian Body Odor?!" Billy shouted and he and his boys burst out laughing.

"You guys are jerks, you know that?" Lance said.

"Don't you have to be stupid somewhere else?" I said to Billy.

Billy scoffed at me. "Wow. You still watch Spongebob? What a loser." He sniffed the air and made a face like he was smelling a dirty diaper. "Ill, what are you eating? Is that from Haiti? Why does it smell like that?"

His friends chuckled and I wrapped my arm around my plate to shield it from him. He could tease me all he wanted—I was not trading my banging Haitian food for some napkin flavored cafeteria food. But in protecting my plate, I left my backpack exposed and Billy swiftly swiped it up from the floor. Like a pack of hyenas, he and his friends rummaged through it, flinging out my books, gym clothes, my new CD, and my Rite Guard body spray.

"What is this?" Billy laughed, pulling out my cell phone.

Yeah, back then a lot of us kept our phones in our backpacks because the only thing they could do was call and text. So there was no point in carrying some extra slab of metal around when you already had pens, pencils, and petty cash in your pockets.

He held up my silver motorola like a trophy for his boys to see.

"You still have a flip phone?" he jeered. "What a peasant."

I stood and reached for it, but he held it out of my reach. "Give it back, William."

"I heard these things are indestructible," Billy said. Then, without any warning or further threats, he threw the phone on the floor and stomped it into two pieces.

"Whoa!" he and his boys cried in amazement.

I made my hands into fists as I stared at my snapped phone. I wanted to punch him in the face.

"I guess that was false advertising," Billy snorted. "Too bad your parents are too poor to buy you another one."

I growled and took a step forward to shove him. But before I could, a voice suddenly interrupted.

"Hey, Billy! Why don't you pick on someone with your own IQ?" Laura glided in between us with her hands on her hips. "I hear there are jellyfish in the lab. They might be a match for you."

Billy snorted as he looked down at her. "You think something small and soft would be a match for me?"

"Is that what she said?" Laura replied, quick as a whip.

Dean and Gary chuckled briefly, but Billy shot them both a look before glaring at Laura again.

"Get outta here, Wood," he ordered her.

"Make me," she challenged him. She stood her ground, daring him and his friends to make a move. But a minute passed with nothing and they eventually huffed and walked away.

I didn't know if I should feel grateful or embarrassed that my crush had to step in and save me from my bully. I knelt down and her and Lance helped me collect my clothes, books, and my phone.

"That guy's a real dirtbag," Laura said to me.

"He is," I replied nervously. This was the first time she'd spoken to me and for a second I thought that maybe this was going somewhere. Maybe she had a powerful urge to help me out. But she handed me one of my books, smiled at me, then went back to her seat. And that was that.

"You should tell the principal," Lance told me as we sat back at our table. "Billy should pay for this. Literally."

I sighed. "Just drop it, man." Because this was the way things were. Billy was the apex predator in Hamilton's jungle and I was his prey always on the run. So since I couldn't leave there was nothing to do but take my parents' advice and suck it up and keep moving. Until something big came along that could flip the whole jungle upside down. Something like what my parents would tell me later that night.

Chapter five:
"The Reason"

"*Nous avons de mauvaises nouvelles,*" my mother told us at dinner.

She had bad news. And the fact that she was starting off in French meant that whatever this was it was really bad and my parents were trying to dress it up in French to soften the blow.

"What is it?" Fabi asked. "Are you sick?"

"No," my Mom shook her head.

"Did something happen in Haiti?" I asked.

"Not that we know of."

"Then what is it?" asked Fabi.

My mother sighed and rubbed her hands as she went on. "As you know, we've had the restaurant for as long as both of you have been alive. And after God it's been the reason we've been able to provide for you, send you to good schools, and buy you nice things. And even though it's been hard work, it's…"

"Mom, please," Fabi interrupted. "Get to the point. You're stressing us out."

My parents looked at each other briefly then my mother looked at us and said, "We might have to sell the bakery."

"What?!" Fabi and I shouted at the same time.

I must have heard her wrong. Selling the bakery? There was no way. What the heck was happening that would make them do something like that?

"Some big investor is buying all the businesses on our block so he can tear them down and build apartments," my mother explained.

"So just tell him no," Fabi shrugged.

"It's not that simple," said my father.

"You guys built that restaurant from the ground up," Fabi said, her voice rising. "Everyone in the neighborhood loves it."

"We know that," my mother nodded slowly, her voice a lot softer than Fabi's.

"What if we sue the investors?"

"Not an option," my father shook his head.

I stared at him in disbelief. This couldn't be happening. I had to be dreaming. But then the pieces started coming together in my head, like my vision blurring back to focus after getting punched in the face. "Wait…so all that construction that's been going on…that's why? That's the investors building new apartments?"

My parents nodded at the same time.

Fabi sucked her teeth. "These stupid *moun blanc* think they can just come in and take whatever they want. *Bun salop.*"

"Watch your mouth," my father said firmly.

"It's not fair!"

"There has to be something we can do," I said.

My parents looked at each other then my father sighed and leaned closer over the table.

"Mr. Franklin wants to sell so that he can finally retire," he said. "But because he knows that we wanted to buy the building some day, he said he's willing to make a deal with us."

Fabi and I tensed at the same time.

"What's the deal?" Fabi asked.

"If we can come up with enough money for the down payment in time," my father started. "He'll sell the building to us instead."

"How much?" Fabi asked.

"Ninety thousand."

Ninety thousand. I couldn't even wrap my mind around how much money that was. I'd never had a job or had to pay any bills. But from the worried looks on my parents' faces, I knew that was a lot of money.

Fabi sighed. "And how long do we have to get it?"

"June 1st," my father replied.

"June 1st?" Fabi almost jumped out of her seat. "That's eight months. That's impossible! That's basically all of your income. We'd have to starve and live on the street the whole time."

My parents held each other's hands on the table.

"We're thinking of ways around that," my mother said.

I lowered my head. Ninety-thousand dollars in eight months. That was a lot of money in a little bit of time. And according to Fabi we'd never be able to get it all. It felt like the bottom of my world had split open and I was free falling through a black hole of uncertainty. What would happen to us? Were we going to be homeless like Fabi said? Would we have to move? And then a thought occurred to me.

"What if I transfer schools?" I asked. "I could go to Orange High and you guys can put all of that tuition money towards the down payment." A glimmer of hope started rising inside of me. Maybe this was the silver lining. I could finally escape the cesspool of Hamilton High and be a regular black kid at a regular public school, fly under the radar, and live out my senior year in peace and anonymity.

"No, Nick," my father shook his head. "We sacrificed too much to put you in that school."

I was about to raise a counter argument, but the firmness on his face stopped me. My mother mirrored the face and they both stared me down, making it clear that this wasn't up for debate. Even in the midst of this, they were still determined to make sure that my education was intact—even if it meant we would literally have nothing. They had sacrificed so much to put me in that school and now they were about to lose all of it.

"I could take out a loan for school," Fabi suggested. "So you don't have to help with tuition anymore."

"No," my father said, just as firmly. "I already told you, I'd rather us be broke for a little while because of tuition than be broke for the rest of our lives because of debt. And you're not dropping out either. We're gonna figure something out."

I sank into my seat as Fabi started firing up other ideas and venting about gentrification and how much she hated rich people. And as their voices faded into the background of my mind, an idea started to form and I slowly sat up. I tuned back into the conversation just in time to hear Fabi ask, "Then what are we gonna do?"

"God will make a way," my mother said, forcing a smile.

And in a way, maybe He already had.

***

After dinner, I knocked on Fabi's door and she let me in. Fabi was one of those girls that you could immediately tell what kind of person she was just by looking at her room. One wall was covered top to bottom with black and white posters of figures from African-American history: Huey Newton, Fred Hampton, Harriet Tubman, and Malcolm X right in the middle. Another wall had colorful posters of anime including *Dragonball Z, Cyborg 009*, and *Deathnote*. She had two bookshelves against the wall opposite her bed that contained volumes of books on Pan Africanism, womanism, and biographies of civil rights leaders. And on the ceiling was the biggest poster of all of Jean-

Jaques Dessalines and Toussaint L'Ouverture, the main leaders of the Haitian Revolution. So yeah, my sister was basically a Black Panther who loved anime.

She dropped down on the edge of her bed as I sat at her desk.

"I need to ask you something," I said softly.

She leaned forward when she saw the seriousness on my face.

"What's up?" she asked.

"We need to figure out a way to save the restaurant."

"No kidding, Sherlock. That's what I was trying to do before you barged in here."

I rubbed my hands together, still rolling the unbelievable idea around in my head. I should've just come out with it, but I was still terrified of actually going through with it.

"Something weird happened at school the other day," I started. "I wasn't gonna say anything about it at first, but now after hearing about the bakery, I'm rethinking things."

"And?" Fabi waved me on impatiently. "Get to the point."

I scratched my head as I ran the scene at the game over again in my head. "This mom asked me to make her daughter break up with her boyfriend."

"Ok," Fabi replied. "That's a little weird."

"It's Sarah Gibson. She's dating Billy Richardson."

"Billy? The guy who's been bullying you?"

"Yeah. And Sarah's Mom doesn't like Billy and wants Sarah to break up with him, but I guess Sarah won't listen. So she asked me to break them up."

"*Gad on tin tin!*" Fabi scoffed, which was basically, "What kind of nonsense is this?"

"She said she'd pay me $2,000 to do it."

Fabi leveled her eyes at me. "Excuse me?"

"Yeah. She's serious." I pulled out the $100 bill. "She even gave me a down payment."

Fabi jumped from the bed and snatched the bill out of my hand. "Are you serious, Nick? What'd you say?"

"I told her I'd think about it."

"You told her what?!" she shoved me so hard the chair nearly rolled back into Goku on the wall.

"A woman said she'd pay you $2000 for a break-up and you said 'I'll think about it'? What is there to think about?"

"That was before I knew the bakery was being bought out!" I shouted back. "But also…" I paused as I ran my hand over the back of my neck. "I just don't feel right about it. I wanna do it and use that money to help Mom and Dad, but it feels wrong. So I wanted to ask for your advice."

"Here's my advice," she pointed both her hands like blades at me. "Say yes."

I groaned and got up to pace the floor. "But this just feels…unethical."

"Unethical? Billy Richardson is a dog! You're doing Sarah a favor! Plus, think of what you could do with that money. You could split half with Mom and Dad to put towards the down payment and keep the other half to do whatever you want. You're using it for a good cause. What's unethical about that?"

I sat back down and pressed my fist to my lips as I concentrated. Those were good points. As a matter of fact, I'd been thinking of giving my parents more than half.

"So the ends justifies the means?" I said it more like a statement than a question, but Fabi was already frustrated that we were still debating this.

She groaned and lifted her head to the ceiling like she was begging God to smite me. But her eyes fell on the poster of Toussaint and Dessalines and she snickered to herself.

"Do you remember how Toussaint freed the slaves in Haiti?" she asked, fixing her eyes back on me.

"Yes, Fabi," I groaned. "I've heard the story."

"Don't be *frekan*," she snapped.

But I *wasn't* being disrespectful—it's just that I could already see where this was going.

"When France wouldn't free the slaves," Fabi started, pacing methodically in front of me. "Toussaint defected to Spain and used their army to beat France. Then when France finally abolished slavery, Toussaint defected back to France and used their army to kick Spain off the island. He played his enemies in order to get what he wanted. And that's how Haiti became the first successful slave revolt and the first black republic. So yes, I think the end does justify the means."

I scratched my head. "But didn't Toussaint die in the end?"

"That's not the point!" Fabi groaned and pinched the bridge of her nose in frustration. "Listen to me. Billy Richardson is screwing you over. This investor is screwing Mom and Dad over. And you're in a position to screw them both over *and* help the family." She paused to let her words sink in. "You asked for my advice, that's my advice. It's your choice. But whatever you choose…" She walked up to me and pressed the $100 bill against my chest. "…you're gonna remember this for the rest of your life."

I grabbed the bill as she backed away. I couldn't argue with her logic. I *would* be doing Sarah a favor. I didn't owe this stupid school anything for me to be feeling bad about doing something like this. But most importantly, I would be helping my parents save their bakery.

So I asked Fabi to use her phone, called Mrs. Gibson and said, "I'm in."

Chapter six:
"Mission Impossible"

All I was going to need for this mission was a camera. Because remember, this was 2006, so not every phone had a camera and the ones that did definitely didn't have iPhone quality. So Fabi let me borrow her Panasonic.

Now, in order for you to understand how this operation went down, you've gotta know the tea. And the tea was that Billy Richardson was cheating on Sarah Gibson with Emily Reynolds. Everyone knew this—I'm pretty sure even Sarah knew, but she was in denial. I kind of felt bad for her, but like Fabi said, I was doing her a favor. All I had to do was get cold hard evidence of Billy cheating, and it'd be a wrap.

So the next day I had Study Hall in the computer lab with Emily. We were all in there, but no one was studying, of course—everyone was on their computers on MySpace and facebook. Sidebar, I wasn't allowed to have MySpace because at one point a bunch of predators had used MySpace to track down teenage girls and leave their body parts in dumpsters. I'm not sure if that actually happened or if it was just my Mom being overly dramatic and paranoid. Either way, I was only allowed to have facebook.

As usual, at one point Emily and her friends got up and went to the bathroom, like clockwork. Since everyone else was too busy scrolling or playing Solitaire and Mr. Mills was in the front of the room flipping through a *TIME* magazine, I casually slid into Emily's seat and started going through her facebook messages. Lo and behold, I found some between her and Billy and boy were they juicy. Apparently they were into some foot stuff, sucking toes and all that. I pulled out Fabi's camera, snapped a pic of the screen—screenshot before the screenshot—then slipped back into my seat.

After school, Fabi picked me up and brought me to the 1-Hour photo spot where we developed the pic. The next day in homeroom, I slid the pic in Sarah's binder then sat back and watched the dominos fall. By lunch, Billy and Sarah were done. They were screaming at each other in the caf, he was chasing her in the halls, throwing stuff in the locker room—he was furious. I so wanted to tell him that it was me, but I knew for a fact that he would kill me. So I had to enjoy this victory from a distance.

Then Mrs. Gibson contacted me through Fabi's phone and we met up the next day after school behind the bleachers. But this time she was with Mrs. Karla, that racist Mom from the game.

"Oh my God!" Mrs. Gibson squealed and she beckoned me with those suburban Mom hand waves as she pulled me into a hug. "Thank you so much! Thank you! Thank you! Thank you! Sarah dumped him! You're incredible!"

I slowly pulled away from her and nodded. "Thanks. It's a gift, I guess."

She wiped her eyes and I wasn't sure if her make up had gotten smudged from our hug or from her tears.

"She's even talking to me again," she finally said. "She told me I was right and that she was sorry for not believing me." She pressed her hand to her chest and grinned at me. "Thank you."

I nodded again.

"Oh!" she suddenly snapped out of her smile. "I almost forgot! I'm a woman of my word." She reached into her purse and pulled out a white envelope. I took it and my eyes went wide at all the bills inside and I had to remind myself to count them. I had never seen this much money in my life before: $1900.

"And because you fixed my relationship with my daughter," Mrs. Gibson said. "I'm throwing in a little extra for you." She dropped five more hundreds into my palm.

Combined wIth the $100 down payment she'd given me, that came out to $2500.

$2500.

I had made $2500 in less than a week just to make this woman's daughter break up with her boyfriend. My head was spinning. I wanted to scream. I wanted to run around school and wave this money in everyone's face–especially Billy's. But I just cleared my throat and stuffed it all into my pocket.

"Thanks," I said and shook her hand. "It was, uh…nice doing business with you."

"Likewise."

I was about to turn to walk away, but then Mrs. Karla cleared her throat.

"I…ummm…" She looked like she was struggling to get her words out. Like she was allergic to what she was about to say. "I have to admit…I'm impressed with what you did."

"Hmmm," I said. Was she now?

"I too have a problem with my daughter," she went on. "If you're up for it...I might have a job for you."

Chapter seven:
"Complicated"

When I made it home with Fabi, we ran to her room, locked the door, and I spread all the money on her bed.

"Look at this!" I cried. "Can you believe this? That's $2500!"

Fabi traced her fingers across the bills in amazement.

"Wow…" she whispered. "You did it. You really did it."

"I can't believe this," I said, pacing the floor. "I just made $2500!"

We just stood there for a full minute staring at the cash in disbelief. Neither of us had ever made this much money at once. Well, I'd never had a job and Fabi was working part-time at the Rutgers bookstore so she wasn't seeing this kind of money either.

"Well," she finally breathed and swiped a $100 bill. "I'll be taking this. Consider it your sister tax." She snapped the bill in my face, expecting me to grab it from her, but I didn't.

"That's fine," I shrugged. "You deserve it."

She narrowed her eyes at me. "You're not gonna fight me for it? You're so boring."

I started organizing the other $2400. I set aside $1000 for my parents then another $1000 and then the last $400. I pocketed the $400 then handed the second $1000 to Fabi.

She looked at the money then at me. "Wait…you're giving me half your money?"

"Technically it's only forty-two percent," I corrected her. "But yeah."

"No," she shook her head and pushed the money back to me.

"No," I pushed it into her neck. "Take it. I couldn't have done any of this without you. Plus, you need it just as much as Mom and Dad do. Put it towards your tuition. The bookstore's not covering it all and obviously neither are Mom and Dad. Just take it."

She stared at me without blinking and I saw one of her eyes start to glisten. Then she snatched the money, kissed my forehead and spun before I could see a tear fall.

"Anyway," she cleared her throat on her way to her desk. "What's next?"

"Well," I sighed as I sat on the bed. "I got another client."

Fabi raised an eyebrow. "Really?"

I nodded. "Mrs. Karla's daughter is dating another bad boy and she wants me to break them up. She's offering $2000 too."

Fabi whistled. "Well, I guess you gotta get to work then."

So I did.

First things first, we told my parents that I got a job at school and that Fabi got a second job and that we'd be giving them some of the money to put towards the down payment. Fabi's job was a lie, but a necessary one because there was no way my parents would take $1,000 from us at a time without thinking we were selling drugs. After the typical back and forth and a few tears of disbelief, I gave them the money and told them we'd pay them every week. Next, I bought a new phone and had money left over to finally get myself an iPod. I stocked it with my very first homemade playlist, complete with Usher, Paramore, Tupac, Eminem, and Disney classics. I know—my musical tastes were all over the place.

After that, I got to work on breaking up my next two victims, which took all of one day. I got paid the two grand plus tip and word spread to the rest of Mrs. Gibson's friends. Soon, every single mom in that group was giving me assignments. I had to buy a prepaid cell to use as a burner phone to keep my parents from wondering why all these calls kept showing up on the bill. And since the only people who had the burner number were the moms in the "Gibson Circle", I didn't have to worry about picking up the wrong call at the wrong time. Over the next month I was breaking up a girl and her abusive boyfriend over here and hooking another one up with a Yale prospect over there. I ended up making over $12,000 in one month from these moms. $12,000.

I kept giving half to my parents and forty-two percent to Fabi and kept the remaining eight percent for myself. I know you're probably thinking, "Wasn't it tempting to take more of that for yourself?" Yes. Yes, it was. But like I said, my family needed it more. And plus, as much as I wanted to splurge and stunt on everyone at Hamilton with some new Jordans or LeBrons, showing off that sudden wealth would definitely set off alarms.

I kept racking up clients all the way through November and only got a break the week of Thanksgiving when we didn't have school. All that to say, things were looking really good for me. Until one day, I got a phone call from Mrs. Gibson that changed everything.

"I need Sarah to be this year's valedictorian," she explained. "She has a 4.0 and she's on track for it if she keeps it up—especially since Billy's not distracting her anymore. But there's one student who might catch up and ruin her chances."

I paced my room as I listened. This was different from the usual tasks. We were moving from relationships to grades. But I was up for it.

"Okay," I replied.

"I need you to make sure that student doesn't become valedictorian so that my daughter will."

"Alright," I shrugged. "Who's the student?"

I already had a few possibilities in my head of who she was thinking of and was piecing together a game plan tailored for each of them. But when she said the name, I dropped the phone.

"Laura Wood."

Chapter eight:
"Oh No"

"Hello?" Mrs. Gibson asked.

I scrambled to pick up the phone. "Uh…uh…sorry…I just…that's…that's a little different from what we've been doing. I don't think I can do that."

"But my daughter, Nick," she said.

"Isn't there something else I can do?' I tried. "Maybe I could just, I dunno…?"

"There is nothing."

I sighed. "Then I'm sorry. I can't do this."

There was a long silence on the other end. So long that I eventually had to make sure she hadn't hung up.

"Hello?"

"It would be a shame," she started. "If everyone at school found out what you've been doing."

My heart froze in my chest. I opened my mouth to say something, but nothing came out. All I could think about was what would happen if my secret got out. It was one thing for Billy Richardson to know that I'd made his girlfriend break up with him. But now I had almost a dozen bodies to my name. If the rest of the school knew, they would rip me to shreds.

But at the same time, this was Laura we were talking about. Could I really do this to her? Could I ruin her chances of being valedictorian for some cash? My stomach twisted in a knot and I sat down at the edge of my bed.

Now it was Mrs. Gibson's turn to check on me.

"Are you still there?"

I lowered my head and took a deep breath. "Yes…" I took a few more seconds to think then finally said, "I'll do it. But it'll cost you extra. My going rate is $2000, but for this it's gonna be $3500."

"$3000," she responded.

"$3300."

"$3200."

"$3250."

"Deal."

I hung up and felt sick to my stomach. The worst part wasn't just that I was about to destroy my crush's academic life. The worst part was that I already knew exactly how to do it. I knew that we had AP English together and I knew that we had a 15-page paper due next week that was worth 15% of our grade. And I knew that Laura had been going ham and bananas working on it in the library every day after school for the past month. And I knew that she loved the candies the librarian left at the counter because there was a regular bowl and a lactose free bowl because Laura was lactose intolerant. I wasn't a stalker—just observant. All I had to do was wait until the day before the paper was due, switch the candies in the bowl, wait for Laura to use the bathroom, then delete the paper off her flash drive.

So that's what I did.

I made it to the library before Laura. But before I went in, I sprayed on some of my Rite Guard body spray. You know, on the off chance that we bumped into each other, I wanted to make sure I smelled good. It was stupid, I know. But I was seventeen and I was dumb. Anyway, I walked into the library, switched the candies, then sat in the back and waited. Laura came, got a candy, logged in, got started on the paper, and about ten minutes later, left in a hurry. I got to work and within a minute had deleted her paper on both her flash drive and the backup she'd saved to the desktop. As I was doing it I felt something drop next to my foot, but before I could check on it, I saw Laura's silhouette appear behind the glass of the door. I rushed away and vanished into one of the aisles.

When I made it back home that night, I couldn't stop thinking about it. I couldn't believe what I had done. But it wasn't the end of the world, right? Laura was a smart girl, she would bounce back. Besides, colleges only looked at junior year, right? She'd be fine. She could still get into Harvard without being valedictorian. She'd be fine. But then, as I was emptying out my backpack I realized something was missing—my body spray. And I realized that must have been the thing that had dropped when I was sitting in Laura's seat.

Frick.

Chapter nine:
"Toxic"

Mrs. Gibson paid me for Operation: Sabotage Laura. But even after taking the money, I felt sick, like this was blood money. This was the price of my disloyalty to my crush. But I still gave my parents their share for the down payment. And I started wearing Old Spice just in case Laura started sniffing around for anyone who smelled like Rite Guard.

Meanwhile, I could tell Laura's mood had changed. She didn't come out and announce that she'd failed the paper, but I could tell she was tight. For a few days at lunch she didn't play any songs during her chess games. She went from playing three kids at a time to just one and destroying them in two or three moves each time then announcing, "Next!" after each slaughter. Maybe she was just venting. Maybe she was plotting. I didn't know. But a few days later she went back to normal and graced the caf with Disney songs during her matches. And I thought all was forgiven. Boy was I wrong.

Anyway, I got my next assignment a little while after. Lisa Peters' mother wanted me to break up Lisa and her boyfriend Mike Taft. This was my first assignment that ended up being a little trickier than expected. For starters, Mike wasn't cheating on Lisa so I couldn't just show her pics of him and the side chick. However, I did know that Lisa hated drugs. I didn't know if it was because a family member was an addict or someone she knew went to prison for possession or something else. I just knew that in the past she would have very public fights with her exes over not wanting them to smoke. Coincidentally, Mike had a taste for the finer powders in life. And I was assuming he wanted to keep his culinary preferences a secret from Lisa. I just had to figure out how to expose him.

***

"Earth to Nick," Lance said, snapping his fingers in my face.

I blinked several times and it was like waking up from a dream. I was sitting in the caf across from him and hadn't touched my baked ziti.

"Sorry," I said.

"Are you okay?" he asked. "You've been a little out of it lately." Then he glanced over at the chess table and whispered, "You stressing out about Laura?"

"What?" My eyes went wide, but then I realized he didn't know. "No. No. She's...that'll never happen. I'm not worried about that."

"So what is it, then?"

I took a deep breath as I poked my ziti. I obviously couldn't tell him the truth that I was distracted because I was focused on unraveling the very fabric of all social life at Hamilton High. But Lance was also really good at sniffing out lies. Being best friends for four years had made it almost impossible to lie straight to his face. So I just gave him a different truth instead.

"My parents are having money trouble," I said. "Some big shot investor is trying to buy the building where their bakery is so he can build some fancy new apartments. The landlord said that if my parents can come up with $90,000 by June, then he'll sell it to them instead. But we don't have that kind of money. If the bakery goes, then everything goes. So yeah...it's got us all on edge." I finally took a bite of the ziti. "Gentrification 101. Another problem you don't have to worry about."

Lance swallowed nervously and didn't say anything. He always got awkward whenever I mentioned anything vaguely race-related. But I didn't feel like helping him navigate his white guilt today so I changed the subject.

"Have you seen *Wrath of the Dragon?*" I asked.

His eyes lit up and soon we were debating the best *Dragonball Z* movies.

***

That day during P.E., I went back to the guys' locker room, which looked like a tornado had vomited clothes and backpacks all over the floor. I found Mike's backpack, which he had stupidly left in the corner. I could understand the rest of the guys being messy and leaving their stuff lying around, but you've got illegal drugs in here, bro. I mean, it's like these kids *wanted* me to expose them. I checked the pockets and lo and behold there was a plastic bag swelling with white powder. This was ridiculous. This kid had a whole 8 ball of coke sitting in his backpack out in the open. He deserved this.

Anyway, at Hamilton, the guys and girls had P.E. at the same time, but separately. So while we were playing badminton in one gym, the girls were playing racquetball in another. So I snuck into the girls' locker room–praying to God that no one was in there–and moved the coke to the side pocket of Mike's backpack where it was easily visible through the mesh. Ideally, I would've left the backpack right next to Lisa's, but unlike the guys, the girls had actually put all of their stuff in their lockers and locked them. The entire floor was so squeaky clean it was actually pretty impressive. But this also meant that Mike's backpack would be the first thing the girls would see on the bench when they walked in. I was banking on Lisa recognizing it. There was, of course, the chance of someone else getting to the coke first and that opening an entire different can of worms. But that was a risk I was willing to take.

So I left the backpack, headed back to the gym, then waited for everything to fall apart. Mike flipped when he couldn't find his stuff. He went around shoving and screaming at every guy within arms reach, but I was already dressed and gone. Imagine his shock when he finally came out to find Lisa waiting in the hall with his backpack and the bag of coke. Shouting ensued, cursing, crying, threats, yada, yada, yada. I took a casual drink at the water fountain a little way down just to watch my work unfold.

"You lied to me!" Lisa shrieked. "I thought you were different!"

"I *am* different!" he cried back. "It's not what it looks like!"

"Does this mean nothing to you?" And she snatched the necklace off his neck. "This was a promise!"

"I'm sorry!"

I didn't know what that was about, but I guessed that was some sort of special necklace she'd given him? I dunno. But just when it looked like they were done, something stupid happened.

"I'm really sorry," Mike said. Then he started crying. "I didn't mean to. I'm never gonna do it again, I promise."

Lisa stared at him in silence for a second. There was no way she was gonna believe that. But then she threw her arms around his neck and hugged him tight.

"You promise?" she asked.

"I do," he said.

I rolled my eyes and held back the urge to vomit. Then Lisa handed Mike the necklace back–*and* the coke–and said, "Keep *this*. Get rid of *this*. I mean it."

I did a face palm and groaned. Time for Plan B.

***

My last period of the day was U.S. History, which was an easy A. I'd already read through half the textbook and done a quarter of the assignments ahead of time so I usually spent all class doodling or daydreaming. But today I had to figure out a way to solve the Mike problem. So I had pulled out one of my empty composition notebooks from my locker before class and was now scribbling notes on the pages. I wrote down everything I had done for each of my targets up to this point starting with Sarah Gibson, and included sidenotes on what other methods could have also worked. I just needed to get some mental momentum to jog my creativity.

The notes took up about ten pages. And if you're wondering why I was stupid enough to be writing out my evidence in the middle of class for anyone to see, don't worry, I was doing it all in 100% French. I thought of writing it all in Spanish since I spoke that too–perks of having an uncle who married a Mexican woman–but I couldn't take the chance that Hamilton students were actually remembering what they learned in Spanish class. Plus, even if someone didn't know how to speak it, Spanish was phonetic so anyone could piece stuff together if they read something like *"dinero"*. But not only was French less common at Hamilton, but it wasn't phonetic. So a non-French speaker would have no idea that the word *"deux"* was pronounced *dur* and not "dee-uhx".

I looked at the page with the notes I'd just written.

Elizabeth n'aime pas les drogues. Michel fume beaucoup. Comment utilison-nous cela?

I had changed their names because Lisa and Mike had no French equivalent. I stared at the page for several seconds, but nothing came to me and eventually the bell rang.

Chapter ten:
"Paper Planes"

That night after dinner I knocked on Fabi's door and she answered, taking a bite of a cookie.

"What's up?"

"I need your help," I said, marching in past her.

"What's new?" She took another bite and I realized it was *bon bon amidon*, a Haitian cookie that looked like an ivory-colored biscuit, but would crumble more than a Nature Valley bar. You'd start off with a regular crunchy cookie and by the end have a pile of powder that looked like crack. And it tasted just as good.

"Lemme get some," I asked, reaching for her.

She slapped my hand away.

"C'mon!" I begged.

"Stop it!" She slapped my hand again then walked to the other side of the room. "What do you want?"

"I need to break up a girl and her boyfriend," I explained. "But it didn't work today. She got back together with him."

"Huh," Fabi scoffed. She took another bite and a small trail of powder rained onto the floor. She was halfway through the cookie so it was starting to fall apart. "*Ket.*" That was the Kreyol version of "frick" or "damn".

"So I'm gonna try again, but I'm gonna need a ride and some photography."

"What's in it for me?" she teased.

I rolled my eyes.

"Fine," she agreed, taking another bite. More powder fell and the cookie finally fell apart, breaking in two. She caught the second piece in her other hand, but before she could pop it in her mouth, I tackled her onto the bed and wrestled her for it.

"*Visye!*" she screamed. "Get off me, you greedy little jerk!"

And we kept wrestling until we ended up on the floor laughing. Half of the laughing was because of Fabi and the other half was because I'd come up with an idea.

***

The next day, I followed Mike into the bathroom and while he was taking a dump, I set my plan in motion. With an erasable marker, I wrote my burner number on the mirror over every sink with the note: call me for a good high. Then I got into the next stall and waited.

All of a sudden, I heard a camera click beneath me and I looked down to see a flip phone staring up at me from the bottom of the adjacent stall.

"What the heck?" I jumped out then kicked that stall door open to see Waldo Mills, a skinny, freckle-faced sophomore, crouching on the floor, holding his phone up at me.

"Gotcha," he said.

I was too dumbfounded to even say anything at first. Had this kid just taken a picture of me in the bathroom? This was why they called him Waldo the Weirdo.

"What were you doing?" he asked me, looking at his phone in disappointment.

"What was *I* doing?" I snapped at him. "What were *you* doing?"

"I was trying to take a picture of you pooping, but you were just sitting there."

"What?" I couldn't believe what I was hearing. And he was saying it like all he'd done was try to give me a high five. "Why would you want a picture of me pooping?"

"Don't flatter yourself," he shrugged at me. "I do it to everyone."

My head was spinning trying to keep up with this nonsense. "Why?"

"For blackmail," he said. "You know…just in case."

I squinted at him. I had never even had a conversation with this kid, let alone done anything to him. I just knew everyone thought he was weird and made fun of him—because he went around doing stuff like taking pictures of people pooping.

"You better delete that," I told him.

"You're not even doing anything in it."

"Exactly. So what do you need it for? You're gonna blackmail me with a picture of me sitting on the toilet with my pants on?"

He shrugged and said, "Good point." Then he pressed a button. "All gone."

"You're a weirdo, you know that?" I said to him.

"No," he shook his head. "I'm just ahead of my time." Then he turned and walked out the bathroom, just like that. Like it was all normal. But I didn't have time to dwell on it because I heard Mike flush. So I slipped back into my stall and shut the door. Mike started washing his hands and I could hear him pausing to read the mirror.

That night, I got a call from him. I couldn't have him recognizing my voice over the phone and I couldn't just try to sound more hood than I really was. And using a Haitian accent would risk him being able to trace it back to me. So instead I used the next best thing–a French accent. Who knew that growing up speaking French would one day help me stage a drug deal? I told him to meet me at the pull up bars at Verona Park, about a fifteen-minute drive from my house and from Hamilton. If Mike was willing to drive out in the middle of the night for this, then I knew I'd have him. And he did.

We met at the bars, cloaked by the shadows under the trees. It was early December so it was a little chilly so I was able to get away with wearing a hoodie, gloves, and a Spider-Man mask. Even in the dark, if he saw that I was black, he'd know it was me.

"Are you Mike?" I asked, voice dripping with French.

"Yeah," he replied.

"I believe this is what you want?" I gave the area a visual sweep before pulling out a plastic bag of powder from my hoodie pocket.

"And you said this is some new stuff?" he asked.

"Yes," I nodded. "Brand new. Going to hit the streets soon, but you get to be one of the first ones to experience it."

"And you said the high lasts longer?"

"Yes," I nodded.

He looked around quickly then slipped me a $100 bill, but I looked down at it without taking it.

"What's the matter?" he asked, anxiety creeping into his voice. "C'mon, take it."

"I don't think that will be enough."

"What do you mean? You said $100 over the phone."

"That was before I noticed that," I said, nodding my chin at his collar where Lisa's necklace was hanging, glittering in the moonlight.

"This?" he touched it gently. "My girlfriend gave this to me."

"That is nice. What if I told you I could give you double if you gave me that necklace?" I pulled out a second bag of powder and Mike's eyes went wide. "Double the dope. Double the fun."

Mike stared at the two bags for several seconds then traced his fingers up and down the necklace. He didn't move, but I could see the struggle in his eyes.

"Never mind," I finally said, moving to put the second bag away.

"Wait!" he stopped me. "I'll take it." And with that he gave me the necklace and I handed him both bags.

"Enjoy," I said, then turned and left.

What Mike didn't know was that Fabi had been taking pictures of the entire exchange from her parking spot across the street. Or that the powder was actually crushed *bon bon amidon*. Either way, when I slid the picture in Lisa's locker the next day, along with her necklace, she was inconsolable. They broke up before lunch.

Chapter eleven:
"Assassin's Tango"

When lunch finally came I was on a high knowing that I was gonna get paid for another successful mission. Obviously I couldn't tell anyone why I had a spring in my step, so I just grinned to myself on my way to Lance at our usual table. But along the way I spotted Laura sitting by herself at the chess table and she pushed a chair out with her foot to block my path.

"Sit with me," she said with a friendly grin.

My jaw dropped in shock. Was this really happening? Was Laura Wood asking me to sit with her? I looked over at Lance at our table, whose jaw was just as open as mine and he nodded emphatically. Bro code for the win.

So I sat down, trying with everything in me not to show that I was doing cartwheels inside. Apparently my day was about to get even better. I could smell a faint hint of strawberries that I was guessing was her shampoo and I couldn't help but smile. Strawberries were my favorite. Favorite fruit on my favorite girl. That came out wrong. Never mind.

"So…" I started. "What's up?"

"I'm nervous," she replied, wringing her hands together. "I just need someone to sit with me for a minute." She kept looking around the cafeteria like she was waiting for someone to show up. An ex boyfriend? A stalker?

"What are you nervous about?" I asked her.

She glanced at me and took a deep breath. "You'll see."

I nodded and we sat there for a few more seconds in awkward silence. What could I say? I was sitting with my crush for the first time. She had asked me to sit with her! What kind of luck was this? I had to think of something. I couldn't just let this opportunity slip. Should I compliment her on her shampoo? Tell her I liked strawberries too? No, that'd be weird.

A few of the chess club members finally arrived and sat with us and I wondered if Laura would tell me I could leave now that her friends were here. But she didn't.

I cleared my throat. Maybe I could ask her about chess. If she wanted to play. Would that be too basic? Predictable? Screw it. I was gonna do it. I was gonna do it.

"Do you, uh…" I started. But before I could finish, the TV on the wall flashed on. Everyone in the caf turned in their seats and the chatter slowly died as we all waited for some funny video or some boring announcement to play. Instead, Laura's face appeared on screen.

"Students of Hamilton High," she said. "I have an announcement to make."

I looked at her sitting next to me and she swallowed nervously. Everyone else at the table glanced at her in confusion then looked back at the screen.

"You may have noticed that there's been a lot of drama going on lately," Laura went on in the video. "A lot more than usual—hook ups, break ups, grades messed up. I have reason to believe that none of this is random. I believe that it's all being orchestrated by a single person—a phantom."

A low murmur rolled through the entire caf as everyone started whispering. My throat went dry as I fixed my eyes on the screen in complete disbelief.

"And this phantom has ruined my chances of being valedictorian," Laura went on. "Whoever you are, I want you to know that you messed up. Because you deleted my AP English paper and because you left your Rite Guard body spray at the scene of the crime I now know that you're a senior, you're a guy, and you're dead."

An eerie hush fell over the room.

"Hell hath no fury," Laura said, squinting into the camera. "I will hunt you down, I will find you, and I will ruin you."

And with that, the screen flashed off.

Ket.

Chapter twelve:
"L's Theme"

I. Was. Stressed. When I tell you I was stressed? I don't even remember what happened for the rest of the day. I was literally holding my breath until final period. And when I finally made it home, I barged into Fabi's room to panic.

"She knows!" I screamed. "She knows!"

I paced frantically as Fabi tried to calm me down, but I couldn't stop freaking out.

"What's going on?" she asked. "Who knows? Nick, will you just relax for a second?"

"Laura!" I shouted. "She knows! She made a video and told the whole school that somebody's been sabotaging the student body. She even gave it a name–the Phantom. She doesn't know it's me, but she knows it's someone. She gave me a name!" I ran my hand over my head as I groaned. "I've gotta transfer. I have to. I gotta switch schools. Change my name. Everything. She's gonna find me."

"Nick, Nick, Nick," Fabi tried to reassure me. "You're gonna be fine."

"No, I'm not gonna be fine!" I whirled on her. "This girl is the president of the chess club, on the debate team, AP classes. You have no idea how smart she is."

"Maybe," Fabi shrugged. "But I know how smart my brother is."

"Fabiola! This isn't the time for a touchy-feely moment! She has my Rite Guard body spray! She could run the fingerprints on that and trace it back to me!"

Fabi gave me a swift smack to my face and I froze in my spot.

"Did you just smack me?" I asked, clutching my cheek.

"Do you hear yourself?" she replied. "Fingerprints? Have you ever committed a crime?"

"No…" I said.

"Have you ever been a government employee?"

"No…"

"So why would anyone have your fingerprints?"

I paused for a second as I let that sink in. "Wait a minute…is that…is that how that works?"

"Yes. What'd you think, the government just has everyone's fingerprints on file once you're born?"

I shrugged. "I dunno. Yeah, I guess."

Fabi pinched the bridge of her nose and let out a deep sigh. "Listen to me. You're gonna be fine. Trust me. Just breathe."

I inhaled then exhaled a few times then slowly sat down at the edge of the bed.

"Good," she said. "Now…remember *Deathnote?*"

I nodded. *Deathnote* was an anime about a high school senior named Light who found a notebook that would kill anyone who's name he wrote in it. So he used it to start secretly killing off criminals. But then a detective named L figured out that something was off about these killings and announced that he was hunting down this killer. The whole show was a cat and mouse between Light and L where they were constantly trying to outwit each other. Fabi and I had read the manga last year and the anime had just come out this year. This was before Netflix so we had to actually wait every week to watch it.

"You are Light," Fabi continued. "You've been hired by these Moms to sabotage these students' lives. You've been this relationship assassin moving in the shadows and nobody knows. Laura is L who now wants to hunt you down. And what did Light do when he found out L was coming for him? He joined the police force so that he could get close to L and know what he knew and always be one step ahead of him. That's what you gotta do with Laura. Get close to her. Become friends with her–so you always know what she knows about you and you'll always be one step ahead."

I thought about it for a second.

"But Light dies in the end," I finally pointed out. "Why do you keep comparing me to people who die in the end?"

"That's not the point!" Fabi groaned. "Are you listening to what I'm saying? Get close to her."

"I'm listening, I'm listening." I stood and started pacing again. It was actually a pretty good idea. A *really* good idea. If I just sat back and tried to hide from Laura, she would no doubt eventually find me. But if I had access to all of her intel, I could know how close she was to catching me at all times and use that information to throw her off my tail. It could work. But then there was the obvious wrinkle in the plan.

"There's one problem," I stopped and turned to Fabi. "I like Laura."

"Like…like her, like her?" Fabi asked me.

I nodded. "So if I do this, I'm gonna have two secrets to keep: what I did to her and what I feel for her."

"Okay," Fabi said. "Listen to me very carefully, Nick. You get close to this girl. You befriend this girl. But under no circumstances do you ever tell this girl how you feel. That shouldn't even be an issue because you know you're not allowed to date yet."

"Don't remind me," I groaned.

"No, I will," she smirked. "Because if I'm still not allowed to date, you better believe I'm not letting you start before me."

"Okay."

"But seriously," she said firmly. "You cannot be with this girl. It'll distract you, you'll let your guard down, then she'll catch you. Do you understand?"

I sighed, but eventually nodded. I was already an undercover mercenary. Now it was time to be a spy.

So the next day, the first thing I did in homeroom was go straight to Laura.

"Hey," I said. "I'm so sorry to hear about what happened to your GPA. Sorry your chances of being valedictorian got ruined."

"Thanks, Nick," she said. "I appreciate that."

"But also…" I added. "I wanna help you find the Phantom."

Chapter thirteen:
"Get the Party Started"

Laura's announcement sent a ripple through the whole school and everybody became suspicious of everyone. The phrase "they're the Phantom" kept getting whispered in every single class as everyone wondered which one of us was guilty. It was like a schoolwide game of mafia. Billy and his friends even beat up a theater kid that they thought was the Phantom. It was getting a little wild.

But during lunch Laura and I went to the library to have our first "debriefing". I told Lance about it and he completely understood. He even joked that I was about to break some rules. But Fabi's warning was ringing in my ears. This was all business. I had to stay focused. I wasn't doing this to get with Laura. I was doing this to stay ahead of her.

"Lemme show you what I've got so far," Laura said as she cleared a table. She pulled some notebooks out of her backpack then spread several sheets of looseleaf paper across the surface. "You're gonna think I'm crazy. But I'm not."

"No," I shook my head, eyeing the sheets. "I've got an open mind."

But I wasn't ready.

"Here we go…" Laura pointed at one sheet with a web of words and doodles with the word ORGANIC written in bubble letters at the top. "All of these are things that have happened in school since September that I think happened organically." I scanned the sheet quickly and saw things like "Sean Rogers gets malaria…Leslie Jenkins hooks up with Jordan Nile…"

Then she pointed at the second sheet with similar doodles and words, but at the top in red marker was the word PHANTOM. And I saw things like "Sarah Gibson breaks up with Billy Richardson…Lisa Peters breaks up with Mike Taft…" There were over a dozen events on the sheet and 90% of them were things I'd done. My chest tightened with a combination of dread and admiration. How had she figured this out? She had literally mapped out every piece of drama that had happened in school for the past three months.

"Wow," I said, trying to hide my surprise. "This is…really impressive."

"I'm not crazy," she insisted. "It's all here."

"No, no," I agreed. "I see." I scratched my chin, like I was calculating something–which I very much was. "But…I'm not sure about some of these." I picked up the sheets one by one and examined them. Then I put them back down and pointed at Lisa Peters. "I don't think that was the Phantom. I remember hearing about that. It sounded pretty organic to me. But this one…" I pointed at Sean Rogers. "I think that was him. That malaria was suspiciously random."

She took the sheets from me and examined them then shook her head.

"No, no, no," she disagreed. "That doesn't fit the Phantom's M.O."

"His M.O.?"

"His *modus operandi.*"

"I know what it means…" I stopped myself. "How do you know his M.O.?"

"Look…" Laura pulled out another sheet with more notes and doodles. "The majority of the time, the Phantom leaves some sort of evidence for his 'victims'. Like a photograph. That's how Sarah found out Billy was cheating and it's how Lisa found out Mike was still doing drugs."

I put my fist to my chin to keep my jaw from dropping. She was right. I had been leaving photos after most of my assignments. I didn't even realize how obvious that made it that someone was behind all of this. How had I been so stupid?

"Plus," Laura went on. "Whenever the Phantom attacks, there's always another student that's affected. So with the breakups and hookups, obviously both students involved are affected. And with my paper being deleted, apparently someone else wanted to be valedictorian. But when Sean got malaria, it didn't affect anyone that I could tell. He's not on the honor roll, doesn't play any sports, and isn't even in a relationship. Him getting malaria didn't affect or benefit anyone. So it couldn't have been the Phantom."

I kept my fist to my chin calmly, but inside I was running like a chicken with its head cut off. She was good. She was really good. This was gonna be a lot harder than I thought.

Chapter fourteen:
"I Need to Know"

"I have something special for you," Laura said as I followed her into the library the next day.

"Special sounds good," I said, wondering what surprise was waiting for me.

"If I'm gonna keep working with you, I need to make sure that I can trust you. You know, because every male senior is a suspect and you're a male senior, so…"

"Makes sense," I shrugged, still wondering where this was going.

She stopped in front of the conference room door then turned to me. "I don't know you that well yet so don't take this personally."

"I'm won't," I said, but I was secretly getting nervous. What was this about?

"If you don't have anything to hide, then this will be completely harmless."

What was she getting at?

"But if you *do* have something to hide…that'll be a different story."

"What are you talking about?"

"I want you to take a lie detector test."

My heart sank and I swallowed nervously. I waited for her to burst out laughing and say that she was joking, but she just opened the door and waved me in. When I walked inside, I saw a laptop sitting on the table with a bunch of wires and electrodes hooked up to it and a bunch of other gizmos I couldn't really identify. It was a lie detector. She had a freaking lie detector and she wanted to hook me up to it. This was bad.

"Whoa," I chuckled. "You're serious."

"Very serious," she said, shutting the door behind her. "Of course the choice is yours. But if you say no, I'm gonna have to assume you have something to hide. If you say yes, then we can move on."

I shrugged as casually as I could. This was bad. So, so bad. But like she said, I couldn't say no. That would make her even more suspicious of me. But if I said yes, she'd find out I was the Phantom. I'd never taken a lie detector test before in my life. I didn't even know these things still existed. And with Laura of all people? She'd fry me hotter than a plantain.

I swallowed again and scratched the back of my neck.

Think, Nick. You gotta think your way outta this one.

I couldn't back out. But there had to be a way to beat a lie detector test, right? I'd seen people do it in movies before so hopefully there was some truth to it. But how did they do it? From what I knew the machine would measure your physiological reaction to questions like your sweat and your heart rate. So in theory then, if I could make myself nervous and calm at the right times, I could trick the machine.

In theory.

"Let's do it," I finally said.

Laura smiled.

It took a couple minutes to set everything up and hook me up to the machine.

"Where'd you even get this?" I asked her.

"My uncle works for the FBI," Laura said casually. "He gave this to me as a birthday present last year."

"Hmmmm," I said. That was doing nothing to keep me calm. I was about to be interrogated by the niece of an FBI Agent.

"Alright," she said, clapping her hands. "First, I'm gonna establish a baseline. I'm gonna ask you some questions and I need you to lie."

I raised an eyebrow. "You *want* me to lie?"

She nodded. "I need to see what you look like when you're not telling the truth."

I nodded. That made sense. This was what she was going to use to measure my lying reactions for the rest of the test. If I could make my reaction as wild and obvious as possible now then make my reaction calm later, she wouldn't be able to tell because the difference would be so great. So how could I increase my heart rate at will?

"You ready?" she asked as she stared at the laptop.

"Ready."

"Is my hair red?"

I looked at her short red hair bright as flames around her head. Wow. It was really beautiful. Like a crown of autumn leaves. I imagined her letting me run my fingers through it and what it would feel like. The sweet strawberry scent of her shampoo wafted into my nose and I had to force myself not to inhale. Then I thought of her smiling at me and instantly felt my heart thumping in my chest.

"No," I replied.

I heard the needle scratching wildly.

"Is *your* hair red?" she asked, eyes still on the laptop screen.

I looked at her hair again and thought of her smiling at me and my heart kept pounding.

"Yes."

The needle danced across the sheet and Laura laughed.

"You're a terrible liar," she said.

"I am," I replied.

"Now I need you to tell me the truth."

"Okay." I needed to calm down. No more thinking about Laura and her pretty face smiling my insides into nervous jelly. Instead I reached into my childhood for one of my favorite memories. It was my first time visiting Haiti. I was six and Fabi was nine. My parents had brought us to our grandfather's chateaux in the countryside. I remembered laying in the grass with Fabi while we ate mangos we had just picked from one of the trees. The Sun beamed down on us, kissing our skin with warm light as the sweet juice ran down our faces. I smiled just remembering it.

"Is your name Nicholas Toussaint?" Laura asked me.

"Yes," I replied.

The needle barely moved.

"Are you a senior at Hamilton High?"

"Yes."

Nothing.

"Okay." She did some shuffling on her end of the table then cleared her throat. "Now for the real questions. You ready?"

I shut my eyes and took a deep breath, still staring up at the Sun in my mind's eye. I could even hear Fabi giggling next to me. "Ready."

"Have you ever been bullied by anyone at school?"

"Yes."

"Have you ever bullied anyone back?"

"No."

"Are you aware that a 'Phantom' has been targeting students at Hamilton High?"

"Yes."

"Do you know anyone who's been targeted by the Phantom?"

"Yes."

"Have you been targeted by the Phantom?"

"No."

"Do you know who the Phantom is?"

"No."

"Are you the Phantom?"

"No."

"Do you have a crush on anyone at school?"

I almost opened my eyes. The Sun froze like an image on an old VHS tape and my heart started banging in my chest. What was that about? Where did that question come from? I could hear the needle skating across the sheet. It was too late to fake it now.

"Yes," I said as calmly as I could.

"Hmmmm," I heard her say. Then she laughed. "I'm just messing with you."

I sighed and lowered my head.

"You're so annoying," I muttered.

"All done!" she sang.

"Did I pass?" I grinned.

Laura shrugged. "Actually, these things don't even work."

I blinked several times. What did she just say?

"I mean, they're not actually good at finding out if you're lying. But they can make criminals so nervous that it forces a confession out of them."

I tightened my lips as I glared at her in disbelief.

"So my hope was that if you *were* the Phantom, this would scare you into confessing that. But instead, all I know now is that you're either not the Phantom or just a really good liar."

"Huh," I said. "Good to know."

Chapter fifteen:
"Naughty Girl"

One night, after finishing my homework, I cracked open my notebook to check our financial status. In addition to all my notes on my victims, I'd also started recording all the money I was making. Just like with the victims' notes, I kept the financial notes in code in case someone ever found this. But since numbers were the same in English and French and the names of months weren't that different, I kept the numbers the same but didn't include dollar signs and I changed the month names to different fictional character names.

Octavius(12.000)
  -2.500
  -2.000
  -3.000
  -2.500
  -2.000

M&D: 6.250
F: 5.000
N: 0.750

Ninetails(9.000)
  -3.000
  -3.000
  -3.000

M&D: 5.250.
F: 3.000
N: 0.750

Decepticon(7.000)
  -3.500
  -3.500

M&D: 4.000

F: 3.000

N: 0

Jane Porter(???)

Total M&D: 15.500

Total F: 11.000

Total N: 1.500

Grand total: 28.000

November had been a low one because we had Thanksgiving break. December would've been even worse than it was because we were gone for a week. But I'd had the foresight to institute an increased "holiday rate" to counteract that. Regardless, at this rate, I was averaging around $9,300 a month. Which, obviously, is a crazy amount of money for a seventeen-year-old. But since part of that was going to Fabi, it was really only $6,250 a month, which was still crazy. But with a goal of $90,000 in 8 months, I'd only have $50,000 by the deadline in June. Granted, by next month, I would have Fabi's tuition for next semester paid off so we could probably stop paying that and focus more on the down payment. Either way, if I didn't make some changes, we wouldn't be able to save the bakery.

I pulled out my calculator to figure out how much I'd have to make for the next five months to hit the goal when my burner phone rang. I picked it up and it was a mother--Kyle Johnson's mother to be exact. Like I said before, Kyle was one of the very few kids besides Lance at Hamilton that didn't radiate complete douchebaggery. Which was why this phone call was a little concerning.

"I need you to make Kyle break up with his new girlfriend," his mother said.

I sighed as I sat down on my bed. I had an inkling who he was dating, but had to confirm. "And who is she?"

"Vanessa Diamond," his mother replied. "I'm worried that she's just trying to take advantage of him. I've heard rumors, but I don't know for sure. He's just such a good kid, you know? I don't want to see some…some…tramp ruin him."

I lowered my head. It was exactly what I was afraid of. Vanessa Diamond was a problem. I'm not one to slut shame, but Vanessa wasn't a slut. She was a sexual psychopath who made Regina George look like Mother Theresa. Her nickname at school was the Virgin Killer because she would go out of her way to have sex with boys who were virgins then move on to the next one. She apparently got off on being a guy's first. But what made her so sadistically good at what she did was that she tailored her approach to each specific victim. She would watch them and study them until she could tell them exactly what they wanted to hear to make them feel like she actually liked them. So even though every one of them knew that she just wanted to have sex with them, they all thought that they were different.

And how did I know all this? Because Vanessa had tried to take my virginity junior year. The only reason I resisted was because I was trying to save myself for marriage. That and the fact that I was more afraid of my parents than I was attracted to her. I wasn't even allowed to date, let alone have sex. They would split my Haitian cheeks apart if they found out.

"Please," Mrs. Johnson said. "I don't want her to ruin my boy."

I shut my eyes and took a deep breath.

"I know it's weird to put a price on my son's innocence," she went on. "But I'm willing to pay you $3,000."

I opened my eyes. It *was* a little weird to put a price on a boy's virginity, but here we were. $3,000 was fine with me.

"You got it, ma'am," I told her.

***

The next day at lunch, the plan was underway. Since Kyle most likely already knew that Vanessa wanted to take his virginity, just convincing him that she wanted to have sex with him wouldn't make him break up with her. I'd have to be a little more…resourceful.

The first step of the plan was going to be to slip some laxatives in Vanessa's coffee. I stood in line at the drinks section where the seniors usually restocked on their fill of caffeine for the day. I was right behind Vanessa and watched her tap her foot impatiently as we waited for the senior boy pouring the hot water into his cup in front of her. Finally it was her turn and she grabbed a cup. Then I reached into my pocket for the laxative and someone punched my shoulder from behind.

"Hey, bro," Lance said.

Frick.

I glanced quickly from Vanessa back to Lance and forced a nervous smile. "Hey. What's up?"

"You sitting with me today?" he asked. "Or you still talking to Laura?"

"Uhhhh…" I looked over my shoulder at Vanessa as she poured her hot water. "Uhhhh…I'm…gonna be with Laura…"

He frowned. It had been a while since we'd sat together at lunch. We still had classes together and still talked, but lunch had been our thing and that hadn't been happening. So understandably, he probably felt like our friendship was hanging in the balance. But he didn't know that my social life as I knew it was also in the balance because I had to make sure Laura never knew my secret. There was a lot to juggle. And speaking of which, Vanessa had just finished making her coffee and was walking past us.

Frick!

Without thinking, I stepped in her way and bumped her so hard her cup spilled all over the floor.

"I'm so sorry!" I cried.

"You klutz!" she screamed. But when she looked up and saw it was me, her entire body relaxed and a seductive smile curled onto her face. She pulled a strand of her blonde hair behind her ear and flashed a brilliant smile. "Hey, Nicky."

"So sorry, Vanessa," I said. "I didn't see you there."

She looked down at the stains on her white blouse. "A boy should never apologize for getting me wet."

I cleared my throat as I grabbed some napkins and handed them to her. "I'll make you another one. How do you like it?"

"I'll take it any way you give it to me, Nicky." She watched me pour and I could feel her eyes boring into my back. With my body shielding her and Lance from what I was doing, I stirred in the laxative then turned to find her leaning inches away from my face. She was close enough to see the blue of her eyes and the specs of hazel around the irises. The scent of apples wafted into my nostrils and I held my breath. She stayed there, inches from me, and inhaled, like she was breathing me in. I had heard that there were people who could smell virginity. Vanessa Diamond was probably one of them.

I held the cup up to her and she slowly traced the length of my body with her eyes before finally grabbing the cup, making sure our fingers touched when she did. Then she held me there, gently gripping my fingers.

"The offer still stands, Nicky."

"That's good to know," I nodded then forced a smile.

She took a sip then finally turned away. "Later, boys."

Once she was gone, I let out a breath I didn't realize I'd been holding in.

"Sorry, Lance," I said. "We…really have this thing going on right now…but I promise, I'm gonna start sitting with you again soon."

He raised an eyebrow then looked over his shoulder at Vanessa who had just sat next to Kyle. "Yeah, it looks like you've got a 'thing' with a lotta people."

"It's not like that," I frowned. "You know she's still tight that I rejected her."

"And I'm still confused why you did."

I groaned. "Is it so bad that I actually wanna wait until marriage?"

"No. But it is a little weird when you've got girls like Vanessa willing to—"

"Can we not talk about it?"

"Okay…" he put his hands up in surrender. "Just checking to make sure we're still friends."

"We are," I assured him. Then I dapped him up before heading over to Laura at our new table in the corner of the caf.

"What took you so long?" she asked me when I sat down.

"Nothing. You got anything new today?"

"Not much," she said, opening her notebook. "But I've been working on this theory of how to predict who his next victim is gonna be…"

She went on spilling out her ideas, but I was checking on Vanessa a few tables over, sipping her coffee and running her hand through Kyle's hair.

"…so if that were true," Laura was saying, tossing a cherry into her mouth. "It would mean he was targeting only guys. But we've seen him get girls too."

"Yeah, yeah," I said absent-mindedly.

"Are you listening to me?" Laura said, patting the table.

"Yes!" I snapped to attention. "Yes. I'm listening. You thought he might just be targeting guys, but he's obviously not."

"Right…" She went back to her notebook and tapped her pen on her lips. "But I know there's some kind of pattern to the victims, even if it's not their gender."

Then Vanessa stood and hurried to the bathroom. Good. It was in motion. "Do you think he's working with someone? Or is he riding solo?"

"I think he's got a team," I said. "I mean, how could one kid be taking on the whole student body like this? He's gotta be working with someone."

"That does make sense," Laura nodded. "But what group would be willing to sabotage the whole school? All of the victims are from different cliques. Billy was a jock, Mike was…"

Vanessa came back from the bathroom holding her stomach. She grabbed her backpack then hurried towards the back entrance of the caf—the entrance nearest the nurse's office.

I pulled my phone out under the table and called Fabi. But I didn't pull it to my ear until I heard her pick up.

"*Alo?*" I said.

Laura looked up at me.

"It's my sister," I mouthed to her. Then, in Kreyol, I told Fabi, "She's on her way to you. Is everything ready?"

"Yessir," Fabi replied in Kreyol. "Nurse Judy just left, I'm heading into her office right now."

"Okay. Good luck."

I hung up and slid the phone back in my pocket.

"That's so cool that you speak another language," Laura said. "Is everything okay with her?"

I nodded. "I forgot part of my lunch at home so she's coming to bring it to me."

"That makes sense," she said. "Kreyol and French are a little similar, right? I heard you say '*en route.*' That's 'on the way.' So she's on her way?"

My heart stopped as my head snapped in her direction. "What? How…how do you know that?"

"I'm fluent in French," she shrugged, like she was just telling me she had gum in her purse.

Laura Wood spoke French? And all of a sudden I realized how lucky I was. Fabi and I usually switched between French, Kreyol, and English when we spoke with each other. If I had just decided to speak French to Fabi just now, I would have handed Laura my secret on a silver platter. I had dodged a bullet and didn't even know it.

"My Dad used to be a Latin professor," Laura went on. "So he taught me as a kid. Which made it a lot easier to pick up French when we'd go to Paris every summer."

I smiled at her, but inside I was screaming. Why was this chick so smart?

"Is there anything you can't do?" I asked her.

She pursed her lips as she thought about it for a second. "I can't do that thing where you tie a cherry stem with your tongue."

I squinted at her. "I was joking."

"So was I." She stuck her tongue out and revealed a cherry stem tied in a knot. Then she pulled it back in her mouth and winked at me.

"Well," I cleared my throat. "*C'est tres magnifique ça.*"

"*Beaucoup plus magnifique que le Phantom, n'est-ce pa?*"

I nodded slowly, caught somewhere between terror and admiration.

We went back to talking about the Phantom. Did he have a team? What was his motive? Could we predict his next victim? Then my phone rang again.

"Is it your sister?" Laura asked, eyes wide with excitement. "Pick it up! Pick it up! I bet you I can guess what you're saying."

I held the ringing phone in my hand and forced a smile. This was bad. I had to make sure that I didn't use any Kreyol words that sounded like French that Laura could pick up on. What if something had gone wrong and Vanessa hadn't actually gone to the nurse's office? If Fabi asked what Vanessa looked like, I couldn't just say she's white with blonde hair and blue eyes. All of those words were the same in Kreyol and French and had nothing to do with a forgotten lunch. Laura would immediately know I was lying. My heart was banging like a drum against my ribs in time with the rings and I finally answered.

"It's done," Fabi said in Kreyol. "I got the recording. She's heading back to the caf. Meet me in the parking lot."

I breathed a sigh of relief then replied, "*Map vini.*"

Then I hung up.

"Mop...vee-nee," Laura repeated. She furrowed her brow as she thought then eventually sighed. "I got nothing."

"It means 'I'm coming'," I translated. "She's outside. I'll be right back."

A minute later I was meeting Fabi by her car in the parking lot and she handed me her voice recorder. Once again, this was before every phone had a voice memo app so we had to record stuff on separate devices. College kids all over the country were using these things to record their professors' lectures. She gave me the recorder and I pressed play.

"What seems to be the problem?" I heard Fabi say.

"Where's Nurse Judy?" Vanessa asked.

"She stepped out for a second. I'm Nurse Kendra, her intern for today. How can I help you?"

"I'm sick," Vanessa replied.

They went back and forth about what she was feeling then Fabi asked her some "routine" questions. When was her last period? Was she sexually active? Did she have any STD's she was aware of? And to the last question, Vanessa paused before naming several.

"Nice," I said, stopping the recording. Then I continued in Kreyol, even though there was no one outside, but just in case. "This is perfect. Now I just gotta get this to Kyle."

"*Merci beaucoup,*" Fabi said with a dramatic curtsy.

And the French jogged my memory and I realized how stupid I was. This wasn't going to work.

"Crap!" I groaned. "I forgot!"

"What?"

"Laura's figured out that I leave evidence for the victims. If I give this to Kyle, she'll trace it back to the Phantom."

"You didn't tell me that."

"I forgot. And apparently she speaks French too. So we gotta stick to Kreyol at all times."

"Dang. Is there anything this chick can't do? So how are you gonna let Kyle know his girlfriend is a walking STD?"

I fiddled with the recorder in my fingers.

"Time for plan B."

Chapter sixteen: "Bye Bye Bye"

After school, everybody poured out of the classrooms into the hall as usual. I made sure to slip some small talk with Lance every period I could just to keep him from getting too suspicious of me pulling away from him. But once we were all rubbing shoulders on our way to our lockers, I tracked Kyle and followed him into the boys' bathroom. We both made it to the urinals at the same time and of course we kept the customary empty urinal between us. But I had to break guy code by striking up a conversation in order to set my plan in motion.

"Thanks again for the CD, man," I said without looking.

"No problem," he replied, eyes straight ahead.

Awkward silence.

"I like your backpack," I said, indicating the keychains hanging from the pockets. Each of them was a bobblehead of a different anime character: Luffy, Goku, and Vegeta.

"Thanks," Kyle replied.

"You know Mr. Jamison has a stash of manga in his classroom?"

I saw him pull his neck back from the corner of my eye. "Really?"

"Yeah," we both flushed at the same time then headed to the sink. "I go there every now and then to read after school. He's pretty cool about it."

"You can just…walk in?"

"Yeah," I nodded as I dried my hands. "C'mon, lemme show you."

And just like that, we were on our way to Mr. Jamison's class on the second floor. Because everyone was too busy rushing to go home there was no one in the halls up here but us. I kept Kyle busy the whole way by talking everything anime. Who'd win in a fight between Goku and Superman? When would Luffy find OnePiece? Basic stuff.

"I'm just saying, it's been on since the 90's, bro," I was telling him. "There's no way OnePiece will still be going in the next ten years. That's like–"

Kyle stopped when we walked past a door and heard Vanessa's voice behind it.

"…are you sexually active?" Fabi was saying.

"…yeah," Vanessa replied.

"Do you have any STD's?"

Kyle leaned his ear towards the door as he listened to her rattle them off.

"Is that…" I whispered. "Vanessa?"

Kyle nodded. "I'm confused. She told me she always used protection."

I frowned as I listened, pretending to feel bad for him—but technically I did. "Were you guys planning on…you know…?"

"Well…" he lowered his eyes as he thought. "I dunno now…"

I grabbed his arm gently and pulled him further down the hall. "We should probably go before they see us."

"She lied to me," he said as we walked on.

I shrugged. "She was probably embarrassed. I wouldn't wanna tell anybody if I had herpes."

He stopped suddenly. "Herpes? That's not what I'm worried about. You didn't hear her?"

"What?" I asked him.

"She's in the nurse's office because she's feeling sick."

I stared at him in confusion.

"She's pregnant," he finally said. "If I have sex with her now, she's gonna think I'm the father."

I blinked several times as I tried to put the pieces together. Her being sick. Her being sexually active. I could see how someone would connect those dots. But I wasn't about to correct him so I just nodded.

"Yeah…that's messy, man."

And just like that, the thought of reading manga was suddenly the farthest thing from Kyle's mind.

"I gotta go…" he said absent-mindedly.

He turned and left—probably to go wait outside that door for Vanessa. But by now Fabi was long gone with the speaker and recorder. But Kyle would eventually find Vanessa anyway and break things off. She didn't go down without a fight, but Kyle Johnson was apparently a lot more stubborn than he let on because he didn't cave. The next day at lunch Vanessa poured a bag of mini hot dog wieners onto Kyle's head and all the upperclassmen called him "Tiny Johnson" for the rest of the week. I felt bad for him, but I still made that $3,000.

Chapter seventeen:
"Intuition"

The following day was Friday so I got permission from my parents to stay out late with Laura at the library after school. So while everyone else was either at practice or pregaming for a party, the two of us were scrawling conspiracy webs on whiteboards and devouring Doritos.

"Hey," I snapped suddenly with a mouthful. "Ummm…Vanessa and Kyle broke up. Organic or Phantom?"

"They broke up?" she spun on me mid-pace and her eyes darted back and forth. "When?"

"Yesterday. Organic or Phantom?"

"How'd you find out?"

"Did you not see her pour that bag of tiny wieners on him at lunch?" I asked.

She shrugged. "I must've been in the bathroom when that happened."

You might be wondering why I would volunteer this info. Wasn't I risking getting caught? Maybe. But it was also a good way of testing how good I was at hiding and how good she was at finding me.

She narrowed her eyes then started skipping across the room and whistling the Inspector Gadget theme song.

"That's a good one…" She stopped all of a sudden and gripped the back of a chair. "I need to focus…uhhhh." She took a deep breath then shook the chair. "Ok, I'm gonna teach you a game to help me focus."

"What?" I asked.

"I'm gonna teach you a game to help me focus," she repeated. "I focus better when I'm multitasking so I'm gonna teach you a mental game so I can focus."

It took me a second to process what she was saying, but it suddenly made sense. She needed her brain to be busy with multiple problems at once in order for her to focus better. That was why she was always doing something extra whenever we met like juggling, or pacing, or doodling. And it was probably why she was so good at beating three people in chess at a time.

"Alright," I said. "What's the game?"

"I call it 'funky monkey,'" she replied. "I'm thinking of two words that rhyme, but aren't associated with each other. So I'll give you two words that don't rhyme and each of those words go with each of the two words that do rhyme. You get it?"

"Got it."

"So if I say 'smelly chimp', you say…"

"Funky monkey," I said with a grin.

"Exactly," she clapped. "Smelly goes with funky, chimp goes with monkey, and they both rhyme." Then she started running in place like she was trying to get rid of this mental energy rising up inside her. "Hit me."

"Uhhhh…" I scratched my chin for a second then snapped. "Female globe."

"Girl world," she said immediately. "C'mon, Nick. Do better."

My jaw dropped. That was fast. "Okay…um…useless money."

She paused for exactly one second. "Broken token."

"What?!" I cried. "How did you—"

"Are you even trying, Nick?" she said, pacing again. "C'mon, hit me!"

I drummed my fingers against the table as I tried to come up with one that would stump her. I was lowkey excited and nervous at the same time. On the one hand, this was actually a really fun game and I couldn't wait to teach it to Fabi. I was also intrigued to see how quickly Laura could figure out a really tough one. But on the other hand, if I did give her a tough one, it was going to help her focus and possibly be able to figure out that I had just struck again. Either way, I would know just how smart Laura Wood really was and what to watch out for in my next assignment.

"Tiny paper," I finally said.

She turned to me, pursed her lips, then said, "…little…tittle?"

I laughed. "No."

She smiled then went back to pacing. She mumbled to herself as she went along, stopping every so often to write on the whiteboard or draw another arrow connecting something. She'd stop and snap at me randomly then mutter to herself and go back to pacing. All the while I sat there watching her, mesmerized by the whole process. Finally, after almost exactly two minutes, she stopped with her back to me and let out a deep sigh.

"In the case of Vanessa Diamond and Kyle Johnson," she said, folding her arms behind her. "I find the Phantom…guilty."

I swallowed. "How do you know?"

"I'm not one-hundred percent certain yet," she admitted. "I'll have to interview them both on Monday. But from what I know about Vanessa's track record, she's almost undefeated. And I can't think of any reason why a sophomore like Kyle Johnson would all of a sudden break things off with her out of nowhere."

I lowered my head, simultaneously impressed and disappointed.

"Oh and by the way," she said, looking at me over her shoulder. "Particle article."

Chapter eighteen:
"Hollaback Girl"

On Monday, I met Lance at his locker and we caught up on anime and shows.

"*Smallville* has been getting really good," Lance was saying. "We already saw Flash and Cyborg and now Green Arrow is on. I bet you they're gonna have the whole justice league by next season."

I shook my head. "I dunno, man. They've been moving real slow. Lois came two seasons ago and her and Clark still haven't even started dating yet. It's been two seasons of the friend zone. What are they waiting for?"

Lance was about to counter with something when suddenly we heard some murmuring down the hall. When we looked, we saw students pointing and laughing as they walked past Vanessa Diamond's locker. There was a tiny pink onesie taped to the locker door and above it in big red paint were the words: MOTHER SLUT.

Vanessa finally arrived and froze when she saw the onesie and the words. There was a sudden hush as everyone watched her, but then some kids started whispering.

"What a slut."

"She's such a whore."

"It's a girl!"

Billy, Gary, and Dean walked past her hollering at the tops of their lungs and Billy grabbed his crotch seductively as he made kissy faces at her.

Vanessa was still standing at her locker and hadn't moved. I couldn't see if she was smiling, crying, or straight-faced. But she eventually ripped the onesie off then marched past before stuffing it in a trash can as the hall erupted in a mix of boos and laughter. I swallowed uncomfortably as I watched her go. These kids were ruthless. And this nonsense was nothing new. But this time it was kind of my fault. But was it, though? I didn't tell Kyle to think she was pregnant. He assumed that on his own. But did Kyle spread this rumor? It was hard to imagine him doing that.

"Well, I guess it's a good thing you said no to her," Lance whispered to me.

I winced. I knew he meant well. But it just made me feel worse.

That night I got a call from a mother.

"Is this…Nick?" the voice said.

"Yes it is," I replied.

"I got your number from…" the woman paused for a second as if she was debating whether or not to reveal this. "…from Serena Gibson."

"I know," I said coolly. "What can I help you with?"

"My name is…Valorie Diamond."

I raised an eyebrow. This was interesting. "Vanessa's Mom?"

"Yes," she answered softly. "I need your help with something."

"Okay," I said as I shifted to the edge of my bed. Had she found out what I'd done? Was she angry? Was she going to report me? Press charges?

"There's a rumor," she explained. "That my daughter is pregnant."

I tightened my fist around the phone, waiting for the shoe to drop.

"It's not true," she went on, her voice shaking softly. "I know it's not true. It can't be. We did multiple pregnancy tests."

There was a short silence.

"These kids are so mean," she said softly.

Another silence.

"But I know who started the rumor," she said. "And I know it's the same girl who spray painted that ugly word on her locker." She sniffled. "Angie Clarkson."

I shut my eyes and breathed a sigh of relief. This wasn't about me. I was in the clear. I felt kinda bad about it, but still, it was relieving to know she hadn't traced this all back to me. Plus, Angie Clarkson was another typical spoiled Hamilton brat. She was a Cartesian, a straight A student, and rumor had it that she'd gotten accepted into every Ivy League school. But she spent her time gossiping about everyone on campus.

One time when half the cheer squad got mano, Angie convinced everyone that I had cast a spell on the girls. It was insane how many people believed her and the teachers even searched my locker for voodoo dolls for a week. Another time she started a rumor that a girl was sleeping with Coach Hayes, the P.E. teacher. Not only did Coach Hayes get fired, but the girl had a mental breakdown and had to be admitted into a psych ward. And Angie just carried on like nothing had happened. So it wasn't a surprise that she had sniffed out this rumor and sent it spreading through Hamilton faster than Vanessa's STD's.

I waited for a few seconds as Mrs. Diamond went silent. Then I finally asked, "So what do you want me to do?"

Mrs. Diamond took a deep breath then said, "I want you to make Angie pay for that rumor."

"What do you have in mind?"

Mrs. Diamond cleared her throat before answering. "Angie has a secret. And I want you to expose it."

I raised my eyebrow at that. A secret? This was interesting. "What's the secret?"

"She cheated her way through her junior year."

My jaw dropped. There was no way.

"How do you know this?" I asked her.

"I have proof. I can tell you how to get it and you can use it to expose her."

My mind was flipping as it connected the dots. If Angie had really cheated then that meant her acceptance into all those schools was based on lies. If I exposed this, she'd most definitely lose all of that. I didn't *really* feel bad because like I said this was Angie Clarkson, the same girl who happily ruined a teacher's career and a girl's mental health. But I wanted to be sure Mrs. Diamond understood.

"Don't you think this is a little overboard?" I asked. "This could ruin her chances of getting into a good college. Or into any college at all."

"She deserves it," Mrs. Diamond spat. "She ruined my daughter's reputation with a lie. It's only fair that I ruin hers with the truth."

That was an interesting take.

"I'll pay you $4,000," Mrs. Diamond eventually announced.

Holy crap.

I was silent for a few more seconds as I thought this over. Even though, like I said, I didn't feel too bad about exposing Angie, the fact that this was so close to what I'd done to Laura made me a little uneasy. I'd already ruined one girl's academic career. Could I really do it again? But then I realized something. Angie had spent all of high school ruining people's social lives with gossip and no one had ever been able to get any dirt on her. And all the while she had this intellectual skeleton in her closet. This wasn't just revenge. This would be justice.

So I nodded and replied, "Deal."

Chapter nineteen:
"Tearin' Up My Heart"

"What've we got today?" Laura asked me once I sat down at lunch. She was twirling her pencil through her fingers like a propeller while popping skittles into her mouth. We were in the caf this time and not the library—the downside of the library meetings was that we couldn't eat there. So whenever we were really hungry we'd opt to just stay in the caf.

I shrugged as I started opening up my bag.

"I talked with Vanessa," Laura explained without looking up at me. "She's not pregnant. But somehow Kyle is convinced that she is and she doesn't know how or why. So I was right. The Phantom was behind it—and he might be better than we thought."

I took a sip of my water bottle then nodded. "Yeah. This guy's good."

We talked a little for a few more minutes, theorizing how the Phantom had managed to start the rumor about Vanessa, what he would gain from it, and who we thought could be next. Then, out of nowhere, Laura suddenly got deep.

"Why do you think he's doing this?" she asked me. "Like, what's his philosophy?"

"I don't know. Maybe he's just tired of this school. He probably doesn't like anyone and thinks everybody here is a bunch of self-absorbed, snotty rich kids."

She squinted at me and stopped twirling her pencil for a moment. Then she leaned back and resumed twirling. "Well, if that's the case, I think he's wrong."

"Why?"

"I know these kids aren't…the best," she admitted. "But deep down, I think everyone's basically good. We just get taught to be bad by our friends, family or society."

I sucked my teeth, not able to keep the Haitian from coming out.

"That doesn't make sense," I countered. "Society's made up of individuals. So if society's bad it's because individuals are bad. That's like saying your body's sick, but your body parts are healthy. I think everybody's basically bad and we have to be taught–by our friends, family, society or church–how to be good."

She scoffed then leaned forward in her seat. She had a fierce look in her eyes like I was at bat and she was getting ready to send a blazing fastball my way.

"That's pretty grim, Nicholas," she said.

"Well, it's life, Laura. What do you think, everyone's born with a halo on their head?"

"Not necessarily," she smirked. "But I don't think they're little demons either. Take Billy for example." She nodded across the caf and I glanced at the football players where Billy was giving one of the Cartesians a noogie. "He's been bullying you since freshman year. But you don't know what he's been through. You don't know what he's got going on at home. Every bully is just a wounded kid."

I shook my head. "That's cute. But look at the whole school. You told everybody that there's a Phantom. And instead of working together to find this common enemy, they start fighting each other. Because deep down we're inherently selfish."

Laura raised an eyebrow, but was grinning mischievously at me. "Who hurt you, Nick?"

"Nobody hurt me. I'm just being realistic."

"I think life makes more sense when you assume the best of everyone."

"Well, Mark Twain said life makes more sense when we remember that we're all mad."

Her eyes flew open at the quote and she bit her lip before covering it with her fist. "You know Mark Twain?"

"Not personally," I replied. "But I've read him."

"Well," she replied, pulling a strand of hair back behind her ear. "Mark Twain also said that the best way to cheer yourself up is to cheer someone else up. And it sounds to me like your outlook on life needs some cheering up."

"We can agree to disagree," I said. "You think everyone's born good. I think everyone's born bad."

"What about me?" She leaned forward across the table. "Do you think I'm bad?"

I don't know what came over me. Maybe the momentum of the debate injected some confidence in me. But without thinking, I leaned in too, looked her up and down, and said, "Yeah, I think you're *bad*."

Her eyebrows went up and her cheeks flushed. It was the first time I'd ever seen Laura Wood genuinely surprised. She sat back then popped a skittle into her mouth as she looked away and grinned sheepishly.

Smooth, my friend, I thought to myself. But as much as I wanted to relish in my game, I realized my mistake. I wasn't supposed to let her know that I liked her. Fabi's warning came ringing like an alarm in my head again. I couldn't be with Laura—not just because of my parents, but because of my secret. I had ruined her chance of being valedictorian and she was hunting down the Phantom, not realizing that I was the Phantom. But I couldn't get her flustered, blushing face out of my mind. That had been the cutest expression I'd ever seen on her and I wanted to see more of it. It was making my stomach swell with butterflies just remembering it.

I was so swept away by what had happened that I completely forgot about my deal with Mrs. Diamond. Days later, Laura and I kept meeting up as usual, but little by little, Laura started texting me and even calling me—but only after 9 p.m. because that's when everyone had free minutes back then. And these texts and calls started becoming less and less about the Phantom and more and more about random stuff like Mark Twain, Disney movies, and anime. And the more we talked the more I liked her. But the more I liked her the more I hated myself because I wanted to come clean and confess to her, but I couldn't. It was like a love story between fire and water and it was tearing up my heart. And then one night, she messaged me on facebook and said: "This has been really cool. I've never met somebody like you that I could match wits with like this. I just want you to know that I think…"

And my entire world froze to a stop when I read the last three words.

"…I like you."

Chapter twenty:
"Things I'll Never Say"

It took me a whole three minutes to finally respond. During which, Laura hit me with two "?'s" and a "you still there?" Then I finally typed, "Can I call you?"

She said yes and I took another two minutes to dial her number, my fingers shaking nervously. I knew what I wanted to say and I wanted to hear her voice instead of just hiding behind the screen. But that also made it scarier. But hearing her would make it better. I was confused. I just wanted to get this out.

"Hey," she said when she picked up.

"Sorry," I apologized. "I just didn't feel like responding over messaging…"

"No, sure whatever…"

I paused for another five seconds, squeezing my nose between my thumb and forefinger. I finally took a deep breath and said, "I'm not allowed to date."

"What?"

"I'm not…allowed to date. My parents won't let me."

She chuckled. "Are you serious?"

"Yes. My parents are super strict when it comes to stuff like this."

"Wow," she laughed. "But you're about to be eighteen. You're basically an adult."

"Yeah, but I'm still Haitian."

"What does that have to do with anything?"

I slammed my hand against my face. I hated explaining this to people. This was why I didn't talk about it. Our cultures were so fundamentally different—at least when it came to stuff like parents. The dialogue was always the same: "But you're–insert age." "Yes, but I'm also Haitian." "Why does that matter?" And round and round we went.

"I'm just not allowed, Laura," I sighed.

"That's lame," she scoffed.

I didn't say anything for a while and then it hit me that this all probably sounded like an excuse. I should probably tell her that I actually did like her. And I was about to when I thought, "Then what?" She said she liked me then I'd say I liked her. But there was nothing we could do about it but sit in a romantic tension that ultimately went nowhere. Not to mention Fabi's warning—I couldn't let Laura know that I liked her. If I let my guard down, I could slip up and she could find out I was the Phantom. So I settled for an awkward silence instead.

"I don't want you to think I'm making this up," I finally said. "Cuz I'm not."

"I believe you," she answered. "I still think it's lame. But I believe you."

Another silence and I shut my eyes as I breathed several sighs of relief. My heart was still pounding in my chest, though. Laura Wood—my secret crush for the past four years–had just told me she liked me. This was wild. This was absolutely wild. Even though we couldn't date and even though she didn't know I liked her too, this was the next best thing. Now I just had to hope that she didn't come out and ask me if I liked her back.

"Well, if you like someone…" she eventually added, as if she was waiting for me to cut in. My heart caught in my throat for a second then she said, "…you don't have to tell your parents. It can be our little secret."

I laughed at how ridiculous the thought was. I didn't go behind my parents' back. Now don't get me wrong, I wasn't a prude goodie-too-shoes. I just didn't go out of my way to disobey them. I mean, I was out here getting paid by Moms to sabotage kids' social lives. But in my defense, my parents never explicitly told me not to do that. So technically, I wasn't disobeying them. I know. My morals were all kinds of messed up.

"I can't do that," I replied. "I just can't."

She sighed. "That's a shame, Funky Monkey. You'd make a really good boyfriend. For whoever you do like."

"Is that your nickname for me?"

"Yeah. It's my favorite game. You're my favorite guy. I think it fits."

My stomach flipped. I was her favorite guy. I couldn't take it. This was too much. I was overwhelmed. I had a nickname!

"Cool," I said, conveying much more calm than I was actually feeling. "I'll call you…um…Princess Jasmine." I immediately regretted it. That was so stupid.

She giggled again. "*Aladdin*'s my favorite Disney movie!"

"Mine too!" A wave of relief rolled through me.

"So maybe I should call you Abu instead of Funky Monkey."

We both laughed. And on and on we went, talking into the night about nothing and everything. Until eventually, my mother knocked on my door and let me know it was too late to be talking on the phone. So we hung up. But I couldn't sleep, knowing that I had to be the luckiest boy alive.

Chapter twenty-one:
"Breakaway"

The next night at dinner, I decided that I'd ask my parents the question that had kept me up all night.

My mother had made white rice and *sauce pwa* with some *legume* and of course fried plantains. My parents were talking about how great things were going at the bakery and how grateful they were for the money Fabi and I had been bringing in. So I figured this was the perfect time to bring it up.

"Um…" I cleared my throat. "Mom? Dad? I have a question…"

Fabi looked up at me silently from her seat.

I cleared my throat again as I picked at my rice. "There's a girl at school that I've become friends with."

"Oh yeah?" my mother smiled. "That's nice. Another friend? Good for you."

"What's her name?" my father asked.

"Laura," I replied, looking up briefly. "She's really cool. She's on the chess team. She plays softball. She's really smart. And she's a really good friend."

Fabi narrowed her eyes at me and the look in them said, "Don't you dare do it."

"Well, that's good," my mother nodded. "You should invite her over sometime."

"Yeah…" I said slowly. "I'd like that. But also…"

Fabi tightened her lips and I could tell she was winding up her foot to kick me under the table.

"…also…" I continued. I was about to tell them that I liked Laura, but a realization suddenly hit my mind like a wrecking ball. See, remember how we actually speak Kreyol at home and I'm just translating for you? So in Kreyol, the word for "like" and "love" are the same exact thing. If I told my parents that I liked Laura, they would literally hear that I loved her.

I cleared my throat again. "She's really smart and really pretty. And she told me that…well…"

My father titled his head forward and raised his eyebrows, patiently waiting for me to just spit it out.

"Can I have a girlfriend?" I finally blurted.

Fabi dropped her fork and sighed.

My parents looked at each other.

"Come on, Nick," my father said. "You know the rules."

"I know," I said. "I know. But she's so cool. And she told me that she…" I cleared my throat once again. "…she told me that she wanted to be my girlfriend too. And I really want her to."

"You know the rules," my mother reiterated. "No dating. The three L's. *Legliz—*"

"*Lekole. Lakaye,*" I finished. "I know, I know."

"You have to focus on school," my mother continued. "School and love are like matches and gasoline. They don't go together."

I rolled my eyes. They were always so dramatic.

"Do you love her?" my Dad asked.

"Well…I…uh…" I stuttered. "I…I like her."

"You love her?" my mother almost shrieked. "You can't even spell love."

"No," I said. "I like her, like her. Not love her like her."

"So you love her?" my mother added.

"No. I like her."

"You love her."

"Like her."

"You're gonna marry her?"

"No," I groaned. "Just…"

Fabi snickered. She was enjoying this.

"Is she Haitian?" my mother asked me.

Here we go. "No."

"Is she black?" asked my father.

"No," I told them. "She's white."

"Oh-oh!" my parents said at the same time.

"What did you think? I'm the only black person at Hamilton. What else would she be?"

My mother sucked her teeth. "How are you gonna marry a white girl? You want me to stick together the two English words I know to talk to her?"

"Nobody said anything about marriage."

"That's gonna be my only daughter-in-law and I won't even be able to talk to her."

"She's…" I sighed. This was exhausting. "She's not your daughter-in-law. And besides, she speaks French."

"Didn't you just say everyone there is racist?" my father pointed at me. "And now you're trying to put yourself into one of those families?"

"She's not like the rest of them," I argued. "They're not like—I'm not marrying her!"

"But you love her," Fabi said.

"You're not helping!"

"Love and school don't mix," my mother reminded me.

And now was the time that they'd launch into some story about someone they knew who's life was ruined because they dated in school.

"Remember Sister Nancy?" my mother started. "Her son started dating when he was twelve and his girlfriend went to jail."

"That's because his girlfriend was his teacher," I reminded them. They always went for the extreme examples.

"Or Brother Carl's daughter?" my father chimed in. "She got pregnant and had to drop out of school."

"Or Sister Baptiste's son?" my mother went on. "He started dating and got herpes and AIDS and all the other ones."

I pinched the bridge of my nose as they kept rattling off all the outlier horror stories.

"Not everyone who dates has sex," I tried to explain. "I just want to have a girlfriend. That's it. I wouldn't be doing anything with her."

There was a long silence as they watched me closely. I let the silence play out a little longer as I got ready to play my trump card. Somehow Fabi saw it coming and kicked me under the table. But I ignored her.

"Plus…" I started. "I thought that maybe you'd know I was responsible since I've been…helping with the down payment."

My parents stopped chewing at the same time and Fabi stabbed her fork into her plantain while locking eyes with me. My parents looked at each other briefly then slowly leaned back in their seats.

"First of all, Nicholas," my mother said. "That was uncalled for."

"I'm sorry," I said quickly. "I'm not trying to bribe you. I just…I just want you to know that I'm different from all those other kids. You've taught me well. I'm not gonna make stupid choices like them. I'm responsible."

"You are responsible," my mother agreed. "And we really appreciate your help. We really do." Then she looked at my father before turning back to me. "We just don't think you're ready yet."

I sighed and lowered my head. Even without looking, I could tell Fabi was smirking.

"But…" my mother said and I looked up. "I'll tell you what. You can start dating when you're eighteen."

"Are you serious?!" Fabi cried. "Eighteen?! I still can't date and I'm twenty!"

"Fabi," my father said, raising his hand to calm her down. "Why are you yelling?"

"You told me I had to get a bachelor's before I get a bachelor," Fabi snapped. "And now you're letting him get a girlfriend before he even graduates high school? His birthday is in four months!"

"Your mother has a point, Fabi," my father explained.

"What point? That he's responsible? I'm responsible too! I have a job. I have a car. I have a 3.7 GPA. I've never done anything wrong, but I still can't date. You treat me like a baby because I'm a girl."

"Fabi," my father said. "You know we just want to protect you."

But Fabi wasn't having it. She threw her napkin onto her plate then stormed out of her seat. She was halfway out the living room before she stopped abruptly with her back turned to us and her fists at her sides.

"Can I be excused?" we heard her mutter.

"Yes," my father said.

Then she stomped upstairs to her room.

And I was left there feeling a sickening blend of relief and regret. In a few months I'd be able to date Laura. But in the meantime, I may have just lost my sister.

Chapter twenty-two:
"Love Will Find a Way"

The next day Fabi still dropped me off at school, but it was a silent car ride. She didn't even turn on the radio. Just twenty minutes of stinging, suffocating, sullen silence. She hadn't said a word to me or anyone since dinner last night. On the one hand I thought she was being a little dramatic. All I had done was ask to start dating and my parents had said in a few months. It wasn't like they'd said, "Oh sure! We'll pay for the wedding right now!" You would've thought I had burned her favorite dress or something.

But on the other hand I did get it. Fabi had spent her whole life working twice as hard as me to get half the things I had. She didn't get her own room until she was thirteen while I got mine when I was ten. She had never been allowed to even go over any of her friends' houses growing up, but last year I slept over Lance's house for the first time. My parents had even bribed her with a brand new car to have her live at home while in college, but we all knew that they were probably gonna let me live on campus. Every time I got something she never had it ate away at her. And now I was gonna have a girlfriend years before she'd ever been allowed. I felt bad. Did she have her eye on someone? Was there a guy at Rutgers she liked? Or at work? I wanted to ask her, but with her eyes drilling into the windshield and her hands gripping the steering wheel like a vice, it was obvious now was not the time.

When she pulled into the parking lot, I got out then turned back to her before shutting the door.

"I'm really sorry, Fabi," I said. "I didn't mean to—"

But she drove off before I could even finish.

I texted Laura during homeroom that I couldn't meet up today. And afterwards I realized it was horrendous timing because now she definitely thought I didn't like her. But she said that she needed to catch up on AP Calc anyway and I wasn't sure if she was lying or not. Either way, Lance was excited to see me at lunch.

"Welcome back," he said as I sat down.

"Thanks," I sighed.

He studied my face and frowned. "What's the matter?"

Then it hit me that in the hurricane of ups and downs between yesterday and today I'd never even called or texted Lance about any of it.

"Oh!" I said suddenly. Then I looked around to make sure Laura wasn't nearby. "Laura said she likes me."

"What?!" Lance cried. "No way! Way to go, man!" He dapped me up over and over again. "That's awesome! So wait…why are you so down?"

"That's the thing…" I started. "I asked my parents if I could date her…"

He rolled his eyes. "Here we go again."

"It's not what you think," I stopped him. "They said I could date her when I turn eighteen. Which is in May."

"Wow," he raised his eyebrows. "They changed the rules for you. Sweet."

"Yeah," I looked away. "But my sister wasn't happy about it. She's three years older than me and they still won't let her date. So…now I'm pretty sure she hates me."

Lance made a face like he'd just smelled a dirty diaper. "Your sister is twenty and she's still doing what your parents tell her? She's an adult!"

I rubbed my forehead in frustration. "We've been through this before, Lance. There's no such thing as being an adult when you're Haitian. The point is that my sister's really mad at me and now I feel like I have to choose between her and the girl I like."

Lance scoffed. "Sounds like Laura's making you choose between her and a lot of people."

I shrugged weakly. "See? That's the point. I don't want to have to choose. Why can't I have a girlfriend *and* a best friend *and* a sister? Why is this even a big deal?" I buried my face in my hands. The worst part about this was that the only reason all of this was even happening was because I was the Phantom. And the only person I could talk to about all of it was the one person who didn't want to talk to me right now. Not to mention that I didn't think I could even keep being the Phantom without Fabi's help.

That afternoon Fabi picked me up and we drove in silence again. I made it ten minutes in before I couldn't take it anymore.

"I'm sorry, Fabi!" I blurted as I turned to her in my seat. "I shouldn't have done that last night. That was a super privileged little brother thing to do and it wasn't fair. I was being selfish."

She didn't take her eyes off the road.

"I really, really like Laura," I went on. "And I've had a crush on her for four years. But you've been my sister my whole life. And if I had to choose between her and you…" I paused and took a deep breath. "I'd choose you. I like Laura, but I love you."

"Don't make it weird, Nick," she smirked as she stopped at a red light.

I smiled and felt my chest lighten like I'd been holding my breath. That was the first thing she'd said to me in almost a day.

"I'm fine," she added. "I just needed some time to be dramatic about it. This is all a part of being in a traditional, patriarchal culture. You're always gonna get treated better than me because you're the youngest and you're a boy. And there's nothing I can do about that until I graduate and move out. So I just suck it up for now. But that doesn't mean I'm gonna hate you for it."

I smiled. I would've hugged her if we weren't in the car.

"Besides," she went on. "You know good and well you wouldn't be able to be the Phantom without me."

"I know!" I shouted. "I was stressing all day about that!"

We both laughed as the light turned green.

"Also," she said as she started to drive. "You don't ever have to pick between me and a girl. You don't always get the chance to be with the person you love. But I'll always be your sister."

I smiled and pretended I was about to hug her.

"Don't touch me, *frekan*," she snapped.

"Love you too," I said.

"Whatever."

"Just say it back once."

"No."

"Please???"

"If you don't–"

Suddenly my phone rang.

"Hello?" I answered.

"Nicholas." It was Mrs. Diamond. "Have you done the thing yet?"

My jaw dropped in shock. This whole time I had forgotten about everything. I banged my head on the glove compartment and almost made Fabi swerve. How long had it been? I'd let myself get swept up in my feelings for Laura and the drama with Fabi that I'd almost let this slip away.

"I'm so sorry, Mrs. Diamond," I said quickly. "I just got caught up with some things. But don't worry. I'm gonna do it." Then I looked at Fabi and she winked. "I'll get it done tonight."

Chapter twenty-three:
"Cry Me a River"

Now that Fabi and I were back on good terms, I could get back to Mrs.
Diamond's mission. Angie Clarkson had confessed to cheating in a therapy
session earlier this year. Mrs. Diamond didn't tell me how she knew that and I
didn't ask. But this was 2006, when everyone—students, teachers, and school
therapists—still kept hard copies of their notes. All I had to do was get my
hands on the file containing Angie's confession, take a picture of it with
Fabi's camera, then get out. I chose to do this on a Friday night during a
home swim meet so not only would the school be empty, but it wouldn't be
all that suspicious to see a student on campus. But regardless, I couldn't risk
being seen so I'd come up with my own disguise: an all black hoodie, black
cargo pants, black boots, black leather gloves, and a white skull mask. It was
the middle of January so all of this doubled as not just a disguise, but kept me
warm too. Not only that, but my usually red backpack was reversible and the
inside was black so I'd turned it inside out and packed an extra set of clothes
just in case. It was my very own Phantom suit.

Fabi parked in the back parking lot of the school and I slipped out and
jogged to the rear entrance. The building would be locked, but there was a
window in the teacher's lounge that was always loose. Students would use it
to sneak in after dark to hook up in the locker rooms, smoke in the
bathrooms, or steal test answers from teachers' offices. I slipped inside then
made my way out of the lounge and into the halls and immediately realized
something was wrong. I had fully expected the halls to be dark. But instead
they were blazing bright like it was the middle of the day. Then I heard voices
around the corner and I slipped back into the teacher's lounge. What was
going on?

I waited behind the door and peered through the narrow window as three
girls walked past laughing. Why was the building still open? And then it hit
me how stupid I was—the meet. They left the building open because the
teams were using the locker rooms and so that everyone else could still use
the bathrooms.

Frick.

Now I had a decision to make. If someone saw me sneaking around these
halls with my Phantom outfit on it'd definitely look suspicious. But if

someone saw me leaving Mrs. Porter's office in regular clothes that'd be just as suspicious. What should I do?

I thought about it for a second and reasoned it'd be better to not waste more time changing outfits and to just get this done as soon as possible. So I peeked out of the lounge, made sure the coast was clear, then headed into the hall. I climbed to the fourth floor and made it to Mrs. Porter's office with no incident. I got to her door and pulled out one of Fabi's old debit cards and used it to jimmy the lock loose. It was one of those old doors where this trick actually worked and it took me literally three seconds to get in. Once in, I left the lights off and used a flashlight to navigate her office. I raked through the files in her filing cabinet and was grateful for how organized she was—everything was labeled and in alphabetical order. It took me a minute to find "Clarkson" and I yanked the file out. It was about as slim as a comic book so I guessed she had just started sessions this year. I flipped through the pages and skimmed them, glancing over my shoulder every few seconds to make sure no one was looking in.

I saw a bunch of irrelevant stuff like her break up with Adrian Robinson, her parents' divorce, her sister's eating disorder, and it suddenly dawned on me how very illegal this probably was. I had to get that confession and get out of there fast. I kept flipping and finally came across a line that said, "Feels guilt over cheating." My heart skipped a beat and I stopped flipping as I read more. "Confessed to obtaining answers to exams of every class junior year." Jackpot.

Angie's full name was at the top left hand corner of the file so a picture of this entire page was all I'd need as evidence. I put the file down on Mrs. Porter's desk then held Fabi's camera over it. I took the picture, but nothing happened. I pressed the button again and nothing happened again. I turned the camera over and over in my hands and a bolt of panic shot through me like lightning—the battery was dead.

You had to be kidding me.

There was no time to come up with another way of taking a picture so I just snatched the file and put it in my backpack. I'd make a copy and bring the original back. I'd have to break in again, but we'd cross that bridge tomorrow. I put everything back, locked the door behind me, then spun to run down the hall and crashed into someone.

"What in the world…?" a girl said, rubbing her head.

I froze in shock and almost pissed my pants when I saw Laura staring straight back at me.

"What?" she whispered. "Who are you?" She looked over my shoulder at Mrs. Porter's office then back at me. Then at my mask. I saw the calculations working behind her eyes then her face twisted into a scowl. "You're the Phantom."

Then I ran.

Chapter twenty-four:
"He's a Pirate!"

I sprinted down the hall like my life depended on it. I was two steps away from the corner when Laura clipped my legs and dragged me to the floor.

"Who are you?!" she shrieked, reaching for my mask.

We wrestled like animals and I gripped her wrists as I fought to keep her hands away from my face. But she was surprisingly strong. But I finally managed to flip her onto her stomach and pulled the bottom of her sweater over the front of her head like a massive wedgie. She was *not* happy about that.

But the time it took her to squirm and flop trying to free her head was enough for me to round the corner and escape. There was no way I could outrun her for long. Not in this outfit. Sooner or later someone would see me and if I hopped into Fabi's car everyone would know it was me. I had to change ASAP. But there's a phrase in Kreyol that goes, "When you're running from rain, you can fall into a basin." The idea is that sometimes while trying to avoid one problem you run into a bigger one. Little did I know that Laura was the rain.

I bust into the stairwell and swung over the railing onto the lower steps. I repeated this for all four floors, threading my way over each railing in a graceful parkour descent before I heard Laura bust through the door at the top. But I was already running through the door into the basement. I dragged the couch nearby and blocked the door—it wasn't super heavy, but it was heavy enough to buy me more time while Laura would be trying to push the door against it. Then I sprinted into the boys locker room and bent over my knees, out of breath from the parkour and the panic. I yanked my mask off and opened my backpack ready for the fastest outfit change in history.

"Nick?"

I looked up and Lance was staring at me on the other side of the room. The basin.

At first he just seemed confused as he kept wiping his hands with paper towels.

"I can explain," I started to say.

"Why are you dressed like that?" he asked, half chuckling.

"I know you're down here, Phantom!" Laura screamed outside. There was a loud thud as she kept banging the door against the couch.

And that's when Lance's expression changed. I saw the same calculations play across his face that I'd seen on Laura's and he pointed at my mask then at the door I'd just run through.

"You're the Phantom?" he whispered.

"I don't have time to explain," I said quickly, already changing. "Please don't say anything." I ripped my clothes off like they were on fire then started pulling on my regular outfit.

"This whole time," Lance said softly. "It was you? How could you be–"

I reversed my backpack and stuffed everything inside just as Laura crashed into the locker room.

"Whoa!" I shouted. "Why do people keep running through here?"

She blinked several times at us then shook her head quickly. "Wait. Someone came through here?"

"Yeah," I nodded. "This kid in a mask. He ran out the back entrance." I pointed behind me.

"Nick!" Laura cried, her eyes wide. "That was the Phantom!"

"Are you serious?!" I shouted back.

"C'mon!" She rushed past me and sprinted out the back entrance and I jogged after her.

I stopped at the door and looked back over at Lance who was staring at me with the worst look of betrayal on his face.

"Please," I mouthed to him.

Before he could respond, Waldo the Weirdo walked into the locker room drinking a soda. He looked back and forth at us then said sheepishly, "Gotcha?"

"Get out," I growled at him and he turned and left. I looked at Lance frowning at me then slipped outside after Laura.

Chapter twenty-five:
"Just Missed the Train"

The back entrance of the boys locker room led directly to the tennis courts, which were wide open with nowhere to hide. But beyond them were the woods, cloaked in thick shadows underneath a blazing white moon.

"Where'd he go?" Laura asked, spinning every direction for the Phantom.

I pretended to look too and put on my best look of confusion. There was literally nowhere else to go but the tennis courts or the woods. "There's no way."

Laura stopped and stared straight ahead. "He must be in the woods. Let's go."

"Uhhh…" I grabbed her arm before she could run off. "I don't know if you noticed, but I'm black. I don't mess with woods—especially not at night."

She yanked her arm away from me. "You're scared of some trees?"

"I'm scared of crazy white people stuff in the woods after dark!" I countered. "I dunno what this kid is into! We could be walking into some weird death cult and I end up on a milk carton. If you wanna go after him by yourself, go ahead."

She turned to the woods and for a second I wondered if she was actually gonna take the challenge. But then she sighed and walked back to the building. She leaned against the brick wall then slid down to the ground and rested her hands on her knees.

"I was so close," she said as I sat down next to her. She sighed and her breath came out in a cold puff. "Frick." She shut her eyes for several seconds then opened them and said, "I had him, Nick. I had him pinned. And I was about to rip his mask off and he gave me a…a…a sweater wedgie."

I swallowed to keep myself from laughing. "A what?"

"He pulled my…he…never mind…" She sighed again then kicked her foot out in front of her. "He was fast. Like really fast."

"Yeah?" I couldn't keep myself from grinning this time.

"Yeah. I think he might be on the track team."

I grabbed my chin to force myself from smiling too hard. I had actually thought of doing track several times. But I could never bring myself to play on a team with Hamilton kids. There was enough drama outside of the locker room as it was. Never needed to add more nonsense to my life. But yeah, I was fast and I knew it.

Laura was staring at the edge of the woods with a weird look in her eyes. She was lifting her chin slightly like she was making some kind of promise to herself, but there was a slight grin curling its way at the corners of her mouth. It was like she was caught between being determined and being impressed.

"Whoever he is," she finally said. "He's good. He's really good."

Chapter twenty-six:
"Bad Day"

"We have a problem," I told Fabi when we got home that night. I had told her about Laura almost catching me on the drive over. But I had left out the part about Lance. I was still shaking from the adrenaline, but wasn't sure now if it was from the dread building up.

"How big of a problem?" she asked me.

I sat down at the edge of her bed as she leaned against her desk and folded her arms.

"Lance knows I'm the Phantom," I sighed.

Her eyes went wide as she came off the desk. "What? How?"

"Well, I was running from Laura," I started. "I went into the locker room to change and…Lance saw me take off my mask,"

Fabi slapped her palm to her face. "*Ket.*"

I ran my hands over my head then plopped back onto the bed.

"What did you say to him?" Fabi asked me.

"I told him not to say anything."

"And…?"

I furrowed my brows as I remembered the scene. "He didn't say anything."

Fabi sighed. "Do you trust him?"

I paused for a second. I did. He was my best friend. We told each other everything. I mean, except for this, of course. But before this, ever since freshman year, we had told each other everything. Girls we liked, dirty jokes we'd heard, stuff we were afraid of. But then again, there was that question I'd asked him earlier this year.

"Do you trust him?" Fabi asked again.

I nodded, but she wasn't convinced.

"How much money do you have right now?" she asked me.

"A couple hundred," I told her.

"Take half and tell him not to say anything."

"You want me to bribe him?" I asked her.

"Yes."

"He won't go for that," I shook my head. And I remembered what he'd said. *I'd rather be poor with a clean conscience than rich with a ruined one.'* "He plays by the books. He's a super rule follower. This is the last thing I should do to make him not talk."

Fabi started pacing in front of me. "So he knows your secret, you don't trust him, and he won't take a bribe."

"I didn't say I don't trust him," I corrected her.

"So you think he'll keep your secret?"

I thought about it for a second. He had kept other secrets in the past. Like my crushes. Or one day I wasn't wearing deodorant. Or the time I farted and he convinced everyone it was him. He'd kept the secrets then. I was able to trust him with those. But could I trust him with this?

"You need to take care of him," Fabi warned me. "Or this is gonna bite us in the butt."

Chapter twenty-seven:
"Mo Money Mo Problems"

I wasn't usually one to brag, but at this point I was starting to feel myself. I'd gotten a few easy clients in between Kyle's Mom and Vanessa's Mom so January was shaping out to be a lot more lucrative than expected. All in all, I had made over $50,000 by now in four months. I was halfway to having all the money for my parents' down payment, I had Fabi's tuition for next semester already covered, and no one had any idea that it was me. Not to mention, I was still on a high from outrunning Laura last night. So even though I looked like the same Nick on the outside, inside I felt like a superhero. I walked through the caf on my way to my usual table with Laura and bumped into Billy and his goons.

"Watch where you goin', Tootise!" Billy shouted, shoving me to the side.

"Don't touch him!" Gary warned. "You might get infected with that Haitian Body Odor!"

The three of them laughed their heads off, but I just ignored them and kept moving. Even they couldn't bring me down today. I looked for Laura, but she wasn't at the table yet. I felt a jolt of pride at remembering how I'd outsmarted her last night and it added to my already skyrocketing confidence. But then I saw Lance and my heart sank to the floor. He looked up at me and the frown on his face felt like a dagger to my chest. How had I forgotten about that? There was no use running from this—I had to deal with it now.

"Hey," I said softly as I sat down in front of him.

He glanced at me once then took a bite of his sandwich. I wondered for a second if he was just gonna give me the silent treatment. But he finished his bite then shook his head at me.

"I can't believe you," he whispered. "You're really him?"

Our table was empty and the nearest table was the chess table and they were all absorbed in their matches. Laura wasn't there either so they were all playing without music. Where was she? I kept my voice barely above a whisper as I responded.

"Yeah. I am. But you gotta understand."

"Understand what?" Lance hissed at me. "You're messing with student's lives, here. You're messing up people's reputations. So that business with

Vanessa's locker? That was you?"

"No," I shook my head. "I didn't do that."

"But everything else? Like…" Then his eyes lit up and his frown got deeper. "Laura. You deleted her paper. You did that to your crush?"

"Shhhhh," I said when his voice started getting louder. "Yes. I did. And I feel terrible about it. But–"

"But what, Nick? What kind of person would do that to someone they like? I can't believe you. This is wrong!"

"Just let me explain," I told him. I couldn't believe we were having this conversation. What was he doing in the bathroom last night, anyway? Why did he have to take a dump right then and there? "I…it's just that…" I took a deep breath as I thought about how much I should tell him. He wouldn't understand unless I told him the whole truth because right now he thought I was just randomly terrorizing our classmates. "A group of Moms is paying me to do this."

He blinked several times. "What?"

"A group of Moms is paying me," I repeated. "And they're paying me a lot of money. Like thousands of dollars."

His frown didn't budge. I don't know why I had expected him to cave after hearing about the money. This was Lance Fairmount we were talking about–if he thought something was wrong, then it was wrong no matter how much you got paid to do it, which was why I wasn't surprised when he made the connection a second later.

"So when you asked me that question a few months ago?" he said. "About doing something wrong if someone paid you $2,000? That's what you were talking about?"

I nodded.

"But it's still wrong," he insisted.

"I know," I nodded. "But this money is helping my parents. I told you there's this stupid investor who's trying to bully them out of their bakery. So I've been giving them this money so they can buy the building themselves and keep the bakery. I'm doing this to help my family, Lance. You gotta understand."

His frown faltered for a little bit and he looked away.

"Nobody's getting seriously hurt anyway," I argued. "And plus…" I looked around at the other tables. "You and I both know most of these kids are trash. I haven't done anything they don't already do to themselves. Like the whole Vanessa thing. That was Angie Clarkson. Or even Vanessa herself–you know how many STD's she's spread through the school. Or all the stuff Billy has done to me and to other kids too. What I'm doing is nothing compared to what they've been doing."

"Is that what you tell yourself?" Lance muttered.

I sighed. I had known this from the start. Lance was a straight arrow–no rules should be broken no matter what. Which meant that his instinct was to snitch on me. But would he? Would he be willing to throw our friendship away for his morals?

"Please," I begged him. "Don't tell anyone. My family needs this."

I saw the struggle play out across his face as he took several deep breaths. Then my phone vibrated and I saw a text from Laura: meet me in the library ASAP.

"Frick," I breathed. What now? I looked up at Lance and he was running his hands through his hair. "I gotta go."

He didn't respond. I grabbed my stuff, but stopped and looked at him one last time. "Please, Lance. I need this."

He looked at me, but didn't say anything and I left without a response. Laura must have made some sort of breakthrough in the investigation she needed me to see. If it was important enough to almost stand me up at lunch it must have been good, which worried me. Did she find out my secret? There was no way. Had Lance told her? I walked into the library still feeling frazzled from that conversation. But when I made it to the section in the back where we would normally meet, the frazzleness morphed into full-on panic.

"There he is!" Laura announced.

She was standing in front of the whiteboard and three other students were sitting at the table: Sarah Gibson, Lisa Peters, and Kyle Johnson.

"I'm sure you already know these guys," she said, waving over everyone's heads. "But one thing they all have in common besides being fellow Hamiltonians is that…"

I finished her sentence before she did. "…they're all Phantom victims."

"That's right," Laura said, clicking her tongue at me.

My mind was racing a mile a minute. I was in a room literally filled with my victims. What in the name of all things sane was going on here?

"So, what is this?" I asked Laura, forcing my voice to stay calm. I kept my eyes fixed on her, like I was scared Sarah and Lisa would somehow be able to see the Phantom on my face if I looked at them.

"After I interviewed them all about what happened to them," Laura explained. "And confirming that the Phantom must have been behind their stories, I figured it'd be a good idea to invite them in to help us find him. You know, since two heads are better than one, why not have five?"

"I still haven't ruled out that you're not the Phantom," Sarah said flatly, crossing her arms over her chest.

"Even though we all know the Phantom is a boy?" Laura countered.

"According to you," Sarah replied. "I know you're jealous of me because I'm the only player who's ever gotten close to beating you. So you ruined my relationship to spite me."

"By that same logic, I could argue that you're the Phantom," Laura said, unamused. "Because you were jealous that I was going to be valedictorian. But I won't because once again I'm 99% sure that the Phantom is a boy."

They went back and forth for a little and the rest of us just sat there like awkward third wheels. Sarah and Laura were in the chess club and were rivals—or at least as close to rivals as you could be with Laura Wood. Sarah was clearly second to Laura in chess and academics so the rivalry was mainly one-sided. But Sarah was super smart regardless.

I glanced at Lisa, who yawned then started braiding her black ponytail. She was a Cartesian and her Dad was a Philosophy professor at Columbia University. Rumor had it that she read Confucius and Plato for fun. So she was also super smart .

Then there was Kyle, who had stood and started tracing his finger across the book bindings on the shelf. Like I said before, he was a nice guy that only a psychopath would ever hurt, but he was also part of the A/V Club. And from what I knew they spent their time after school figuring out ways to hook up their gameboys to projector screens. So again, another super smart kid in the room. But not only that, Kyle was my only victim that I'd actually interacted with face-to-face. If push came to shove he could place me at the scene of the crime and it wouldn't be long before everyone else pieced it all together.

This was not good. It was bad enough trying to stay ahead of one Laura Wood. Now I was gonna have to outsmart a room full of them.

Chapter twenty-eight:
"Hit 'Em Up Style"

"I've got some pretty interesting intel on the Phantom," Laura announced and everyone turned to her. She leaned forward and pressed her palms onto the table. "I saw him last night."

I heard the others murmur around me.

"Wait," said Kyle. "No way. Who is he?"

"He was in disguise," Laura replied. "Had a hoodie and a mask."

"Whoa," Kyle breathed. "Like a…like a vigilante."

"Or a criminal," Lisa muttered.

"Tomato tom-AH-to," Laura said.

"Wait," Sarah cut in. "How do we even know you saw him? You could be making this up to send us on a wild goose chase."

"Nick saw him too," Laura nodded at me.

I nodded back. "I did. Hoodie and the mask and everything. I didn't know it was him, though."

"How'd *you* know it was him?" Sarah grilled Laura. "And not some random kid playing dress up?"

"I caught him sneaking out of Mrs. Porter's office. And when I said he was the Phantom, he ran."

Sarah narrowed her eyes at her, but didn't say anything. It was so crazy to me that she was here, trying to figure out who the Phantom was, when her mother was the one hiring me to be the Phantom. This was some poetic level of wildness.

"From our interaction, I was able to gather some more clues on who he is," Laura went on. "He's definitely a guy–like I said. Just from how strong he was." She must have seen the confused looks on everyone else's faces because she quickly added, "We wrestled a little while he was trying to run away. And he was fast."

"How fast?" Kyle asked. And it was obvious that he was more impressed than anything. I had to force myself to not smile at his fanboying.

"Really fast," Laura answered. "Disappeared-into-the-woods-before-we-got-outside-fast."

"Whoa," Kyle breathed again.

"So he must be an athlete, then," Lisa said.

Laura nodded. "Exactly. None of the basketball or baseball players are good sprinters and the soccer players were watching the meet. So that narrows our search to senior boys who are in AP English and either play football or are on the track team."

That was gonna be a pretty small list. AP classes and varsity sports were almost mutually exclusive groups. Only a handful of kids belonged to both at the same time.

Lisa swiveled in her chair as she thought. "Troy Rogers is on cross country. And he's in AP English."

Laura snapped her fingers at her then turned and wrote TROY ROGERS on the board. "Gimme more."

"Anthony Thompson is a quarterback," Kyle added. "I mean, he's like ALL the way down on the bench, but he's in AP English too."

Laura wrote his name. "Who else?"

"That's it," Sarah scoffed. "Troy Rogers and Anthony Thompson. No one else fits your criteria, Laura."

I scratched my chin. On the one hand, I was impressed because this did seem like a razor sharp process of elimination. I could sit back and watch Laura stalk Troy and Anthony while I kept racking up more victims. But on the other hand, with only two suspects it would take Laura a lot less time to figure out they weren't the real Phantom.

"Do any of these guys have a motive to ruin our lives?" asked Lisa. "I've never even talked to Troy."

"Well, Anthony doesn't get much playing time," I offered. "And Billy was the first victim."

I saw Sarah tense up at his name.

"Maybe he was jealous," I shrugged. "So he targeted Billy."

"That tracks," Laura pointed at me.

"Uh, hello!" Sarah sang. "Billy wasn't the victim. *I* was."

"Possibly," Laura countered. "But you could also argue that Billy was the real target and you were collateral."

"Collateral?!" Sarah gasped. "I was humiliated!"

"And Billy lost his girlfriend."

"And got a new one in two days!" Sarah screeched.

"But you gave him Hell first, didn't you?" Laura winked at her.

Sarah pursed her lips and couldn't resist a sly grin.

"So did my Dad," she added.

I looked at her. I wondered what Mr. Gibson had done to Billy. Had he threatened him? Cursed him out? I would've loved to have been there to see that.

"Even still," Lisa chimed in. "That doesn't explain us. Why would Anthony want to break up my relationship with Mike?"

No one had an answer for that. But I was starting to feel really good about all this again. As long as they were stuck on trying to prove Troy and Anthony guilty, I was good. But then Laura shifted gears and put me on edge all over again.

"I almost forgot!" she cried, spinning to face us. "I was supposed to ask all of you about your takedowns."

"Our what?" Sarah asked.

"How the Phantom targeted each of you," Laura clarified. "I know I interviewed you briefly before inviting you, but I wanna go through it all again to see if we can find any patterns."

The hair on the back of my neck stood up. I wasn't worried about the girls—none of them could possibly trace their events back to me. But if Kyle even whispered a word that he was with me when he overheard Vanessa talking to the nurse, one too many questions and the story would unravel. Plus, Laura had already interviewed Vanessa too so if she probed Kyle enough, she'd find that their stories didn't fully match. I did a quick sweep of the room then ran a mental calculation. Kyle was on my right, Sarah was on my left, and Lisa was next to her.

"That's a great idea," I nodded, leaning forward. "Sarah, you should go first since you were the first victim."

"Thank you for acknowledging it," she said then rolled her eyes at Laura. "I was already a little suspicious that Billy was seeing someone else from the start. But then one day in—"

"Wait," I cut her off. "What made you think he was cheating on you?"

She told us about a bunch of little things Billy did like texting during their dates, picking her up late etc. then went back to her story. I kept asking follow up questions every so often to keep her talking as long as possible until ten minutes later she was done. The whole time, Laura took frantic notes on the board. Then we moved on to Lisa and I patiently probed her with questions. She was less of a talker than Sarah so it took a little more to draw things out of her. She was done in three minutes.

"Alright," Laura announced. "Last but not least—Kyle. The floor is yours."

My heart was pounding in my chest and I hoped no one could hear my foot nervously tapping the carpet as I counted down.

"Well," Kyle started. "It was after school. I was—"

Suddenly the lunch bell rang and I breathed a sigh of relief.

Laura sucked her teeth then said, "We'll pick this up tomorrow."

Everyone else stood and I lowered my head as I grinned to myself. I lived to lie another day.

And that afternoon, I made copies of Angie's file, slipped it back into Mrs. Porter's office, and left with Fabi without anyone seeing me. The next morning, before school started and while the halls were still empty, I taped a dozen copies to the lockers. Then, when everyone eventually poured into the hall half an hour later, the wildfire began.

Chapter twenty-nine:
"What Goes Around...Comes Around"

"I can't believe Angie Clarkson cheated her way through junior year," Kyle said when the group met at lunch.

We were all sitting in the library's conference room, processing the newest Phantom news. Tensions were high and it seemed that everyone had their own unique reason to be seething over it.

"I knew she wasn't as smart as everyone thought she was," Sarah scoffed.

"How can you say that?!" Lisa screeched. "That's my cousin!" She sniffled and wiped her nose with her sleeve. "All the schools revoked her acceptance. She doesn't know where she's gonna go now. And I heard she might even be getting investigated or something."

She threw her head onto her arms and started sobbing. There was an awkward silence as we all looked at each other. None of us really cared about Angie, being that most of us had been at the end of her gossip at one point or another. But it was a little disconcerting to see Lisa so torn up over this.

"But that's what she gets, Lisa," Sarah finally blurted, ruthlessly. "What goes around comes around."

"Shut up," Lisa muttered.

"I would feel bad if she hadn't been spreading so much gossip. Last year, she told everyone that I gave Larry Hicks a blow job and I'm still living that down."

"Wait, so you didn't give him a–" Kyle started.

"No!" Sarah cried. "And that's the point! She scarred everyone's reputations with lies while all the while she had this big skeleton in her closet. What a hypocrite. I'm glad the Phantom did this to her."

Lisa suddenly shrieked like an animal and dove over the table to claw at Sarah's face. She would've done it too if Laura hadn't been quick as lightning and yanked her back by her arms.

"Go to Hell!" Lisa bellowed, spitting at Sarah.

"Stop!" Laura shouted, forcing Lisa's elbows together behind her back. "Stop it!"

Lisa struggled for a few seconds as Sarah wiped the spit off her face in shock. We all watched in stunned silence until Lisa finally let out a deep sigh and crumpled into her seat. I had to admit that even I was surprised. I knew this was gonna be bad, but it hit different seeing Lisa Peters actually try to fight Sarah Gibson over something I'd done. If Laura hadn't been here to stop her, they would've definitely fought and what would have happened then? A catfight between a Cartesian and one of the top chess girls. It might not unravel the social structure, but it was enough to set some dominos falling.

"This is the kind of stuff the Phantom wants—to see us all going at each other's throats. We need to stop fighting each other and figure out why the Phantom did this."

"How do we know it was him again?" Kyle asked innocently.

"Because it was photo copies of Mrs. Porter's therapy notes," Sarah explained. "And…" She glanced at Laura and rolled her eyes. "…and Laura saw him come out of Mrs. Porter's office."

"Exactly," Laura pointed at her. "So this must have been why he was there that night—to get that confession."

"Although it's still possible you're lying about seeing him," Sarah added.

"But I saw him too," I chimed in. "I mean you can argue that both of us are lying, but the chances get slimmer with each liar you add."

"Whatever," Sarah shrugged.

"It was the Phantom," Laura said definitively. "Plus the whole displaying the copy thing fits his M.O. It's just that this time instead of giving the photo to his victim, he gave it to all of us."

"But something's not right," Kyle pointed out. "Why target Angie?"

"Because he's a monster!" Lisa screamed.

No one replied for a second. Then Kyle said very carefully, "That might be true, but…I'm pretty sure Angie is the one who told everyone that Vanessa's pregnant."

"I heard that too," Laura nodded.

"Three," Sarah added.

"Is it true?" Laura asked Lisa.

Lisa sniffled and hugged her elbows on the table. She refused to look at any of us, but after an uncomfortably long silence, she finally whispered, "Yes."

"I would say it's unbelievable," Sarah said. "But you know…it isn't."

"So Angie spread the rumor," Laura said as she started pacing. "Are you saying this was some sort of justice?"

"It looks like it," Kyle replied. "I mean, look at the timing. It happened just a few days after Vanessa's locker got vandalized. No other Phantom acts have happened so closely together."

There was a short silence and I started rapping the table to make it look like I was thinking. But I wasn't. I was planning. I already saw where Kyle was going and I needed to figure out how I'd steer the group away before he got there.

"I admit," Sarah said. "That actually does make sense."

"No it doesn't," Lisa said with a sniffle. "Why would he get revenge on Angie for something that *he* did to Vanessa?"

Everyone looked at each other and I could see them playing with these two pieces that didn't fit, trying to come up with an explanation.

"Unelss," I cut in. "Vanessa wasn't a victim."

"What?" Laura looked at me. "What do you mean?"

"Lisa's right," I went on. "Why would the Phantom target Vanessa and then get revenge for Vanessa? Angie only spread the rumor that the Phantom allegedly started. It would make no sense for the Phantom to get justice for that since he's responsible. Unless he wasn't responsible for Vanessa. He just wanted Angie."

The others looked at each other and even Sarah pursed her lips with a look of mild affirmation.

"But I'm sure that he targeted Vanessa," Laura insisted.

"How sure?" I pressed.

Laura paused before answering. "90%."

"So there's a 10% chance that he didn't. And in that case it would make sense that he would target Angie. Otherwise we have a Phantom acting for and against himself at the same time."

"Maybe," Laura said, leaning across the table towards me. "He just wants to watch the school burn."

"That sounds pretty psychotic," I said with a grin. "And I thought everyone was basically good."

There was a short pause as she slowly grinned back at me. Everyone else looked back and forth from us awkwardly.

"Should we leave?" Kyle said, clearing his throat.

"There's another explanation," Laura said, turning to everyone else. "The Phantom could have targeted Vanessa and Angie because he wasn't acting on his own behalf."

"What do you mean?" asked Kyle.

"What if the Phantom's victims look like contradictions…" She paused for dramatic effect before finishing. "…because different people are hiring him?"

Chapter thirty:
"Kryptonite"

I rubbed my chin as I thought Laura's theory over. She thought that other students were hiring the Phantom to sabotage other students. On the one hand she was too close to the truth for comfort and that didn't sit well with me. But on the other hand, I could use this to my advantage.

"I second that," I said, raising my hand.

The others looked at me briefly and Laura nodded.

"So let's test it out," I suggested.

"How?" Sarah shrugged.

I stood and started walking around the room as I spoke. "If there are students hiring the Phantom to target other students, then depending on how big this group is, there has to be a chance that one of us knows one of those 'clients'."

"Or *is* one of those clients," Kyle added.

I pointed at him. "That too."

Sarah rolled her eyes and Lisa sniffled.

"So how about it?" I asked. "Have any of you contacted the Phantom?"

No one said a word as one by one everyone shook their heads. And as I watched them reply, a startling realization suddenly hit me and I almost gasped.

"Do any of you know anyone who's contacted the Phantom?" I forced myself to ask, ignoring the revelation.

And as each of them shook their heads again, my discovery crawled up my spine like a giant foreboding spider.

I snapped my fingers in mock frustration. "Dang it. Back to the drawing board."

"That doesn't prove anything," Laura disagreed. "For one, everyone here could be lying."

"Oh, of course we are," Sarah said. "We're the liars and not you. How do we know you're not in cahoots with the Phantom just to throw us off your scent?"

"Once again," Laura aimed praying hands at her like blades. "I wouldn't ruin my chance at being valedictorian just to be in 'cahoots' with some random maniac. But also..." She turned to me. "It's possible that the Phantom's clients just aren't in this room. I'll need to talk to more students. Starting with Vanessa."

"Makes sense," I said as I sat back down. I cleared my throat and slowly drummed the table with my fingers to keep the spider at bay. The thing I had realized was that I was the only person in the room who wasn't a victim.

***

"I need to target myself," I explained to Fabi on the car ride home that afternoon. "I'm the only one in the group who hasn't been a victim. Sooner or later they'll realize that and be able to figure it out by process of elimination."

"Wow," she replied. "I didn't even notice that. So it's like in mafia when people start getting suspicious of the two people who never get accused."

"So the only way for the mafia to throw the group off..."

"Is to kill one of their own," she finished. "So what are you gonna do?".

"I don't know yet," I replied, staring out the window as I thought. "It has to be something that ruins my reputation. But I don't really have a reputation to begin with. There's nothing to ruin."

"It's not just about rep," Fabi corrected. "The Phantom also ruins goals. So think about something that you want. How could the Phantom get in your way?"

"Hmmm," I said. What did I want? Since I was getting paid thousands of dollars on a weekly basis, there wasn't much that I wanted that I couldn't just get. I mean, I wanted my parents' bakery to stay intact. But not only would I not want to sabotage that, even if I did, no one at school would know so it wouldn't make a difference. I also wanted Billy to stop bullying me so maybe the Phantom would do something to make him bully me more, like reveal that I'm actually the Phantom that ruined his relationship. But that was obviously out of the question. But then it hit me. There wasn't really some*thing* I wanted. But some*one*.

Laura.

And all of a sudden, I knew what I had to do.

Chapter thirty-one:
"She Will Be Loved"

Getting Vanessa to meet up with me was easy. All I had to do was message her on facebook that I felt bad about everything going on and that I was there if she needed someone to talk to. She said she did and we met up one afternoon for pizza after school. The hard part was going to be not leading her on too much. I couldn't tell her that I finally wanted her now. Not only did I not trust myself to be able to keep resisting her if she put the seduction on full throttle for the rest of the year, but if I did succeed in rejecting her, the last thing I needed was for Vanessa Diamond to put me on her vengeance list. All I needed was to sit with her in that pizza shop long enough for Fabi to get a picture of us. Nothing more. Nothing less.

"This pizza's pretty good," Vanessa said, taking a bite of her chicken bacon ranch slice. "Not as good as New York, but pretty good."

I shrugged as I picked up my plain slice. "I don't know. Jersey pizza is pretty close, in my opinion."

Vanessa rolled her eyes. "I grew up on the Lower East Side. You have no idea what you're talking about."

We went back and forth about the best pizza spots in the city versus the ones in Jersey. I snuck a peek out the window every chance I got to see if I could catch Fabi. The street was packed with no spots so she had been circling the block the entire time. I had to keep stalling.

"When did you leave New York?" I asked.

"When I was ten," Vanessa replied. "My Dad got laid off. And my mom's salary wasn't enough for rent in Manhattan. So we moved across the bridge."

I nodded slowly. It was weird thinking of Vanessa Diamond's family not being able to afford anything. It was weird thinking of any Hamilton student not being able to afford anything for that matter.

"Do you miss New York?" I asked her.

She pouted as she thought about it. "I miss the pizza." She winked at me as she took another bite.

I grinned back as I took a bite too.

"Don't get me wrong," she went on. "We're fine now. Dad's got a new job paying him twice as much, we've got seven bedrooms, a pool, and three cars. We're fine. More than fine." She paused for a second. "It was just weird having to leave at first. Especially when you're so used to having everything and then having…not everything."

She held her slice in front of her face like she was about to take a bite, but just stared at it instead. I had never seen her like this before. There was a time when the infamous Vanessa Diamond hadn't been able to live in a penthouse suite. Had they been in a regular two bedroom apartment? Were they in public housing? I couldn't picture that, but I also realized I didn't really know Vanessa that well. This was the first time I was talking to her about anything other than sex. This was the first time we were actually talking at all, really.

"Sorry…" I finally said. "I know how that feels." I looked out the window again. Still no sign of Fabi. None of the cars on the street had even changed. Not a single spot had opened up.

"What do you really want?" Vanessa suddenly asked me.

"What?" I looked back at her. "What do you mean? You said you needed someone to talk to. So…I'm here."

Vanessa narrowed her eyes at me and I expected her to flash me her signature flirtatious smirk, but she didn't. "We both know that isn't true."

I swallowed, but kept my face even.

"You said I could talk to you, but you haven't asked me once about how I feel about what Angie did to me. And I know this isn't a date because you didn't pay for my slice. Not to mention you keep looking out the window every five minutes."

I sighed. She was right. Those were rookie mistakes. I should've been paying attention to her more. "I'm sorry. I'm…I'm just a little nervous, that's all."

She raised an eyebrow as she kept her gaze fixed on me. For a second I thought she was about to slap me.

"I don't like being played, Nick," she finally said.

"I'm not playing you," I told her. "You're just really sad and I wanted to make you feel better but you're also really pretty so I'm really nervous."

There was a short silence.

"You're right," I admitted. "I should've paid for your slice. But I didn't want you to think this was a date. Because it's not. I'm not trying to play you." All of a sudden I felt like I was hooked up to Laura's polygraph again.

Vanessa rolled her eyes. "Do you wanna know how I get every guy to do what I want? Well…every guy except you."

I glanced to the side then looked back at her.

"It's all about the smile, style, and scent," she explained, grinning mischievously. "If you wanna make a guy blush, compliment his smile. If you wanna make him feel good about himself, compliment his style. And if you wanna get in his head, tell him that he smells good. Because guys who smell good are trying to get our attention."

I nodded slowly. I had to admit—that was pretty impressive. I had flashbacks of different girls complimenting those different things about me. I could even remember Vanessa herself giving me all three. That was probably what aggravated her even more about not being able to get with me.

"You changed your scent a few months ago, Nick," she continued. "*Before* I bumped into you."

My chest tightened. She had noticed that?

Vanessa leaned in across the table closer to me. "So who are you really trying to attract? Or should I ask…who are you trying to throw off your scent?"

I blinked several times, but kept my breathing and my face even. This girl was good.

"I don't know what you're talking about," I told her.

She stared back then finally flashed that flirtatious smirk, as if she had me right where she wanted me. "You can't con a con girl, Nick." Then she stood and slung her backpack over her shoulder. "Thanks for the talk." And with that she walked out the pizza shop. But as I watched her leave, I spotted Fabi's car parked across the street.

Chapter thirty-two:
"I Don't Wanna Know"

Fabi took me to develop the picture and I had to admit—it was pretty good. She had captured the exact moment Vanessa had leaned in close to ask me why I had changed my scent. Her face was determined and mine was slightly uncomfortable. This would be perfect. But I still couldn't shake what she'd said to me: *Who are you trying to throw off your scent?* How did she know? Was Vanessa watching me?

"You think Laura's gonna buy it?" Fabi asked me.

I swallowed nervously at her name. In the midst of everything, I'd forgotten why I was even doing this. And now I was uneasy. I held the picture in my hands as I sat in the passenger seat. I was about to hurt Laura again. Just to keep her and everyone else from thinking I was the Phantom. Was it worth it? Well, if this worked, it wouldn't hurt her that much. The point was that it looked like I was on a date with Vanessa, but I wasn't. The plan was just to show that the Phantom had targeted me. Whatever emotional damage this caused Laura would be minimal. Right?

"Nick?" Fabi interrupted my thoughts.

"Yeah," I said quickly. "I think she will."

The next day at school, I slipped the picture in Laura's locker before homeroom. Then I waited at my locker down the hall while everyone lingered. Laura eventually made it to hers and I watched behind my locker door as she opened hers. The picture slid out and fell at her feet and she picked it up slowly. She was smiling at first, probably thinking it was some sort of surprise. But then her face fell as she frowned. Guilt sliced through my heart like a knife as I watched her hand shake and I could almost swear that I saw a tear well up in her eye. Then she crumpled the picture in her hand, slammed her locker, and marched down the hall. She was coming my way.

I shut my eyes and took a deep breath. This was it.

"Hey, Lor," I waved as she came. But she didn't even look at me. She just walked straight past like I wasn't even there. I winced in the wake of it, like someone had just hit me in the stomach with a baseball bat.

Was it worth it?

I looked up through the mess of students and saw Vanessa leaning against the wall with her arms folded across her chest. She pointed two of her fingers at her eyes then aimed one at me. Then she turned and disappeared in the crowd. What was going on?

I sat next to Laura in homeroom, but she turned in her chair to face away from me.

"Laura," I said. "Is everything alright? What happened?"

This went on for several minutes with me just asking questions to her back until she finally spun and glared at me.

"Do you think I'm stupid?" she snapped.

"What are you talking about?" I asked her.

"I thought you weren't allowed to date," she said.

"I'm not."

"Then what is this?" She slapped the picture onto my desk.

I stared at it and even though I had to pretend I was surprised, the pain was real. Laura was genuinely hurt and because of that *I* was genuinely hurt. All of a sudden, I regretted doing this. Was it really worth it to hurt the person I cared about again?

"Where did you get this?" I asked softly.

"Take a wild guess, Sherlock."

I stared at the picture for a few more seconds, fumbling over my words. I had rehearsed what I would say, but in the moment my brain was malfunctioning. I had actually hurt her again. And she was actually mad. "It's not what you think."

"Don't tell me what to think," she spat at me. "If you didn't like me, you could've just told me that. I'm a big girl–I could handle it. Don't lie straight to my face."

"Everyone settle down," Mr. Jones said at the front of the class. "I have a few announcements to make."

The class started to quiet down.

"I'm sorry," I whispered as Laura turned to face the front. "I can explain. It's not what you think–I promise."

"Is there a problem back there?" Mr. Jones called.

"No, Mr. Jones," Laura said sweetly. Then she slowly looked over at me and said, "There isn't."

I sighed then turned and slouched in my seat. Laura ignored me for the rest of the day and I felt so horrible I couldn't speak. It didn't help that Lance was giving me weird looks too, like he was trying to avoid me. On top of that, every other class I'd see Vanessa winking at me. I was suffocating. And it was all my own fault. I felt like I was about to implode.

The minutes crawled each period and it felt like it took days for lunch to come. But when it did, I wasn't sure I even wanted to meet up with the group. But I had to. This was all a part of the plan, even though I was regretting every bit of it.

I walked into the conference room and everyone was already there.

"Well, if it isn't Romeo himself," Laura said from the board. "Come. Join us."

The rest of the group immediately sensed the hostility and Sarah whispered something to Lisa. I sat down next to Kyle and took a deep breath, preparing myself for whatever Laura had planned.

"Good news," she announced. "The Phantom struck again."

"Really?" Sarah asked. "Who was it?"

In one swift move, Laura nailed the picture to the board with a thumbtack. It took a second for it to register to the group, but when it did, the girls gasped and Kyle put both his hands on top of his head.

"No way," Lisa breathed.

"Yes way!" Sarah cackled, looking back and forth between me and Laura.

"Are you kidding me?" I jumped to my feet. "You won't talk to me all day, but you wanna do this in front of everyone?"

"So we have witnesses for any more of your lies," she replied.

I rubbed my hand over my face and Sarah spun her chair towards me, chewing her gum ecstatically.

"We can leave, if you want," Kyle said, moving to get up.

"No!" Sarah and Laura cried at the same time and he sat back down.

"I can explain," I started. "It wasn't a date. I didn't even pay for her pizza."

"Oh!" Laura squealed. "Glad to hear you're not a gentleman."

"What a loser!" Sarah instigated.

"She's bad news, bro," Kyle told me.

"I'm not a loser!" I shouted. "And I know she's bad news! This wasn't a date! I'm telling the truth. Can't you see that the Phantom is doing this?"

"Don't blame this on him," Laura shook her head. "This is all on you."

"No, listen to me," I pleaded. "This is exactly what he wants."

"For you to hook up with Vanessa?"

"We didn't hook up!" I shouted. "Nothing happened!"

Laura stared at me without blinking, just huffing softly, like she was containing a seething pot of anger inside her nose. I'd never seen her like this and I didn't like it. Why had I done this? But it was too late to back down now.

"The Phantom is using this," I said.

"How exactly?" Laura squinted at me. "Please. Enlighten me."

"The Phantom must know that we're friends," I said carefully. "And he knows that we're trying to find him. So maybe he's using this to tear us apart so we'll stop looking for him."

There was a short beat of silence and I saw Laura's eyebrow twitch.

"That actually makes sense," Lisa admitted.

"Don't encourage him!" Sarah shoved her in the shoulder. "Let the drama unfold."

"He is kinda right, though," Kyle said. "I mean…" He gestured between Laura and me. "If you guys keep fighting like this, are you really gonna work together?"

No one said anything for an uncomfortably long time.

"It does make sense," Laura finally said as she looked away. Then she glared at me again with fresh fury in her eyes. "But it still doesn't explain why you were on a date with Vanessa in the first place."

"It wasn't a date," I said.

"Prove it."

"What?" I blinked. "How?"

"Call her," Laura nodded to my backpack. "I wanna hear her say it."

My heart was suddenly beating in my throat. This wasn't part of the plan. The plan hinged on the fact that it looked like I was on a date when I wasn't. Once I convinced Laura that it wasn't a date, everything would be okay. But *I* was supposed to convince Laura–not Vanessa. If I called Vanessa and for some reason she said that it was a date, Laura would believe her and everything would be ruined. This was not supposed to happen.

"That's ridiculous," I laughed nervously. "I don't even have her number."

"I do," Kyle spoke up.

I had never wanted to smack him so hard.

"Kyle for the save!" Sarah cheered. "Finally, you did something useful."

Kyle held out his phone to show me Vanessa's number. But I just stared at it, trying to think of a way out of this. I couldn't call Vanessa. The last thing I needed was to invite the most deceptive, conniving seductress in Hamilton

High into this fiasco. She already wanted me. Even though she herself had said it wasn't a date, there was no telling what she'd say if she smelled that I was up to something funny. She might make up a whole hookup story just to spite me.

"Call her and put her on speaker," Laura said.

"What am I supposed to say?" I shrugged. "'Hey, did we go on a date?'"

"Figure it out." She stared me down and waited.

If I didn't call, Laura would think I had something to hide. But if I did call, there was no telling what Vanessa would say.

"Did you forget how to use a phone?" Laura asked me.

I sighed then pressed "CALL". With each ring, I prayed that she wouldn't pick up–that she wouldn't be able to hear it over the noise in the cafeteria or the bathroom or wherever she was. But then it stopped ringing and a sultry voice came on the other end.

"Hello?"

Chapter thirty-three:
"We Belong Together"

"Hey, Vanessa," I said, pinching the bridge of my nose. "It's Nick."

"Oh hey, Nick," she said. Her voice was dripping with honey. "I didn't expect to hear from you."

I looked over at Laura to see her standing with her arms folded and an unamused look on her face.

"I have a quick question for you," I said into the phone.

"Anything for you, my little Nicky," she replied. And I could literally see her wrapping her tongue around my name. Laura's lips tightened as she squinted at me.

"Funny you should call me that, actually," I said, forcing out a laugh. "Uh…because, uh…remember when we hung out yesterday? What did you say that was? Can you say that again for me?"

"I said a lot of things yesterday, Nick. You're gonna have to refresh my memory."

"Well, I wouldn't wanna put any words in your mouth."

"You can put whatever you want in my mouth."

Kyle choked.

Sarah and Lisa gestured at him and screamed silently for him to shut up.

"What was that?" Vanessa asked.

"Nothing," I said quickly, walking away from Kyle. "My laptop."

"Where are you?"

"The library. Listen, I just need you to answer the question. What did you say about what we were doing?"

Vanessa was quiet for a few seconds and even though I was avoiding Laura's gaze, I could feel her eyes boring into my skull from across the room. When Vanessa finally spoke again, something had shifted in her voice. It was the sultriness. She had cranked it up.

"I remember now," she said slowly. "I said that you're the most incredible and desirable guy at school."

I shook my head at Laura. "That's not what she–that's not what you said."

"Yes, it is," Vanessa insisted. "And I said that all I've ever wanted was to be with you and to feel you holding me in those long, strong arms. Because we belong together."

Laura's face was turning red.

"That's not what you said at all, Vanessa," I said. This is what I was afraid of. She was taking over and turning this into her own little game. And now was not the time.

"It is," she said. "And when you asked me out, I couldn't wait to see you."

"You're lying," I begged her.

"I couldn't wait for you to hold me. To squeeze me. To kiss me."

I shut my eyes. I heard Sarah gasp and this time Kyle and Lisa were the ones whispering for her to shut up. But it didn't matter. This was it. I was a dead man.

"But when we finally met," Vanessa went on. "I felt something unexpected pulsing, throbbing, and sinking inside of me."

You've got to be kidding me.

"Do you want to know what I felt?"

I didn't answer.

"It starts with a D."

I sighed and wondered what object in the room Laura would use to kill me.

"Disappointment," Vanessa said.

My eyes flew open.

"What?" I asked.

"Because you weren't there to be with me, were you, Nick?" Vanessa went on. "You were there to be there *for* me. You felt bad because of what Angie had done to me. And you just wanted to be a friend."

I let out a heavy sigh of relief. It felt like I was finally coming up for air after Vanessa had held me underwater.

"As sweet as it was," she continued. "I was still disappointed."

"Yeah..." I said, smiling at Laura. She slowly dropped her hands to her sides. "...that's what you said."

Lisa and Kyle looked at each other with surprised looks while Sarah snapped in frustration.

"She's a lucky girl," Vanessa added.

"Who?" I asked.

"The girl you actually like," she said.

My body went rigid and I forced myself to not look at Laura.

"Tell her I said hi," Vanessa said. And I could swear that she was winking on the other end. Then she hung up.

We're All Savages
121

Chapter thirty-four:
"My Boo"

The bell rang and Sarah threw her head back and groaned.

"Ugh!" she complained. "It was just getting good. This should be a movie!"

I was still holding the phone in my hand, still in shock at what had just happened. Leave it to Vanessa Diamond to take me on a heart-thumping joy ride before bailing me out.

"See you guys in class," Lisa said as she followed Kyle and Sarah out.

Laura stood in her spot holding one arm at her side. She was staring at the floor and the fury was gone from her eyes. The fiery redness in her face was replaced by a softer pink blush in her cheeks.

"I'm…" she said softly. "I'm…I'm sorry."

I swallowed. Technically I was the one who was supposed to be apologizing. I had done this to her. But she couldn't know that.

"It's not a big deal," I shrugged.

"I should've trusted you," she said, still staring at her sneakers. "I overreacted."

"Well, I should've told you that I was gonna hang out with her," I offered. "That would've made it look less suspicious."

"Maybe…" she said, still not looking at me.

It felt like the room was filling up with a suffocating cloud of awkwardness. But for some reason I couldn't move. I didn't want to. Not until I had some kind of closure. I knew I didn't deserve it since I had done this to her and I was gonna deal with the guilt later.

"I'm sorry for hurting you," I said. "There's nothing going on between me and Vanessa. It was stupid. I was just trying to help someone, but I should've known what it would look like to you."

"No," she shook her head. "It was…I mean, yeah, it *did* look weird. But…I get it. And that was sweet of you. Besides, it's not like we're…" She shook her head.

I nodded. "Are we…we still friends?"

She looked up and smirked. "Yeah."

I smiled and it felt like the weight of the world came off my shoulders. I hadn't realized how anxious I'd been that I might actually lose her.

"Besides," she said. "We still have to catch this guy."

I nodded.

We were running out of time before we'd be late to class.

"So what was that she said at the end?" Laura asked hesitantly.

I swallowed and made a face like I was trying to remember.

"Did you tell her who you like?"

I looked at her briefly and melted at the innocent look that flashed across her face, like she was hoping I'd say it.

"No," I replied, with more strength than I felt. "Still my little secret."

She rolled her eyes and the innocent look rolled away with it. Then she grabbed her backpack and punched me in the arm as she walked past. When I got home that night, I had a facebook message from Vanessa. It was three simple words:

You owe me.

Chapter thirty-five:
"A Whole New World"

Now that Laura and I were cool again and my parents had had time to simmer over the idea of her as my friend, I had asked them if she could come over. They'd agreed and today, Saturday, was the day. It wasn't the first time I'd be having a friend over, but it was definitely the first time I was having a girl over. And everything had to be perfect. My room was a mess now, with some of my clothes on the floor, my Phantom costume hanging over my closet door, and the PS2 wires snaking a fire hazard across the carpet. But I'd have it spotless by 2 when Laura was supposed to come. It was 11 now so I had time.

I showered then brushed my teeth, already running through what Laura and I would do when she got here. Some video games, some anime, walking through the park, then come back in time for some mouth-watering Haitian dinner.

Then suddenly the doorbell rang. I froze mid brush and listened as Fabi shouted, "I'll get it!" from downstairs. Then, five seconds later, "Oh hey! You must be Laura."

My whole body went cold. She was here? I ran into the room and looked at my alarm clock. It was barely 12. Why was she here so early?

"Nick!" My mother shouted. "Your friend is here!"

Frick. Frick. Frick frick frick!!!

I had to stall her. She could not come up when my room was looking like this, not to mention with every conceivable piece of evidence that I was the Phantom lying out in the open for the world to see.

I ran to the edge of the hall and shouted, "Gimme a minute! I just got out the shower!"

I rushed back to my room and shut the door as I dove into the fastest room clean the world had ever seen. I stuffed my Phantom outfit into my backpack then locked it in my closet. I scooped up every snack off the floor and tossed them into the trash then shoved all my clothes into a drawer. Then I made the bed, moved the controllers out of the way, and sprayed some Old Spice around the room.

I stood back and took a deep breath as I inspected my work. It wasn't perfect, but it was orderly. This would have to do. I turned to open the door when I realized I was still in my towel. I hadn't even changed!

A minute later I was in jeans and a graphic tee, gave my hair a few quick brushes, and finally made my way downstairs. Laura was sitting in the living room with my Mom and Fabi.

"There's the Funky Monkey," Laura said and Fabi's neck nearly snapped looking at her.

"Sorry," I said, forcing my breathing under control. "I didn't expect you to be here yet. I thought you said you were coming at 2."

Laura shrugged. "I did. But my Mom had to run some errands in the area first so I figured I'd surprise you. Is that okay?" She looked at Fabi and my Mom.

"No, that's fine!" my mother insisted, ever the host. "This is perfect, actually. My husband is making *fritay*. You'll love it."

"What's that?" my Dad called from the kitchen. "She said she wants *fritay*?"

"What's free-tie?" Laura asked.

"Something that's too spicy for you," Fabi said sharply.

"It's a whole bunch of fried stuff," I explained, shooting her a look. "Fried plantains, fried *akra*, fried sweet potato, and fried pork."

Laura nodded approvingly. "Sounds good." She sniffed the air. "And it smells even better."

"We'll call you down when it's ready," my mother said. "Go have fun."

I turned to walk away with Laura, but Fabi grabbed my arm and said in Kreyol, "You letting this little white girl call you a monkey?"

"It's just a nickname," I whispered back in English. "It's a game we play…it's not what you…I'll explain later."

She gave me a look then said, still in Kreyol, "Remember. Don't let your guard down."

I nodded and she finally let me go.

My mother headed into the kitchen, but not before calling over her shoulder, "Remember to leave the door open!"

"Yes, Mom," I replied.

I gave Laura a quick tour of the house then we went to my room.

"Your family's funny," she said as she walked around.

"Yeah," I agreed. "A bunch of comedians."

I wanted to jump right in and tell her what I had planned for the day. But then I realized, what if she wanted to do something else? Should I tell her I had an itinerary? Or should I just ask her what she wanted to do? Why was I overthinking this? It wasn't a date. But still, Laura Wood was in my house. In my room! I couldn't wait to tell Lance.

"Is this your first time bringing a girl home?" she asked.

My brain tripped over my own thoughts. "Well...I'm not 'bringing you home', in the traditional sense. Like...this isn't..."

She held her hand up to stop me. "I know, Romeo. You're not into me. You've made that very clear."

My mouth opened as I tried to explain, but then stopped.

"I meant am I the first female friend that's come here?" she went on.

I rubbed the back of my neck nervously. "Yeah."

She walked around the room, examining the anime posters and paused at my dresser to play with my hairbrush. "What about that girl you like? She's never been here?"

I rubbed my arm as she glanced over her shoulder at me. "Yeah...actually, she has."

She looked me up and down then went back to strolling through the room. "Huh."

She stopped at my desk as something caught her eye. And my heart nearly exploded when I realized it was my notebook—the same notebook I'd been writing all my Phantom notes in. She picked it up and I was across the room in a blink and snatched it out of her hands.

"Don't touch that!" I screamed, stuffing it behind my back. "That's my journal. I write all my...thoughts and stuff in there."

A wicked smile curled across her face. "You have a diary?"

"A journal," I corrected her. "I write my thoughts...and feelings...and stuff in it."

That wicked smile curled even more and she chuckled at me. "Is that girl in it?"

"Yes," I said quickly. "As a matter of fact."

"Can I see?" Laura asked. "I promise I won't tell."

"No," I shook my head. "Listen, do you wanna talk about my crush or actually hang out?"

"Why can't we do both?" Laura shrugged. "We can—" Then her face lit up as something caught her eye. She ran over to the PS2 and picked up one of the games. "You have NBA Street?! Volume 2? Ohhhhh it's on!"

"Are you good?" I asked, relieved that the subject was changed.

She scoffed, already turning the Playstation on. "I'm better than good. I'm nasty."

But she wasn't. We played and I destroyed her. Over. And over. And over again. To the point that I ended up using the Grizzlies—the frickin' Grizzlies—and still washed her 21 to 5. But she was a good sport about it and we both had fun. Then my Mom called us down for the *fritay* and it turned out Fabi was wrong—it wasn't too spicy for Laura. She finished her whole plate and asked for more.

Then we watched *A Goofy Movie* and danced to "Eye to Eye". Then we watched *Aladdin* and recited all the lines—I was Aladdin, Sultan, and Iago and she was Jasmine, Genie, and Jafar. And then because she wanted to redeem herself from the NBA Street massacre, we played chess and she annihilated me. She played "Prince Ali" from her iPod and beat me before the song ended every time.

"It's all about planning," she explained to me as she set up another game. "You gotta be able to think three moves ahead of your opponent."

"I'm usually good at that," I said. "But it just falls apart in chess."

"Obviously," she said.

"You got jokes."

"And w's," she replied, waving her hand over the board.

I laughed and almost snorted. She squinted at me.

"Did you forget I was funny?" she asked. "Don't let the Phantom focus fool you. I'm all jokes all day."

"No," I chuckled. "I didn't forget." But that did make me think of something. I cleared my throat as we went back to setting up the board for another match. "Speaking of the Phantom…why are you so determined to catch him? I mean, I know he made you fail, but…" I shrugged. "Why not just let it go?"

She dropped a pawn onto its square then looked up at me. At first I wasn't sure if she was upset or not. Had I phrased it wrong? Did it come out suspicious?

"You probably don't know this," she finally said. "But I wasn't always a straight A student."

I did know that, but I didn't say anything so that I wouldn't look like I was obsessed with her.

"I just wanted to do everything under the Sun—softball, gymnastics, clarinet, drama, hacking." She snickered to herself like she was remembering something. "But I never focused on one thing long enough and definitely didn't focus on my actual classes that I was actually taking. But I was still getting B's. You wouldn't believe how many times I got the 'if you only applied yourself' speech." She made her voice deep like she was imitating a man and it was so cute I laughed. "Especially from my grandpa. He graduated high school at fifteen, went to Cornell, joined the marines, became a criminal investigator, then went to med school, and became a brain surgeon."

"Wow," I said. Sounded like a pretty intense guy.

"He said I got my smarts from him but I was too busy to actually see my full potential," Laura went on.

I nodded as I listened. I didn't know much about Laura's family, just that her Dad was a professor and her family would go to France in the summer. I'd never heard her talk about her grandparents before. "What's he doing now?"

"Nothing much," she shrugged. "He's dead."

I blinked at how bluntly she'd said it. I didn't know if I was supposed to laugh or say sorry.

"But while he was, you know, dying," she went on. "I told him that I would start applying myself and become valedictorian. I made a promise to my grandpa and I'm gonna keep it. Don't want a supergenius haunting me in my sleep, you know what I mean?" She winked at me.

I swallowed nervously and suddenly felt sick to my stomach. I had no idea. Laura's promise to her dying grandfather had been to become valedictorian and I had ruined that. I was a terrible person. If I didn't want her to know I was the Phantom before, I definitely couldn't let her know now.

We finished setting up the board in awkward silence until she finally put me out of my misery.

"Speaking of dead white men," she said, twirling her king in her fingers. "Here's a tip for you. If you can't think ahead, you can try moving faster."

I nodded, grateful for the change in subject.

"Sometimes," she continued. "Especially if you're playing someone who's not that great—if you move quickly enough, it makes them move quicker too and you can force them to make a mistake."

"Hmmmm," I said to myself. But how could I ever hope to move faster than Laura Wood? I didn't know anyone who could think on their feet like she did.

And then, as we started a new game, a thought hit me like remembering a homework assignment was due today. What if Laura had shown up early on purpose—to catch me making a mistake? What if she was still suspicious that I was the Phantom and this was all a set up? I shook my head and brought my focus back to the game. I was being ridiculous. But later that evening after Laura's parents picked her up, I noticed that my brush was gone.

Chapter thirty-six:
"Feel So Good"

That Monday I was still on a high from hanging out with Laura. I couldn't wait to tell Lance all about it. He was gonna be so jealous. The first thing I did when I got into homeroom was look for where he was sitting. But before I could find him, Laura punched me in my arm so hard I thought it was Billy at first.

"Ow," I said, rubbing where she'd hit me.

"What's up, Funky Monkey?" she said.

"Hey," I said, then I punched her in her arm—obviously not as hard—and she laughed.

"I had fun on Saturday," she said. "We should hang out more often."

"Yeah," I nodded. "Me too. And…we should."

There was an awkward silence where we oscillated between looking at each other then at our classmates shuffling past us.

"Oh!" she finally said. "This is so embarrassing." She ruffled inside her backpack. "I accidentally took this with me when I left." Then she pulled out my brush.

My jaw dropped as I stared down at it.

"I'm so sorry," she shrugged, still holding it out. "It looked so much like mine I didn't even realize it was yours."

Time froze as I stared at the brush without taking it.

Allow me to explain something. In Haitian culture—at least, Haitian-parents-raising-their-kids-in-America culture—if someone borrows something and accidentally takes it home with them, you're not supposed to take it back. Ever. My parents were constantly telling me stories of people casting spells on stuff under the guise of "forgetting to give it back". I always chalked it up to classical immigrant paranoia. After all, what would a bunch of suburban white kids in America know about voodoo? If someone forgot to give me my pencil back they just forgot—it wasn't because they were trying to put a curse on me. But for the first time, I was grateful for my parents' paranoid training. Because this time I had three legitimate reasons to not take this brush back.

For starters, I had never seen Laura brushing her hair at school or at the house. Ever. So there was almost zero chance she would confuse my brush with a brush she never used in public. Second, why didn't she text me about it once she saw that she'd taken it? She had two whole days before today and not a word. What had she been doing with it the whole time? Which led me to three: she must have done something to the brush. She was already suspicious that I was the Phantom. So she could have installed a hidden camera or microphone somewhere in the brush to spy on me and catch me in the act. And she would've gotten me too, if it wasn't for that good old-fashioned Haitian paranoia.

I smiled and shook my head. "No worries. You can keep it."

She squinted at me. "Why would I wanna keep your brush?"

"Safekeeping?" I shrugged. "Something to remember me by."

"Don't flatter yourself," she shoved the brush into my chest.

I took two steps back so she was now holding the brush against empty air. "No offense. It's just that…I'm really weird about stuff like this. That brush never leaves my room so I don't feel comfortable brushing with it now that it's been outside. I'm just gonna throw it away if you give it to me."

She squinted at me then at the brush. "You know what? Now that you mention it…you really are weird."

I stuffed my hands in my pockets as I shrugged then sat in my seat. I was in the clear for now, but I kept my eyes peeled for the next several periods to make sure she didn't try to sneak the brush into my backpack or my locker. She didn't. But just when I thought I had outsmarted Laura Wood, we all met up at lunch and she dropped a bomb on us.

Chapter: thirty-seven:
"Just Lose It"

"What if they're not random?" Laura said, staring at the names she'd written on the board.

"What do you mean?" Kyle asked. He looked from the board to her then back to her. "Are you seeing something we're not seeing?"

Laura kept her eyes on the board as she tapped her chin with her pen. "It looks random at first. But the more victims the Phantom gets the more it starts to paint a bigger picture."

Kyle and I looked at each other. He was confused, but I was trying to hide my nervousness. What was Laura talking about?

"The victims," she went on, still staring at the board. "Sarah, myself, Lisa, Angie, Kyle, Vanessa…" She paused then slowly turned to us. "They're all from different cliques."

Sarah let out an exasperated sigh. "We knew that, Sherlock!"

Laura ignored her. "They're all from different cliques. And we thought that made them random because it looked like no one specific was being targeted. But what if it's the opposite?"

Lisa narrowed her eyes as she tried to follow and Kyle scratched his head, but I already saw where this was going.

"What if we can't find a single target because everyone's the target?" Laura asked.

There was a short silence as everyone looked at each other.

"You mean he wants to destroy the world?" Kyle wondered then shook his head quickly. "I mean…the school? Like, destroy the school?"

"But why?" Lisa asked. "What does he gain from that?"

"He's a psycho," Sarah scoffed. "He probably gets off on this stuff."

"Or he's not a psycho at all," Laura pointed at her. "And he's trying to remake the school…by destroying it first. By making all the most powerful and most popular students turn on themselves until the whole social structure of Hamilton comes crashing down. And then from the ashes he can build something better. So all these attacks, pranks—whatever we want to call them—are all a part of his conspiracy. His agenda. His very own…"

"…Project Mayhem," I finished for her.

Kyle looked up at that, but Lisa and Sarah just glanced at each other blankly.

"Uhhhh," Sarah said. "Project what now?"

"Fight Club," Kyle answered quickly.

Lisa and Sarah looked at each other again then back at us with more irritation than confusion this time.

"And?" Sarah said.

"It's from a movie with Brad Pitt," I explained.

"But what's Project Mayhem?" Sarah asked, her voice rising as she got more irritated. "What are you nerds talking about?"

"It's…"

"No!" Kyle stopped me, half laughing. "The first rule of fight club."

"Is we don't talk about fight club," Laura finished. And the three of us grinned at each other. But Sarah and Lisa looked like they were about to get up and walk out so I put them out of their misery.

"Project Mayhem was Brad Pitt's plan," I started.

"Tyler Durden," Kyle corrected me.

"Tyler Durden's plan," I said. "To break down modern civilization. He and the members of fight club would do these pranks and attacks on big corporations as a way of protesting capitalism and consumerism. The goal was to break down society into anarchy and then rebuild a better one."

Sarah made a face like she had just smelled someone's fart.

"And you guys all watched that?" she scoffed. "You like that 'eat the rich feed the poor' crap?"

Kyle lowered his eyes like he was embarrassed.

"You wouldn't get it," I waved her off.

"And you think that's what the Phantom is doing?" Lisa asked.

Laura nodded. "I think he sees himself as some type of Tyler Durden character and thinks he can make a better school by destroying it first."

The others started murmuring to themselves as they chewed the theory over. I had to admit I was a little confused too. Not by the theory, but by the probability. Laura was actually onto something. Why did it look like this was some sort of anarchist blueprint? I mean, if I really was Tyler Durden, I really would target these students—or students like them—as a way of dismantling Hamilton's social structure. But I wasn't Tyler Durden. And this wasn't Project Mayhem. So why did it feel like it?

But then I remembered Vanessa's case. I had intended to make Kyle think that she had an STD. But instead he assumed she was pregnant. And that rumor led to Angie calling Vanessa a "mother slut", which led to Angie's secret getting out. All of that had been the result of a random coincidence. Could it be that this "Phantom Mayhem" was a coincidence too? But the better question was this: whether it was a coincidence or not, would this theory lead Laura to me? And as if the universe was watching me like a chess match, Sarah asked the question that set the bomb off.

"What difference does all this make?" she said, shooting Laura a look.

Laura faced her and leaned forward across the table. "Because I think I know who the next victim is."

Chapter thirty-eight:
"Let Me Blow Ya Mind"

"Stay with me here," Laura said, holding her hands out like she was actually holding us in place. "I have reason to believe that the Phantom is only targeting seniors."

We all looked at Kyle at the same time, the only sophomore in the room.

"No offense, Kyle," Laura continued. "But let's just assume for a second that the Phantom wasn't actually targeting you, but targeting Vanessa."

Kyle shrugged. "None taken."

"If that's the case," Laura spun back to the whiteboard and simultaneously started scribbling while rattling on her theory. "Then we have a Phantom who's a senior who's only targeting seniors. Which means instead of a pool of 400 possible victims in the entire school, we have a pool of only 100."

My chest suddenly tightened as I ran through my victims in my head. Holy crap. That was actually spot on. Laura had written 400 on one side of the board then 100 on the other side and circled the 100 in red. I pressed my fist to my lips like I was concentrating, but it was really to hide the nervousness creeping into my face. I could already see where this was going.

"Not only that," Laura went on. "But we've already established that it looks like he's targeting seniors in different cliques. Cartesians. Travel Agents. Jocks. Muggles. And he never targets the same person twice. So the pool of possible next victims keeps shrinking."

I swallowed and shifted uneasily in my seat, still staring at the board as Laura wrote the different cliques on it.

"Furthermore," she added. "Each of the Phantom's victims were all in a period of some kind of transition. So Sarah, Lisa, and Kyle, you had all been dating your exes for less than a month. And I had, for the first time, finally gotten a 4.0. We were all on the cusp of things we hadn't experienced before. I believe the Phantom likes to strike right when his victims are on that kind of cusp."

I narrowed my eyes at her, secretly impressed and worried. Why was this actually making sense?

"So I think," Laura said, still writing. "That the Phantom's next victim will be a senior, who's an athlete, and who, like Vanessa Hudgens, is at the start of something new. And who better fits that criteria than our brand new cheer captain, Katie Mills?"

Laura had written Katie's name in all caps and circled it three times before finally spinning to face us.

My chest loosened up a bit. She'd had me for a second. Narrowing the pool of victims from 400 down to a group of seniors that numbered less than a hundred had me shaking a little bit. But Katie Mills was a jump. I didn't see her logic behind why the Phantom would target her. Plus, either way, this was wrong anyway. There was no pattern. The Moms were just giving me assignments. It was ridiculous, but if it kept Laura busy, then I was all for it.

"That…" I nodded, fixing my eyes on the board. "That actually makes sense."

"Oh my God," Sarah scoffed. "Are you kidding me? It does not."

"I think it does," Kyle said. "It explains so much. I mean, if he's a senior, maybe he has it out for the rest of the seniors and people like me are collateral."

I snapped my fingers at him. "Exactly."

"But the whole clique thing is off," Sarah shook her head. "If he's targeting different cliques and he's not double dipping, then why target another athlete? He already got Billy."

"I said he isn't targeting the same student twice," Laura clarified. "Not that he isn't targeting the same clique twice."

"It's a reach," Sarah shook her head again.

"What do you think, Lisa?" Laura asked.

Lisa rubbed her chin as she examined the board. "I don't know…it does make sense. But at the same time, I just feel like you pulled Katie out of nowhere."

"Exactly!" Sarah exclaimed.

Laura groaned and was about to add something, but the bell rang and drowned her out. "I'm onto something!" she shouted as we got up to leave. "Trust me! I know it!"

***

That night started off like any other night. We had dinner, some regular family shenanigans–Dad roasting Mom, Fabi roasting Dad on behalf of Mom, and me and Mom just laughing at it all. Afterwards, I headed to my room, popped in Kyle's CD into my desktop, and started my Calc homework while the main theme of *Spider-Man 2* played. About half an hour in, my burner phone rang and I picked up on the third ring.

"Hello?" I said.

"Is this…" the mother said softly. "Is this…Nicholas?"

"That's me. How can I help you?"

There was a short silence and I took the moment to finish the problem I was on before she finally spoke up again.

"I need your help with something," she said. "A girl at school stole something from my daughter. A bag. A YSL bag."

I raised an eyebrow. "YSL?"

"Yes. Yves Saint Laurent."

"I know what it is. I have a sister. That's a really expensive bag for a teenage girl."

"I know." She paused. "It was mine. And Olivia wanted to borrow it to make the other girls jealous, but I told her not to and she took it to school anyway."

"And then it got stolen."

"Correct. And I need it back." She paused again. "I tried talking to the girl's parents, but they don't believe me. She's denying it and making it look like my daughter and I are the crazy ones." She took a deep breath. "So I need you to steal it back for me."

I stood and started pacing the room. "I have a couple questions for you. First. Why come to me? Why not call the police?"

"Because her father is a cop. And he doesn't believe me."

"Huh. Second. How do I know this bag is actually yours and you're not just trying to get me to rob some innocent girl for you?"

"My initials are stitched into the bottom of the bag," she replied quickly, like she had been expecting this. "I. P. For Iris Potter. It's so obviously different from the girl's initials which is why this is so frustrating because if I could just show her parents, they'll see that it's not hers." She paused for a second before going on. "My mother gave me that bag, Nicholas. And her mother had given it to her. And I was planning on giving it to Olivia one day. I need that bag back."

I thought this over for a second. I felt like she was telling the truth. Hamilton Moms weren't the kind to try to steal bags that they could easily afford to buy themselves. Hamilton girls, on the other hand, were known to steal anything from each other—lipstick, grades, bags, and boyfriends. Plus, like Mrs. Potter had confessed, there was sentimental value to this bag. The point was that this story wasn't too far-fetched.

"Last question," I said. "Who's the girl?"

Mrs. Potter cleared her throat then said, "Katie Mills."

Chapter thirty-nine:
"One Way or Another"

I was dumbfounded. Katie Mills? There was no way. I pulled the phone from my ear and checked the screen like I was expecting to see Laura's face pop up on it. How did Laura know? Was she working with Mrs. Potter? Did she know about the Gibson Circle? Or was she really that smart that she'd been able to figure this out? Could it just have been a coincidence?

"Hello?" Mrs. Potter said on the other end and I realized I hadn't said anything for a whole minute.

"Sorry," I replied. "I heard you. Give me a second." I paced the room as ideas ran through my head. Worst case scenario was that this was somehow a trap set up by Laura to force my hand. But if that were the case, why would she go through these roundabout hoops to catch me? Why didn't she just call me out in front of everyone? This didn't fit her M.O., as Laura would put it. But on the other hand, if this really was a coincidence or even if Laura really had successfully deduced this, it meant that I now had the upper hand. Laura knew who the next victim was, but she didn't know when and how it would happen.

"I'll do it," I told Mrs. Potter.

"Thank you," she breathed a sigh of relief. "How much?"

"How much was the purse?"

"Twelve hundred."

"Then it'll cost you twenty-four-hundred. Twelve hundred for the bag and twelve hundred for the grab."

"Deal," she said quickly.

***

When I walked into the conference room at lunch the next day, Sarah and Lisa were huddled around Laura's laptop. Laura was watching over their shoulders with a look of mild annoyance and Kyle was slowly spinning in his chair off to the side.

"This is the dress I'm thinking of getting," Lisa was saying. "What do you think? Too much?"

"Oh my God!" Sarah exclaimed. "That looks so good. You should totally get it. I bought mine already and I cannot *wait* to wear it."

"You already bought it?" Lisa asked. "It's April. Prom is a month away."

"Exactly," Sarah said. "A month away. That's basically tomorrow."

They went back and forth for a little and I was surprised Laura wasn't shutting it down to get us started.

"Hey, Nick," Sarah suddenly said. "Did you invite anyone yet?"

"What?" I asked.

"To prom," she said. "Did you invite anyone?"

I forced myself to not look at Laura, but I could see her looking at me in my peripheral.

"Uh…no," I finally said. "I don't…I don't know if I'm going." That was true. With everything going in with the bakery and being the Phantom, I honestly hadn't even thought about prom. And I honestly didn't really care.

"Not going?!" Sarah scoffed. "That's unacceptable. Even for you. You have to go."

Laura turned and started erasing stuff on the board. But there was nothing on the board—she was just avoiding the awkwardness.

"I think we should protect Katie," I said abruptly, changing the subject.

Sarah rolled her eyes, but she switched with me as she sat down. "You really buy that crap? It's such a Hail Mary. There's no basis."

"Well, hear me out," I said, holding my hands up in surrender. "Let's treat it like an anonymous tip. We follow the lead and if nothing happens, then we don't lose anything."

"Except for time," Sarah disagreed. "Plus, how embarrassing is it gonna be to try to explain to Katie that the Phantom is coming after her and then to find out that it wasn't even her?"

"We don't even have to tell her," I suggested.

"Brilliant," Sarah scoffed. "How do you expect to protect someone from an attack without telling them they're under attack?"

"We could figure out what the Phantom might want from her," Laura suggested. "And work from there. She wouldn't even have to know we were protecting her."

"Exactly," I pointed at her.

"So," Kyle said, scratching his chin. "If he was trying to delete her English paper, then we could get her to print a hard copy so she doesn't fail." Then he stopped and looked at Laura sheepishly. "Sorry. No offense."

"None taken," Laura said. "But you're right. That's how it'd work."

"So what does the Phantom want with Katie?" Lisa asked.

Laura paced the front of the room as she tapped her marker on her chin. "Well, if my theory's correct, then he'd be targeting the new thing in her life—which is becoming cheer captain."

"So he'll probably do something to get her kicked off the team," Kyle suggested.

Laura nodded and wrote "KICKED OFF THE TEAM" on the board.

I resisted the urge to smile. In order for my plan to work, I had to make them believe that they had "figured" this out on their own.

"How would we get her kicked off the team?" she asked without turning to us. "Anyone have any dirt on Katie that could piss off her coaches?" She faced us, but no one said a word.

Lisa shrugged then looked at Kyle who made a don't-look-at-me face. I shrugged too and looked at Laura, who furrowed her brow as she tried to think.

"She's just a regular girl from what I know," she said. "A little prissy and annoying."

"Maybe she's on steroids?" Kyle offered.

"How did she become cheer captain?" Lisa asked.

"Maybe she bribed someone?" Laura tried.

"She's a thief," Sarah announced and we all looked at her.

"What'd you say?" I asked her.

"She's a thief," Sarah repeated, obviously annoyed.

"How do you know?"

"Because she stole my calculator freshman year in the middle of algebra. I could never prove it, but I know it was her. Plus one of my friends said she stole her brush junior year too. And there's other kids who say that she's stolen their stuff. I'm not saying that I think she's a victim, but the girl's a total clepto. She steals like she grew up in a ghetto. No offense, Nick."

"Offense taken," I said.

"So she's a thief," Laura said. "And if she got exposed, then she might get kicked off the team. Or at the very least get demoted from being a captain." She paused for a second as she thought. "Sarah, did you ever get your calculator back?"

"No," Sarah huffed. "My Dad had to buy me a new one. He always buys me things."

My ears perked up at that. That was the second time I'd heard Sarah talk about her Dad. But she had never mentioned her mother. Weird.

"Did your friend ever get her brush back?" Laura asked.

"No. Her parents had to—"

"Did any of the people you know get their stuff back?"

"No. She always figured out a way to steal them without getting caught. But we knew it was her. We *knew!*"

"So she's got a list of victims," Laura went on, twirling the marker in her hand. "None of them ever got the items back that were stolen from them and none of them could prove that Katie stole them. If I was the Phantom, I'd pick one of these victims…"

"And find the thing she stole and expose it to her coach!" Kyle shouted.

"Bingo," Laura winked at him and he grinned from ear to ear.

I grinned too. It was moving along smoothly.

"So who was her most recent victim?" Lisa asked. "I mean we didn't even know she was a thief. How are we gonna find out who she stole from this year?"

"We won't need to," Laura said. "We can start with one we know." She nodded at Sarah. "Does she still have your calculator?"

Sarah scoffed. "Yeah. She uses it every day. But I never wrote my name on it so I can't technically prove that it's mine, you know? But I know it is. What's your point?"

"Maybe the Phantom might try to steal it back for you," Laura said.

Uh-oh.

Sarah made a face like someone had farted on her. "No. I'm fine. I don't need it anymore."

"I know," Laura insisted. "But if Katie's the Phantom's next target, then he might try to take your calculator back to expose her. And if that's true, then you could start instigating her about it to kind of egg the Phantom on. You could be the bait that lures the Phantom out."

Oh no. This was going in the wrong direction.

"I'm not about to be bait for some psychopath!" Sarah protested. "Are you serious?"

"I don't think that's a good idea," I cut in.

"Thank you!" Sarah threw her hands up. "Someone with sense."

"The calculator thing was so long ago. I feel like the Phantom would use something more recent." Then I leaned forward in my chair and stared at the table like I was trying to concentrate. "Now that you mentioned the stealing, I think I remember her coming to school with a real fancy bag earlier this year. It was one of those designer ones. Like, um…uh…"

"Kate Spade?" Laura tried.

"No."

"Coach?" Lisa asked.

"I think it had a Y on it."

"YSL?" Sarah asked.

"Yeah! Is that the one with the overlapping letters?"

"Yeah."

"I think that was it. A YSL bag. I remember her being extra snotty about it the day I saw her with it. I mean she could've just been her regular snotty self, but…I don't know."

"Actually," Lisa nodded. "I remember that day. And Olivia Potter was pisssed at her. I didn't actually hear her say that Katie stole it. But she was definitely pissed at her."

"So you think the Phantom would choose Olivia over Sarah?" Kyle asked.

"I mean, who wouldn't?" Laura winked.

"That was so funny, I forgot to laugh," Sarah said dryly.

"So we've got…" Laura turned back to the board. "Kicked off the team…stealing…Olivia's YSL bag. We have the who, the what, but now we need the where and the when."

I leaned back as everyone stared at the board and thought.

"Maybe in one of the classes they have together?" Kyle suggested. "But I don't know their schedule. What classes do you guys take senior year?"

"I think they have Chemistry together," Lisa said.

"Or maybe during lunch one day when everyone's together in one place," Laura said, absent-mindedly.

I let the silence go on for a few more seconds before humming, "Hmmmm."

"What is it?" Laura glanced at me.

"I think the answer's already there," I pointed at the board. "'Kicked off the cheer team.' If the Phantom wants her to get kicked off the team…" I shrugged.

Laura stared at the board for a second and I saw the moment the thought clicked. "Then he'll strike at a game."

"Ohhhhh," Kyle and Lisa both said at the same time.

"We might not be able to figure out when he's gonna steal the bag," Laura said, going back to pacing. "But he'd probably expose her at a game—where her, her coach, and Olivia would all be there."

"Whoa," Kyle breathed. "That's wicked."

I grinned, but quickly wiped it off with my hand and cleared my throat.

"So when's the next home game?" asked Lisa.

Sarah let out an exasperated sigh.

Laura looked up at the ceiling like she was making a mental calculation. I think this Saturday."

"Yeah," Lisa nodded. "We play Zenith."

Kyle scoffed. "It's gonna be a blowout. Aren't they like number ten in the state?"

"That was only in academics," Sarah corrected him. "They're pretty good in sports. Besides, they were number ten four years ago. They're number three now behind us and Jeffeeson."

"Oh," Kyle frowned. "Well...I guess it might be a good game then."

I covered my mouth with my fist to hide my smirk as everyone looked at each other.

"So is everyone free this Saturday?" Laura asked.

Kyle nodded, Lisa shrugged, but Sarah rolled her eyes.

"Dang it," I snapped my fingers. "I'm not. We have family coming over this weekend so we're gonna be driving them all over the place. But you guys should still do it. If he's gonna strike on Saturday, we don't wanna miss this chance."

Laura nodded. "You're right." Then she put her hands on her hips and took a deep breath. "Well, everybody. Time to catch a phantom."

Chapter forty:
"Bonnie and Clyde"

That Saturday, the bleachers were packed for our home lacrosse game. My stomach was wild with butterflies as I waited beneath a tree nearby. The crowd was cheering as everyone's eyes were on the game on the field. But my eyes were watching Laura as she appeared right on schedule, walking towards one of the bleachers. She stopped short, looked around briefly, then leaned against a tree of her own. She pulled out her walkie talkie and said something into it. She was too far to hear, but I knew she was telling the team something like "I'm in position. Over."

So was I.

And just like that, I was about to set in motion one of the most audacious stunts Laura had ever seen. I took a deep breath and adjusted my hood and my backpack then marched towards her from behind.

"Fancy seeing you here," I said when I was within a few feet of her. I had debated whether or not to change my voice. But the mask muffled it enough that if I just spoke deeper, I sounded like Freddy Kreuger with a sore throat.

She whirled and her eyes went wide when she saw me.

"Ha!" she pointed at me accusingly. "It's you!"

I nodded. "You seem proud of yourself."

"I knew you'd be here," she said and I could see the pride glowing all over her face.

"That makes two of us."

"I knew it." Her smile was a mix of a excitement and rage, which was a scary combination—like she wasn't sure if she should cheer or rip my face off. "I knew you'd be here. Now you're not going anywhere."

"Is that right?" I asked her. "You couldn't catch me last time. What makes you think this time will be any different?"

"This time I have help," she said, tapping the walkie talkie clipped to her hip.

"That's cute," I nodded. "In that case, I won't keep you waiting. The reason I brought you here is because I have an offer."

"Brought me?" I relished in the shocked look on her face. "What are—"

"You're never gonna beat me," I cut her off. "So why don't you join me?"

She scoffed and it looked like she was even thinking about spitting on me. "You must be out of your mind."

"You're a clever girl," I said. "Probably the most clever I've ever met. And I really do enjoy this little cat and mouse game we've got going on. But I think we'd have more fun working together. You could be the Bonnie to my Clyde."

"You do know they both died in the end, right?" she hissed at me.

"And what a glorious death it was."

She narrowed her eyes into angry slits. "Why would I ever team up with you? You ruined my life."

"That's a bit dramatic, don't you think?" I said casually. "I deleted one paper. It's not my fault you didn't have a back up file."

The crowd suddenly cheered as someone scored.

"I'm gonna kill you," Laura threatened me as the noise died down.

"Once again, you'll have to catch me first," I said.

"I already did," she said, looking me up and down. "You're not going anywhere."

I looked around at the bleachers nearby then at the packed parking lot behind us. "Am I? What exactly are you and your friends trying to stop me from doing?"

"We know your next victim is here," Laura said. Then she paused as if she was considering whether or not she should reveal this next piece of information. "And we think it's Katie Mills. You're gonna steal a purse from her."

"Huh," I nodded slowly then pulled my backpack off and reached inside. "You mean this purse?" I pulled out a black handbag and held it for her to see.

Her eyes went big and her jaw dropped. "Whaaat?"

Then her walkie talkie cackled on her hip and Kyle's voice came through loud and clear.

"Laura! We have eyes on the Phantom!"

I didn't think Laura's eyes could open any wider, but they did. She snatched the walkie talkie and said, "What do you mean?"

"He's here!" Kyle replied, and he sounded like he was running. "He just took Katie's purse! We're chasing him down now!"

Laura went to respond and I took my chance to turn and sprint the other direction.

"Hey!" she shouted, running after me.

I led her through the parking lot, vaulting over car hoods like a cheetah. She didn't do too bad herself and went gliding over each hood like she was sliding over first base. Second base. Third base. But little did she know I was about to send her on a wild goose chase.

We reached the end of the lot and I ran through the entrance to the gymnasium. It was completely empty and I hightailed it across the court to the double doors on the opposite end. I went through, exploding into a stairwell just as Fabi was sprinting up the stairs towards me—dressed in an identical Phantom outfit. It felt like time slowed to a crawl like an anime scene as we brushed past each other and she slipped out the double doors behind me and into the gym. The next instant, Kyle and Lisa appeared on the steps and as if we had rehearsed this, I ran across the wall, jumped over their heads, and landed on the landing behind them. By the time they recovered from "me" changing directions so fast, I was already down the stairs and out the door at the bottom.

"There are two Phantoms!" I heard Laura's voice over Kyle's walkie talkie as I left. "I repeat! There are…"

I was out of earshot before she could say it again. Fabi and I gave them all a good run for their money through the empty building until finally losing them and meeting up at Fabi's car parked on a side street. We drove off without seeing even a trace of them behind us.

"Whooo!" Fabi screamed, ripping her mask off. "That's how we do it, baby!"

"That was sick!" I cried. My heart was pumping and my whole body was shaking from the adrenaline. I was surprised Fabi could drive straight. That. Was. Incredible. It was like a fricking movie. But the best part was what Laura and the others would never know: that I'd already stolen Katie's purse earlier that day. The purse I had now and the purse Fabi had were both cheap knockoff lookalikes. So even if we'd gotten caught, the real purse was safe back home. But Laura would never know that. What she would "know" is that she had gotten so close to catching me. But in reality, I was thinking three moves ahead.

Chapter forty-one:
"Slipped Away"

"What happened?" I asked when we met again on Monday.

The awkwardness in the room was palpable. Lisa and Kyle exchanged glances, Sarah's arms were crossed, and Laura stood at the front with her palms on the table and her head down.

"We didn't catch him," Laura said.

I raised my eyebrows, feigning surprise. "Wait. So he was there? We were right?"

"Yeah," Kyle said, almost too excitedly. "He was *really* there."

"What do you mean?"

"There were two of them," Laura said without looking up. "The Phantom was talking to me behind the bleachers and was bragging about how he already had the bag. He even showed it to me. Then I chased him and right when I thought I was gonna catch him…another Phantom showed up."

"With another bag," Lisa added.

"There were two bags?" I asked, looking back and forth between them.

"Yeah," Kyle furrowed his brow. "Which was another weird thing. So does that mean that the Phantom robbed two students? Did Katie steal two bags?"

"More importantly," Lisa cut in. "Are there two Phantoms?"

"Even more importantly," Sarah held up a finger. "How did he know we were coming?"

I sat back as they talked over each other, tossing theories this way and that until frustrations started rising. I forced myself to look concerned and even asked a question here and there, but inside, I was having a blast. I wished that I could record this and play it back to watch with Fabi.

"Someone had to tip him off," Sarah inisted. "And the only one in this room who wasn't with us on Saturday…" She looked at me. "Was Nick."

"Are you kidding me?" I asked her. "I wasn't even at the game. I told you I was with my family."

"And how do we know that for sure?"

"Didn't Nick get targeted by the Phantom?" Kyle reminded her. "Don't you remember Vanessagate?"

"You named it," Laura muttered to herself.

"Whatever," Sarah waved him off. "He could still be in cahoots with him."

"Why would he be in cahoots with someone who tried to ruin his reputation?" Lisa asked. Then she looked me up and down. "Or lack thereof."

"Thank you," I nodded at her. "...kind of."

"I don't think anyone tipped him off," Laura said, palms still on the table. "I think there's a..." Her eyes moved to her laptop screen and her eyebrows suddenly shot up. She moved the laptop and her eyes darted back and forth as she read something. We all watched in anticipation, wondering what was happening.

"Is everything okay?" Lisa asked.

"Is it a school announcement?" asked Kyle. "Is school gonna be canceled tomorrow?"

Laura didn't respond, but she stopped reading and looked up, lost in thought. What had she just seen? And why did it have her hyper-focused?

"We're done," she suddenly announced, shutting her laptop. "I'll let you know when we're meeting again." Then, without another word, she packed up all her stuff and walked out the room.

The rest of us sat there in confused silence, literally frozen over what to say or do. What the heck had just happened?

Kyle looked at Sarah and Lisa. "Was that...girl stuff?"

The girls rolled their eyes as they got up to leave. But I stayed put, suddenly worried. It wasn't girl stuff. Or boy stuff. It was definitely Phantom stuff. And I had to find out exactly what.

Chapter forty-two:
"I Need a Girl"

Laura was MIA for the rest of the day and when I tried to call her later that evening, she didn't answer. I texted her and messaged her on facebook, but got nothing. And for the next few days at school, she acted like the Phantom suddenly didn't exist. She'd be cordial and say hi, even sit with me at lunch, but she refused to talk about anything Phantom related. Whenever I asked, she'd say, "I just need a break. I've got a lot on my mind."

I told her that I understood, but I didn't. Not the way I was pretending to. Something wasn't right. "I just need a break."? That was bull. She was Laura Wood. The girl whose mind could juggle three chess matches simultaneously while timing her moves to Disney songs. She thrived on multitasking and mind-bending puzzles. She was lying to me and I needed to know why. But if she wasn't going to tell me, maybe she'd tell the Phantom.

So one evening I waited for her after softball practice. She would always wait for her parents at the edge of the parking lot behind the school. There weren't many cars out this late and no trees nearby so there was no place to hide. But at the same time, if anyone did see us, from a distance they would just think Laura was talking to some emo kid in a hoodie.

I came up behind her as she was sitting on the curb, doodling in her notebook.

"The weather's been lovely, don't you think?"

She was on her feet and turning to me in a flash and her eyes went ablaze when she saw me.

"You," she hissed at me. "What do you want?"

"The same thing I wanted last time," I said. "You."

She spit at my feet and if I wasn't so amused I would've been offended. She really hated the Phantom.

"I already told you," she said. "I'm never gonna help you. Now leave me alone."

"I don't mean to be forward," I said calmly. "But I know you love the thrill of the chase. You live for it. Imagine how thrilling it would be to have the whole school chasing us? What would it be like to outsmart everyone we knew?"

"I don't need your kind of thrill," she said slowly.

"Is that why you and your detective club stopped meeting?"

She blinked several times as the shock came over her. I could see her trying to figure out how I knew that while simultaneously trying not to let on that she was alarmed. She finally narrowed her eyes at me and said, "Leave. Me. Alone."

I nodded slowly. "As you wish. But to show you that I have no hard feelings…" I pulled out a folded white sheet of paper and held it up between my fingers. "This is a hint on who my next victim is. Yours if you want it."

I held it there between us and watched her eyes go from my hand to my face then back to my hand. The silence swelled for another five seconds then she finally snatched it from me. I had printed out one name in the center of the paper: LOYDE N.B. NICE.

I turned to leave as she was unfolding it, probably confused over who that was. I knew that her curiosity would get the best of her and she'd call the group back together again tomorrow to figure out what this clue was. They'd realize it was an anagram of another name and inevitably Laura would figure it out first. And I couldn't wait for the look on her face when she'd realize that it said—

"Bonnie and Clyde."

I turned back to see her holding the paper open in one hand and glaring straight at me.

"Bonnie and Clyde," she repeated. "You think you're so funny, don't you?"

I was glad she couldn't see my surprise behind the mask. I had spent thirty minutes on that anagram. And she'd solved it in two seconds. Man, she was good.

"You're a lot smarter than I thought," I told her.

She took one step forward and stopped within a foot of me.

"I'm not just smarter than you thought," she said. "I'm smarter than you. Period. And by this time next week, I'll already know who you are. That's why I'm not meeting with my group anymore. Because we don't need to. Because your days are numbered, Phantom."

And with that, she tossed the paper at me before shoving my shoulder as she walked past. And once again I was glad that she couldn't see my jaw dropping behind my mask. Because I was shook.

Chapter forty-three:
"Days Go By"

The next few days was more of the same. No lunch meetings and no real answers from Laura. I was slowly dying from the suspense. What had she figured out? Did she know it was me? The only thing that was able to take my mind off things was a spontaneous family movie night.

Every Friday had been movie night since I was six years old. We'd all go to Blockbuster and my parents would pick a movie and my sister and I would get to pick either a second movie or a video game. Then we'd go home and my mother would make some sort of "TV dinner" and we'd cuddle up in my parents' bedroom to watch the movie. But lately with everything going on with the bakery, we'd all been too busy to keep consistent. But today, my Dad decided we all needed a break so here we were. And for the first time all week, I was hyped.

My Mom and Fabi were downstairs making dinner and I was in my parents' room with my Dad "setting up" the movie.

"It's really not that complicated, Dad," I told him. "You just have to switch these two plugs…" I unplugged the cable cord from the back of the TV then plugged in the DVD player instead and the DVD logo appeared on the screen. "…and that's it."

My Dad shook his head. "No thanks. I need a Ph. D. for that."

I laughed. I was usually annoyed at having to "troubleshoot" the simplest electronic stuff for my parents. But not tonight. I was just happy that for once in the midst of the past crazy six months, we could finally chill as a family, relatively stress-free. It was April now and I'd put over $60,000 towards the down payment. At the rate I was going with the Gibson Circle, if I kept getting a steady flow of clients, we'd have exactly $90,000 by June. So everything was going according to plan. Which made tonight taste even sweeter.

I popped in the *Rush Hour 3* DVD and just as the movie menu appeared, my Mom and Fabi walked into the room with dinner. Fabi was carrying a liter of Brisk and cups and my Mom was carrying a tray filled with *fritay*: fried plantains, fried sweet potatoes, french fries, and *griot* (fried pork). My mom had the cordless phone cradled between her face and shoulder as she carried everything and my Dad spread a blanket over the bed for her to place the tray on.

"*Konsa mem?*" she cried into the phone. "*Gad on tin tin!*"

She was probably talking to one of her sisters about some drama that I didn't care about.

"C'mon, Marie," my Dad said, loud enough for whoever she was talking to to hear. "It's family time."

"Hold on, hold on," my Mom waved him off.

"God should've given women two mouths," my Dad sighed. "Cuz they talk so much."

"And He should've given men four ears," Fabi bounced back. "Because' y'all don't listen."

"*Frekan!*" my Dad said, and he tossed a fry at her.

We all laughed and sat down on the bed as we waited for my Mom to finally hang up. When she did, we turned out the lights, said grace, then I hit play. And with my Mom on my left, my Dad on my right, and Fabi laying across the bed at our feet, it felt like I was a kid again. I gave Fabi a light kick in her back and she reached behind and pinched my foot. I grinned so hard I felt like my teeth were about to fall out. This was what I loved about my family. Being able to sit here together, eating *fritay* and laughing at Jackie Chan and Chris Tucker–there was nothing like it.

And then the phone rang.

"Don't answer it," my Dad warned.

"What if it's important?" my Mom said, already reaching to pick up.

"Then they'll leave a message."

But my Mom answered.

"Who needs four ears now?" my Dad said, flicking the back of Fabi's head.

"Whatever," she muttered.

I didn't bother pausing the movie because I knew my Mom would just say to let it play. But now we wouldn't be able to hear what was happening so it just created this annoying limbo. But weirdly enough, she wasn't saying much. She was just nodding and going, "Oh…oh…but why?" This was a different call. This wasn't her sister. Maybe she was right–this *was* important. And now I couldn't focus on the movie because I wanted to figure out who she was talking to.

"Ok," she said. And then she hung up.

I paused the movie and Fabi and my Dad both sucked their teeth at the same time.

"What's the matter with you?" Fabi demanded, sitting up.

"Who was that?" I asked.

My Mom sighed deeply. "It was the investor."

I tensed.

"What did they say?" Fabi asked.

My Mom paused for several seconds before answering. "He's in a rush to close so he's moving the deadline."

I clenched my fists as I waited for the bomb.

"We have until May."

Chapter forty-four:
"I Write Sins Not Tragedies"

We had until May.

That was next month–a whole month earlier than we'd expected. All of the money I was making was only going to barely get us to the deadline in June. I was pulling in $12,000 every month—which I know is a lot of money, don't get me wrong. But since the vast chunk of that was going towards the down payment, in the grand scheme of things, it wasn't a lot. And now that we had one less month to save that meant I had to come up with another $12,000 out of nowhere. We were screwed.

Needless to say, family movie night was over. My parents made some desperate calls to figure some things out while Fabi and I went to my room to try to come up with a plan. But short of selling drugs, neither of us could come up with any way of making an extra 12 grand in a month. So a few days later my Dad got a part-time job as a taxi driver and as a result we barely saw him. Maybe it would be enough, but maybe it wouldn't.

Then, one night, I got a call from Mrs. Gibson. It had been a while since I'd spoken to her.

"Good evening, Nicholas," she said. "Long time no listen."

"Yes," I agreed. "Good to hear from you again. How can I help you?"

"Do you know my son Aaron? Sarah's brother? He's on the baseball team. But he hasn't been getting any playing time lately. I'm not sure if you've seen him play before, but he's really good."

I looked up at the ceiling as I scrolled through my mind. I knew about Aaron Gibson. He was a pitcher that would come off the bench. He was pretty good, from what I heard. I didn't understand the politics going on there since I wasn't on the team, but apparently there was something–hence why Mrs. Gibson was calling.

"My son has a future in baseball, Nicholas," she went on. "My husband has…what are they called? Boy scouts? Girl scouts? Some kind of scouts coming to see him play, but they can't see him play if he's not on the field. Do you understand?"

I nodded as I listened.

"I want you to make it so that Aaron comes off the bench."

"Okay…" I said. "What do you have in mind?"

"I want you to break the starting pitcher's leg."

My breath caught in my throat. Did I hear that right?

"The starting pitcher," Mrs. Gibson went on. "You know who it is, right?"

I did, but I was still recovering from the savage request to answer.

"Billy Richardson," she answered for me. "The pitcher is Billy Richardson."

I took a deep breath. This was wild. Breaking Billy's leg so Aaron could get more playing time? That was too far.

"Are you still there?" Mrs. Gibson asked me.

"Yes, ma'am," I replied. "Ummm…that's a little different from what we usually do. I don't think I can do this. I'm sorry."

There was a short silence on the other end. Then Mrs. Gibson exhaled and said, "I will pay you $10,000."

My heart skipped a beat. $10,000? That was insane. To break a kid's leg? More importantly, $10,000 would help put us back on track to saving the bakery. In one move I could solve our financial problems. The solution was being offered to me on a silver platter.

But I shook my head.

"It's not even about the money, ma'am," I told her. "This is wrong. I can't do this."

"But my son, Nicholas. He needs this. I told you he has a future in baseball and this coach is playing with it because he has favorites. What about the girl scouts, Nicholas? You take care of me and I'll take care of you."

"But this is wrong," I repeated.

"Look, hasn't Billy Richardson been bullying you?" .

"Yes," I answered. "Billy has been bullying me, but even he doesn't deserve this. I'm sorry. I can't do it."

There was a long silence and I was hoping she would say she understood then hang up. But instead she exhaled again then said, "It would be a shame if the school found out what you've been doing."

My blood went cold. Again with this. My brain immediately formed a montage of what the students would do if they knew I was the Phantom. Not only would Billy kill me, but everyone else would join in on the carnage too. At this point I had over thirty bodies to my name. I would never recover. And Laura. My heart sank as I thought of what she'd do if she found out. Not only would she get her revenge, but I'd lose her. The first girl I'd ever liked and who liked me back—the first girl I genuinely cared about deeply—would be gone because of this. And of course, most importantly, I could kiss my parents' bakery good-bye.

But was I really about to break Billy's leg for this?

"Nicholas," Mrs. Gibson said.

I shut my eyes and took a deep breath. "I'll figure something out."

I hung up and flopped back onto my bed.

$10,000.

I could save my parents.

I could save myself from social homicide.

And just like that my brain started stringing together a plan. I knew that Mike Taft was throwing a party at his house this weekend. He lived in the backwoods and there was a weird bend in a road in the area that kids would usually have accidents on if they drove too fast. A lot of kids avoided it and went the long way to his house, but the daredevils loved pushing their luck. I could set up some detour signs the night of the party when Billy was leaving to force him down that road. Maybe I could even put some stuff in the way and pour some water on the road to make sure he lost control. This was sick.

But the night of the party I went to that bend in the road. I had a couple traffic cones in a duffle bag and a few gallons of water. I stood among the trees off the side of the road, completely cloaked in their shadows as I plotted how I'd do this. My heart was sinking the entire time and my body was shaking.

$10,000.

Save my parents.

Save myself.

But I couldn't bring myself to do it. I dropped down and sat on a boulder. This wasn't worth it. If Mrs. Gibson told everyone my secret, then so be it. I'd have to take the L. Even if it meant losing Laura. And my parents and I could figure some other way to save the bakery.

I called Fabi and asked her to come pick me up then stood to head back to Mike's house. But before I could even step out from behind the trees, I heard a car coming. The engine roared and the headlights flooded the darkness as the pick up truck came barreling around the bend. Billy and his friends were hooting and hollering to rock music and they weren't slowing down. The next thing I knew, the truck skidded out of control, spun off the road, and crashed into a tree.

Chapter forty-five:
"How to Save a Life"

The truck was totaled. The hood was crushed like an accordion, smoke was hissing out of the front, and the airbags were out. My jaw hung open in shock as I watched and waited. There was no way this had just happened. Then Gary grunted and wrestled his way out of the driver's seat, fighting with the airbag on his way. He stumbled to the ground just as Dean flopped out of the back seat. They started cursing and I noticed Gary's words were slurred. He wobbled and staggered a few steps and I wasn't sure if he was disoriented from the accident or drunk.

I stayed crouched in the shadows as I watched. I could see Billy still in the passenger seat. His airbag hadn't deployed. And he wasn't moving. Gary and Dean kept cursing and stumbling around until they finally made it over to Billy. They cursed some more then muttered some things I couldn't hear. But then they looked around and did something I never expected–not even for them. They backed away from the truck then jogged away.

Did they just leave? There was no way. Had they gone to look for help? No. One of them would have stayed behind. Did they really just leave Billy? I was still in shock from witnessing the accident, but I eventually snapped out of it and came out of hiding. I ran over to Billy's side of the truck and was immediately hit with the smell of alcohol. Bud Lite cans were littered all over the front and back seats and beer had splattered onto the radio.

I felt Billy's neck and detected a faint pulse. He was still alive–unconscious, but alive. There was blood trailing down the side of his face and a deep red stain on the side of his shirt. Barely alive. My heart raced and I suddenly realized how bad this looked. I was the only one here with a duffle bag of traffic cones and gallons of water and now this kid was on the brink of death from an accident. If a cop arrived and asked me questions no water would wash me. But I couldn't dip like Gary and Dean. Billy needed help. So I called Fabi again and told her to hurry and she was there a few minutes later.

"What happened?!" she shrieked when she pulled up next to the truck.

"I'll explain on the way!" I shouted. "Help me get him in the car."

We both carried Billy out of the truck then laid him on the back seat of Fabi's Camry. Then we hightailed it out of there and sped to the nearest hospital. We half carried half dragged Billy into the emergency room with Fabi shouting, "He needs help! Somebody help!"

Immediately we were swarmed by blue smocks as nurses intercepted him and pulled him on a stretcher. They wheeled him away and before we knew it we were waiting in the lobby still reeling from everything.

Fabi watched me quietly for a few minutes then glanced at the other people sitting around us.

"Is this what I think it is?" she asked me in Kreyol.

I sighed. My stomach was in knots and I felt like I was about to throw up.

"Yes and no," I replied. "Mrs. Gibson wants her son to get more playing time. So she needed me to break Billy's leg."

Fabi sucked her teeth. "So you made him get into an accident?"

"No," I said quickly. "I was going to, but I changed my mind. I promise. I didn't do it."

"So your duffle bag you threw in my trunk…"

"Traffic cones and water," I explained. And saying it out loud made me shiver. What would have happened if I hadn't had the presence of mind to toss the bag into the car? What if I had left them there at the scene? The police could've found the bag and traced it back to me and once again, no water would wash me. I sighed as relief wrapped me like a blanket.

Fabi pinched her nose, but I couldn't fully read her expression, whether it was disappointment or confusion. "You were gonna injure Billy? By staging an accident?"

"Yes…" I replied softly.

"You realize there's so many other ways to do that right? You could've just punched him in the face. Slammed his finger in a car door. You could've just farted in his pillow and gave him pink eye. But you went straight for a car accident?"

I lowered my head. She was right. This had been stupid.

"Why didn't you tell me?"

I shrugged. "I don't know…" I thought back to the conversation with Mrs. Gibson. I had been so anxious about it all. I hadn't wanted to do it, but she'd blackmailed me. I guess I didn't tell Fabi because I was ashamed. Or scared. I didn't even know anymore. But now we were in the lobby and Billy Richardson might not make it through the night because of my stupidity.

"How much was she gonna pay you?"

I swallowed. "$10,000."

Fabi's eyes went wide. "You're lying."

I shook my head. "She was serious."

Fabi sucked her teeth again. "Wow." She paused for a few seconds then added, "Well, I guess we can use that for your bail money."

"I hate you," I hissed. But it made me laugh.

"Don't worry," she went on. "You didn't do it. So as far as anyone's concerned, you were just in the area and saw the crash after the fact."

I wrung my hands together. Maybe that made sense. But if Billy didn't make it, would that really matter?

We waited for a couple hours and called my parents to keep them from worrying. Fabi told them there was a really bad accident on the turnpike and that we had been parked there bumper to bumper all night. Then, at around 2 a.m., the doctor came out to meet us.

"I have some news," she said and we jumped to our feet. "Billy suffered a mild concussion and a few broken ribs. But he's going to be alright."

Chapter forty-six:
"What About Now?"

Even though it was late and we could technically leave now that we knew he was okay, Fabi and I went in to see Billy. He was sitting up in his bed in a hospital gown, some bandages wrapped around his head, and staring down at his lap. He looked up when we walked in.

"Tootise?" he asked. "What are you doing here?"

Fabi looked at me and mouthed the nickname in confusion, but I waved it off.

"We were the ones who brought you here," I replied. But then I realized how cryptic that sounded. "After the accident. We brought you here after the accident."

"Accident?" Billy furrowed his brow. "What happened?"

"You and your friends were drunk after Mike's party and crashed into a tree. I was in the area and called my sister and we brought you here."

"What?" Billy shook his head in disbelief. "That's...that's crazy..." He looked like he was trying to remember everything. "The party...the truck..wait...Dean and Gary...are they okay?"

Fabi and I looked at each other.

"They're probably fine," I said, turning back to Billy. "They, uh...they left when they saw you were unconscious."

Billy squinted at me. "What do you mean?"

"Your friends ditched you," Fabi said bluntly. "Left you for dead."

Billy's mouth opened to say something, but he stopped.

"They were drinking," I went on. "So I guess they were scared of getting in trouble. And they probably thought you were already gone." I shook my head. Why was I trying to explain what they did to him? They were jerks and I hoped they'd gotten hit by a motorcycle on their way home. Then eaten by coyotes. What kind of friends would do that to someone? Was there no honor or bro code among bullies?

Billy was silent for a long time and just kept staring at his lap. Finally, he smoothened out his bedsheet with his hands and cleared his throat. "So we were drinking at Mike's party, we drove off, hit a tree, they left me, and you found me and brought me here."

"Yeah," I nodded.

"What were you doing out there?" he asked. It wasn't an accusation. He sounded like he just wanted to piece everything together.

"Uhhhh…" I stammered, looking back and forth from him to Fabi. "I was…ummm…"

"Billy!" a woman shrieked as she came rushing into the room, followed by a bald round man. "Billy, are you alright?"

The two of them practically shoved me and Fabi into the wall on the way to the bed.

"Mom, Dad," Billy said. "I think I'm fine."

"Oh my God, Billy," his mother sobbed, tracing her hand over the bandages on his head. "What happened to you? How did this…?" Her eyes fell on me in the corner and a scowl came across her face. "What did you do?"

My body went cold, but before I could answer, Fabi stepped in front of me.

"My brother saved your son's life, that's what he did," she said firmly.

"What. Happened?" Mrs. Richardson demanded.

"Leah, take it easy," her husband said, touching her elbow.

"No!" she snatched her arm away from him. "Aren't you that Haitian kid that's always getting Billy in trouble? You did this, didn't you?"

"What part of 'saved your son's life' did you not understand?" Fabi snapped. "Billy would be dead if it wasn't for my brother."

"He's right," Billy said and his mother spun to him. "I got into an accident on my way from Mike's party."

I noticed he left out the drinking part. He went on with other details that he made up on the spot and Fabi and I quietly backed out of the room. I hadn't done anything and Billy was gonna be okay. But it didn't change the fact that I still felt horrible.

Chapter forty-seven:
"Ordinary People"

The next day Billy obviously didn't come to school and word got around that he'd been in an accident. I guessed his parents notified his teachers because Dean and Gary weren't saying a dang word. They were just going about their day like nothing had happened. Like their friend had just gotten the flu or something. They even called me HBO and shoved me in the hall when they saw me. I was tempted to call them out, but something held me back. So I just kept it moving.

After school, Mrs. Gibson met me and gave me a thick envelope packed with hundreds. $10,000. Even though I hadn't done anything, it was going to take up to six weeks for Billy's ribs to heal, which meant he was out for the rest of the season. So it didn't matter that I literally hadn't done anything–as far as Mrs. Gibson was concerned, this was all me.

And because of that I didn't even want the money anymore. It literally felt like blood money and was a tangible reminder of how close I'd gotten to almost killing someone. I thought about giving it back, but I just stood there stupidly until Mrs. Gibson walked away. So instead I just stuffed the envelope in my backpack and headed to Fabi's car.

"That's a lot of money," she said.

"I know," I replied. "But I don't wanna use it."

"But the bakery," Fabi said. "This will get us back on track."

"But it just…this isn't right." I rubbed my head like it hurt to think about it.

"You and your stupid conscience," she muttered. I expected her to keep going, but she just sat back and sighed. She opened her mouth several times to start to say something, but changed her mind each time. She felt it too.

"I get it," she finally said. "But you better do something with it. You can't just leave ten grand sitting in your backpack like that."

"I'll figure something out," I said.

"Okay. We heading home or what?"

I thought for a second. "Actually, I wanna go check on Billy. Just, you know…to make sure he's doing alright."

"Doing alright? You're doing too much."

"I just feel bad, Fabi."

She shrugged. "Alright. Hospital visit coming right up." And she drove off.

When we made it to the front desk, we told the receptionist who we wanted to see and she directed us to the third floor. But on our way to the elevators, I heard a familiar voice rambling frantically around the corner.

"I just don't understand why you won't cover it," the voice was saying. "Yes, I know it's not in our network, but this is $8,000 we're talking about. How am I supposed to pay my son's medical bills if you're not gonna cover it? What am I even paying you for?"

It was Billy's mother. I looked at Fabi and she looked at me. My stomach sank as guilt weighed me down. The elevator doors dinged and we walked in without a word. But by the time we made it to the third floor, I'd made up my mind about what to do.

We made it to Billy's room and Mr. Richardson was inside.

"Oh, hey," he said, eyebrows raised. He was obviously surprised to see us again. "Well, it's nice to see you. What were your names again?"

"Nick," I replied. "And this is my sister Fabi. We just wanted to check up on him, that's all."

Mr. Richardson smiled and nodded. "That's real sweet of you. We appreciate it."

I glanced at Billy on the bed, who was also staring with a look of surprise etched on his face. There was a long awkward silence where the only sound was the commercial jingle on the TV. Then I cleared my throat and said, "Mr. Richardson, can I talk to you outside for a second?"

He nodded and the three of us stepped into the hallway.

I rubbed the back of my neck then sighed. "I overheard your wife saying that your insurance won't cover Billy's medical bills."

Mr. Richardson frowned and it suddenly occurred to me that his wife might not have told him this yet. And now I was afraid I may have done more damage than good. But he nodded slowly.

"That's true," he admitted. "She's trying to talk some sense into them now, but I don't think it's going anywhere."

"Well…" I continued. "If it's okay with you…I'd like to help."

Mr. Richardson gave a small smile like I was a toddler offering to pay for dinner. "That's sweet, son, but you don't have to do that. We'll find a way."

"No," I insisted. Then I pulled out the envelope and held it out to him. "That's $10,000. Enough for his bills and then some. I want you to have it."

Mr. Richardson stared at the envelope and his eyes started to glisten. He curled his lips in and just when it looked like he was about to sob, the elevator doors dinged and his wife marched out. She took one look at me and hissed like a snake.

"What are you doing here?" she snarled. "Haven't you done enough? You're the one who brought Billy to this hospital that's not even in our network. Because of you we–"

"Leah!" Mr. Richardson said, his voice cracking. "Stop it. He's trying to help."

"We don't need his help," she replied. "This is all his fault, anyway."

"Leah, you don't understand," Mr. Richardson said then took the envelope from me and opened it towards her. "He wants to help."

Mrs. Richardson's eyes went wide when she saw all the bills, but then she immediately clenched her jaw and snorted.

"Where'd you get that?" she asked me. "Selling drugs? We don't need your dirty money."

"Leah!" Mr. Richardson scolded her. "Don't assume that! Even if it was…does it matter? We need this." Then he turned to me. "Thank you so much, son. We will pay you back. You have my word."

I nodded.

Mrs. Richardson's eyes were darting left and right and she kept swallowing like she was fighting back vomit or tears. We never got to see what it was, though, because her husband pulled her away further down the hall to talk to her. When they were gone, Fabi sighed and rolled her eyes at me.

"Well, aren't you St. Nicholas."

Chapter forty-eight:
"Through the Wire"

Later on it was just us and Billy in the room and Billy was just as surprised to see us as his parents were.

"Why…" he started to say. "…why are you here?" He started looking around the room, like he was expecting some ninjas to hop out the corners and stab him or something.

"We wanna check on you," I shrugged.

"But why, though?" he was tensing up, like he was getting ready for me to punch him, which I probably should have. I knew Fabi would.

"I saw the accident," I replied. "I couldn't just leave you there."

He looked at me then at Fabi and stayed tense like he was holding his breath for a full minute. Then he finally exhaled and stared down at his lap.

"You saved my life," he said.

"I did," I replied.

He shook his head. "I don't deserve it."

"You don't."

"You really don't," Fabi added.

I elbowed her in her side.

"You're right," Billy said. I noticed he was avoiding our eyes now. "I'm…uh…I'm sorry, man."

"What was that?" Fabi said, pretending she hadn't heard him. "Could you speak up?"

Billy frowned. "I'm sorry. For all the crap I've put you through."

Fabi scoffed and folded her arms across her chest.

"I'd say it's fine," I said. "But it's not. I didn't do this to make you feel bad. I did it because it was the right thing to do."

"Stupid thing to do," Fabi muttered.

Billy was quiet for a long time. Then he finally said, "How can I repay you?"

"Well, we're down ten thou–" Fabi started and I elbowed her again.

"You can start by not bullying me anymore," I offered instead.

Billy nodded slowly then looked up at me for a second before looking back down at his lap. "That's fair." He took a deep breath. "From now on, I won't mess with you."

"No more HBO," I said.

"None."

"Or Tootsie."

"Nope."

"Or making fun of my food, my culture, or pushing me around."

"Never again."

I held my hand out. "Deal."

He looked at it for a second then shook it.

"For the record," Fabi cut in. "If it were up to me, I would've run the car over you."

Billy swallowed nervously.

"So if you ever pick on him again, I'll finish what they started."

Billy nodded slowly. Now an awkward silence filled the room. What do you say after something like that?

"It must suck that you're out for the rest of the season," I finally said.

Billy sighed. "Yeah. I hate that. Who's gonna hold it down when I'm gone? We're probably not gonna make states now." He sighed again then frowned. "But the worst part is what Dean and Gary did. I thought they were my friends."

I shrugged. "Apparently not."

Billy slammed his fist into the bed then immediately winced as he hugged his side.

"Take it easy, Rocky," I said.

Billy was huffing angrily, but slowly calmed himself down. "I wish I could get them back for what they did." Then he smirked to himself. "You know, I was seriously thinking of trying to figure out a way to contact the Phantom so he could get them back for me."

I looked at Fabi and she rolled her eyes. But I couldn't resist the idea. Getting revenge on behalf of my bully? There was a sort of twisted poetic justice to it. After all, Dean and Gary did have it coming. How could you leave your friend out there to die like that?

"Me and Laura have been studying the Phantom for a couple months now," I said.

"Have you found anything?" Billy asked. "Do you think you could call him?"

I pretended to do a mental calculation. "I think I could figure something out."

Chapter forty-nine:
"Bring 'Em Out"

The next day at school, I waited until third period to ask to go to the bathroom. Then, with everyone still inside and everyone's cars parked outside, I snuck to the parking lot and found Dean and Gary's cars both parked next to each other. Dean had a nice red Mustang while Gary had a jet black Ferrari. Which meant, if you were paying attention, that the pick up truck they'd crashed had been Billy's. Another reason these guys were certified dirtbags and why I felt no remorse for what I was about to do.

I gave the parking lot a quick sweep to make sure no one was around then knelt between both cars. Then I took out my house keys and dragged them across the car doors, leaving a beautiful silver streak tearing through the paint. Then I pulled out a spray can and sprayed the words "I KNOW WHAT YOU DID" on the windows. Then, just to add a little *pikliz* on it, I left two of those half Phantom of the Opera masks on their hoods. This was the first Phantom thing I'd done *pro bono*, but it was honestly the most exhilarating. But little did I know that it would also be the most explosive.

At lunch I sat with Lance to catch up with him since it had been so long. Not to mention Laura wasn't really talking much anyway.

"Glad you remembered me," Lance said bitterly, taking a sip of his Arizona.

"Sorry," I apologized. "I've been really swamped with this whole thing."

"Yeah," he sighed. "I get it. The Phantom's a lot more interesting than your best friend."

"It's not like that," I told him.

"Not to mention you're finally with the girl of your dreams. Who could blame you for dropping me like a bad habit?"

I frowned. I was definitely not going to let him know Laura had gone all stoic on me. He was obviously taking this hard. No need to make him feel worse by thinking I was rebounding. But had I been that bad of a friend lately? Apparently.

"Lance," I started. "I said I'm sorry. I didn't mean to—"

Suddenly, the cafeteria was buzzing with murmuring and everyone started turning to the windows facing the parking lot. A few students got up and rushed outside. Then a few more. And eventually kids were shouting, laughing, and gasping, until half the cafeteria was pouring outside. Lance and I looked at each other then quickly joined the crowd. Everyone was gathered around Dean's and Gary's cars where the two boys were standing there in complete shock. Dean was furious, huffing and puffing like a mad bull. His face was beet red and veins were popping out the side of his head. But Gary's face was pale white like he'd seen a ghost and he was biting his nails nervously.

"What did they do?" people were whispering.

"It's the Phantom," others said.

"He knows," Gary was whimpering. "He knows…"

Dean grabbed him by the shoulders and shook him hard. "Get a grip, man!" Then he lowered his voice. "We didn't do anything. He's just trying to scare us." Then he spun on the crowd and roared, "Who did this?!"

Everyone took a step back and silence fell on the parking lot.

"Who did this?!" Dean screamed again.

"The Phantom," a voice said softly and some kids laughed. It was Tom Simmons and he was one of the Cartesians.

"So you think this is funny?!" Dean shrieked, looking for the voice. "Who did this?!"

But he never got an answer because the bell rang and everyone hurried back to the caf to get their stuff.

I found out later that after school, Dean and a few other football players dragged Tom into the woods, held some sort of mock Salem Witch trial, accused him of being the Phantom, then urinated all over him. This was getting wild.

The next day at school, there were half the normal amount of kids in homeroom. People had stayed home because half of them were afraid the Phantom would target them next and the other half was afraid Dean would and his teammates would accuse them and put them on trial.

"This is crazy," I said to Laura.

She didn't look at me and at first I thought she didn't hear me. I was about to repeat myself when she suddenly said, "Yeah. It is. The Phantom must be a cold-hearted killer to sit back and watch all this happen."

I didn't say anything. At least she was talking. But was that bitterness in her voice?

"By the way," she said, finally turning to me. "You smell really good today."

I grinned uncontrollably. If I could blush I would have. She finally noticed! She had never complimented how I smelled before and when I'd switched from Rite Guard to Old Spice, I'd kind of been worried she never would. So the fact that she still thought I smelled good made me feel good.

The intercom suddenly crackled and Principal Hanes' voice greeted us all.

"Good morning Hamilton High." He sounded hoarse like he'd been yelling all night and all morning. But there was an urgency to his tone that made me sit up straight. Then he delivered one line that dropped on our ears like a bomb. "If the Phantom doesn't turn themselves in by the end of the day…prom is canceled."

Chapter fifty:
"My Happy Ending"

A wave of murmuring rolled through the room as everyone took in the news. Somehow I could feel the same reactions rippling in every other homeroom around campus.

"He's joking right?" Vanessa blurted. "He can't do that!"

"That's not fair!" Sarah shouted.

More and more students started voicing their protest and some even started threatening the Phantom to come out right now. But I was sitting tight. These kids were hazing people in the woods for being accused of being the Phantom. I was the only black kid in this all-white asylum of a school. If they found out I was the Phantom, they'd lynch me. As far as I was concerned, prom was as good as canceled because I wasn't about to say a word.

At lunch I sat with Laura, but she was still quiet and seemed a lot more focused on drawing chess pieces in her notebook than talking. But everyone else was doing nothing but talking. The entire caf was buzzing over whether or not the Phantom was going to turn himself in.

"Are you okay?" I finally asked Laura.

"Yeah…" she said, shading in the rook she'd drawn. "I'm just…stressed."

"Really?"

She kept her eyes on her paper and sighed. "What if we never find this guy? And my grade is never changed?" She paused for a second. "And I never keep my promise to my grandfather?"

I took a bite of my beef patty without a word., feeling the guilt sting me like spice. I still felt bad about this. Well, at least about hurting Laura. But at the same time, I was in way too deep now. There was no telling what the entire student body would do to me if they found out.

"It's not me!" a boy a few tables down cried.

I looked over and three soccer players were towering over a boy with glasses.

"I don't even have the time to do all that stuff!" the boy was explaining.

"We'll find out by the end of the day if you're lying," one of the players said. Then he picked up a bottle of orange juice and poured it on the boy's head.

I looked away and shut my eyes. This was only going to get worse. But coming forward was not an option.

Finally, last period came and it seemed like everyone, even Mr. Jones up front, was waiting in anticipation. For the last five minutes of class, we literally just sat there in silence, listening to each other's heartbeats. Then, a minute before the final bell, the intercom cackled and everyone shifted in their seats.

"The Phantom has not turned himself in," Principal Hanes announced. "So prom is officially canceled."

The intercom cackled off and it was like a bomb detonated. It wasn't just that the kids were pissed that prom was canceled—which they were. But for the past several months the Phantom had been sabotaging everyone's social lives. So for all that time that frustration and anger had been boiling under a pressure cooker of not knowing who this Phantom was. But now that the anger of prom being canceled was being thrown on top of that, it was the final push that blew the top off. But since they couldn't take it out on the Phantom, they took it out on themselves.

It was chaos.

"It was you!" one kid up front stood and pointed at another kid. "Just fess up!"

"How do we know it wasn't you?!" the kid responded and shoved the first kid.

Then other people started accusing and shoving until the whole class was fighting. Then one kid picked up a chair and tossed it through the window, smashing the glass into a million pieces.

"Everyone stop!" Mr. Jones shouted up front.

But even he wasn't safe. One boy actually ran up to him and punched him in the face, knocking him back into the blackboard.

Kids were wrestling on the floor, slamming each other onto the desks, and one kid took out a lighter and set the posters on fire. I had to get out of here. I ran to the door and ducked under swinging elbows and flying fists on my way. I slipped into the hall and my jaw dropped when I saw it was already packed with fighting students. Someone tackled me from behind and I tucked into a roll before they could crush me to the floor. I bounced to my feet and zig-zagged my way through the hall, dodging more elbows and kicks as I went.

I pulled my phone out and called Fabi.

"You gotta come get me!" I shouted over the screams. "It's wild out here! Come now! I don't—"

And then someone pulled the fire alarm. There was a split second where everyone stopped and threw their hands to their ears. But almost instantly they went straight back to pummelling each other. I vaulted over a railing and landed at the bottom of the stairs in a smooth roll. I had to get outside. I could just get a couple blocks away from campus and wait for Fabi at a McDonald's.

I sprinted past a kid spray painting profanities on the wall, another student setting his textbooks on fire, and other students peeing on their lockers. I rounded the corner and suddenly something metal clocked me in the side of my head. I wobbled off balance and pressed my hand to my skull. It felt like someone had just pitched a metal fastball at me. But when I looked down I saw something that was like a kick to my gut.

A Rite Guard body spray.

I looked up and Laura was marching straight towards me with a menacing scowl on her face. She shoved a sheet of paper into my chest then snarled, "It was you."

I barely heard her over the fire alarm, but her face said everything. She pushed me back and I grabbed the paper. There were two sets of fingerprints on both upper corners with a whole bunch of writing underneath them. But near the first one was: PHANTOM PRINT and near the second was: NICHOLAS TOUSSAINT PRINT. And in the middle was one word in bold: MATCH.

My body went cold. My head spun. My ears throbbed.

"You're the Phantom!" Laura screamed at me.

I opened my mouth to say something, but my voice was caught in my throat. My brain was stalling and my thoughts were tripping over themselves trying to figure out what had just happened. How did she do this? When did she do this?

"I can explain," was all I could manage to say.

"You lied to me!" Laura shouted over the alarm.

"Wait, wait, wait," I stammered. "So you were keeping tabs on me?!"

"I didn't trust you from the beginning!" she said and it was like someone stabbed me in the chest. "You came outta nowhere offering to help me find the Phantom. You didn't think that was suspicious?"

I blinked several times and she just stood there snarling at me. My brain felt like it was about to cave in on itself. There was no way. This couldn't be happening.

"So this…" I shouted, waving from me to her. "…this was all fake? This friendship wasn't even real?"

"I could ask you the same thing!" she cried back. "I trusted you! You ruined my GPA!"

Then she started crying. I couldn't hear her sobs over the alarm but I could see her tears clear as day streaming down her face. And before I knew it I was crying too. Something snapped inside of me like the dam I'd been using to hold all of this back had finally burst.

"I'm sorry!" I blurted. "I messed up! I shouldn't have done it. I ruined everything for you. I'm sorry. I'm sorry!"

She squinted at me behind her tears and her lips started to tremble and I saw her mouth the words, "I trusted you."

My heart felt like it had been shattered into a million pieces. I didn't know what to do. Should I keep apologizing? Hug her? Cry more? Everything was literally falling apart around me, in front of me, and inside me. But then something shifted and Laura scowled at me.

"I'm telling everyone!" she shouted.

And just like that, my mind snapped back into focus. No. She couldn't. Kids were still sprinting and fighting around us and even though they could see us, no one could really hear us over the fire alarm. But all Laura would have to do was keep shouting and pointing at me and eventually the message would spread that I was the Phantom. And then I'd be dead.

"No!" I shouted back at her. "Please, don't! I'm sorry!"

"Why shouldn't I?" she screamed back. "You ruined everything!"

"It wasn't my fault!" I blurted. "I didn't mean for any of this to happen. They made me do it."

Laura scoffed. "Who made you do it?"

"Sarah Gibson's Mom! Her and her friends paid me to mess with everyone's social life."

Laura made a face like she had just smelled something rotten. "Are you kidding me? That's the best you could come up with?"

"I'm not lying!"

"Yes, you are!"

"I'm not!"

"You are!"

"Why would I lie about that?"

"I know for a fact that you didn't see Sarah's Mom."

"How are you gonna tell me that? I'm telling you I did. I saw her and she paid me!"

Then she stepped closer to me and said, "Sarah's Mom died five years ago."

My eyes went wide and all the sound around me muted to a muffled hum. Mrs. Gibson was dead?

Then who was the woman who was paying me?

Chapter fifty-one:
"The Real Slim Shady"

"I'm telling you!" I shouted at Laura. "This woman told me she was Sarah's Mom."

"Well you better prove it fast or I'm telling everyone you're the Phantom."

My mind raced to crank out ideas, but the alarm was making it hard to think and it didn't help that somebody was shoving into me every ten seconds. So I finally grabbed Laura's arm and told her to follow me. I brought her to the library and luckily the alarm wasn't as loud in there.

I logged into a computer then went on the Hamilton High facebook page and scrolled through their pictures of the games. Laura watched over my shoulder with her arms folded across her chest and didn't say a word. I found pictures of basketball games, volleyball, soccer, and finally got to the football ones and eventually Homecoming. I slowed down and looked through each one carefully until I found one with a view of the bleachers.

"What are we looking at?" Laura finally said, her voice dripping with impatience.

"Just hang on," I replied. I zoomed in on the picture and breathed a sigh of relief. One perk of being the only black kid in school was that it was always easy to find me in a picture. And there I was in the bleachers sitting next to Mrs. Gibson and her friends.

"There," I pointed. "That's me. And that…" I pointed at the woman next to me. "Is the woman who paid me." The picture was a little blurry but I could still make out her features. So if this was Sarah's Mom, Laura would recognize her.

Laura leaned over my shoulder and stared at the screen for a whole minute in silence.

"I have no idea who this woman is," she finally announced.

"I promise you on everything," I told her. "That's her."

Laura kept staring at the screen then repeated, "I have no idea who this woman is."

I swallowed nervously. Did she not believe me? Was she still going to expose me? But just when I was sure she was about to grab my arm and drag me to the riot downstairs, she stood up straight and said, "But I think I know who might."

She pushed me to the side then printed the picture. A few minutes later, Fabi was outside waiting for us. As we drove off, some fire trucks and police cars came swerving into the parking lot behind us.

"This school is crazy," Fabi shook her head as we drove off.

"Tell me about it," I said.

"So where are we going?" Fabi asked, looking at Laura through the rearview mirror.

"To see Billy," Laura replied, staring out the window.

"Billy?" I asked. "What does he have to do with this?"

"Just trust me."

"Trust you? Why would Billy know that woman?"

Laura snapped her head in my direction and spat, "You're not in a position to question my methods, Phantom."

Fabi glanced at me in shock. "*Li konnin?*"

I nodded. "She knows."

"You knew about this too?" Laura glared into the rearview mirror. "Were you his accomplice?"

"Hold on!" I said, cutting in. "Don't take it out on her. This was all me…and Mrs. Gibson…or whoever she is."

Laura rolled her eyes. "Whatever. Just get us to Billy."

We were in the hospital room half an hour later and Laura held the Homecoming picture in front of Billy.

"Do you know who these women are?" she asked, pointing at Mrs. Gibson and her friends.

"Good to see you guys too," Billy scoffed.

"Do you know who these women are?" Laura repeated.

Billy glanced at the picture and said, "That's the Homecoming game. Hamilton vs. Jefferson."

I tilted my head in surprise. There wasn't a caption or anything on the picture. "Wait. How did you know?"

Billy shrugged nonchalantly. "I remember everything about every game I play."

At first I was skeptical and thought he was messing with me. But then I remembered seeing a video where LeBron was describing in detail every single play of one of his games months after the fact. He apparently had a photographic memory of every game he'd played. Maybe Billy could do the same thing. But he could somehow remember details in the stands too.

Which was pretty wild when I thought about it. But Laura wasn't as mindblown by this and stayed on task.

"Billy," she said firmly. "Do you know who these women are?"

Billy furrowed his brow as he looked at the picture. "Nick, why are you sitting on the Jefferson side?"

"I'm not," I replied, coming around to double check in the picture. "That's the Hamilton side."

"Well, those are Jefferson Moms," Billy responded. "I only see them when we play Jefferson."

"What?" I said. That didn't make sense.

"Why are there Jefferson Moms on the Hamilton side?" Billy asked.

"Better question: why are Jefferson Moms paying me thousands of dollars to ruin kids' lives at Hamilton?"

Billy's head snapped in my direction. "Excuse me?"

I threw my fist to my mouth. "Ahhhhh…" Billy looked from me then to Laura who sighed.

"What did you just say?" Billy asked me.

"Uhhhh…" I started. But there was no point in denying it now. "Don't get mad, okay? Don't get mad…I'm the Phantom."

"What?!" he screamed. He sat up bolt upright in the bed then screamed again from the pain in his ribs. "Are you serious?"

"I'n sorry!" I cried, throwing my hands up in surrender.

"So you did all this?" Billy demanded. "Why would—"

"Billy!" Laura cut in, snapping in his face. "Billy? You can be mad later. But right now we need to figure out how to prove that these women are behind everything that's been happening at school. Because if we don't, I'm still not gonna be valedictorian and Nick is gonna get suspended or worse."

I looked at her. "So you believe me?"

She narrowed her eyes at me then took a deep breath. "Billy would have no reason to lie and had no idea why we were asking about this picture. So it seems logical to assume you're telling the truth."

I gave a sigh of relief.

"But that doesn't mean I'm not pissed at you."

I frowned.

"I'm still lost," Billy cut in. "Are you the Phantom? Or are the Jefferson Moms the Phantom?"

"They've been paying me to ruin everyone's lives at school," I explained.

He furrowed his brow. "Why would Jefferson Moms pay you to sabotage Hamilton?"

"Better question," I added. "How are we gonna prove it?"

"That's what we're gonna figure out," Laura said.

Chapter fifty-two:
"Lose Yourself"

Laura and I paced back and forth in front of Billy as we all bounced ideas off of each other.

"Maybe we could get their real names and addresses from their credit card information," Billy offered. "They were paying you right? That's a paper trail."

I shook my head. "It was always cash."

Billy kissed his teeth. "Of course."

"And you don't know anything about them?" I asked him. "Other than the fact that they're Jefferson Moms."

He shook his head. "Just faces. No names. What if we just told the cops?"

I thought about that for a second. "But what would we even say? These Moms have been paying me to mess with my classmates? We still don't have any evidence."

Laura hadn't said a single word and just kept pacing frantically with her hand on her chin.

"...I can't...but what if...maybe something..." she mumbled to herself. I watched her furrow her brow then run her hands through her hair with a frustrated sigh.

I recognized the signs that she was having trouble staying focused.

"Hey," I finally said to her and she stopped and looked at me. "Mediocre drink."

She smiled then went back to pacing.

"What was that?" Billy asked.

"Inside thing," I answered. "It helps her think."

Billy shrugged. I sat down at a chair near his bed and there was a long silence where the only sound in the room was Laura's footsteps and hushed muttering.

"Teach me something in Kreyol," Billy finally said to me.

I looked at him in confusion then said, "Uhhh...*sak pasé.*"

He rolled his eyes. "Everyone knows that one. Teach me something else."

What was with the sudden interest in my culture? "Ummm...*gad on tin tin.*"

"God a ten ten?" he tried.

I shrugged, ignoring the way he butchered it. "And if you really wanna sound Haitian, you set it up with 'oh-oh?'"

"'Oh-oh'," he said, copying my tone.

I nodded. "Not bad."

"What does it mean?"

"It's like…'look at this nonsense'. Or 'that's some bull.' You usually say it after something you think is crazy or stupid."

"Okay," he nodded.

There was an awkward silence and I watched Laura pace and mutter again for another minute.

"I'm a jerk," Billy suddenly said.

I looked up. "What?"

He winced like he was in pain then sighed. "I've been such a jerk to you."

I glanced at Laura briefly, who was still lost in thought, then shrugged at him. "It's whatever, man."

"No…" he shook his head then sighed again. "It's not whatever. The thing is…" He stared down at his lap and started fiddling with his fingers. He was about to say something that was making him really uncomfortable and by default was making me uncomfortable.

"Listen, Billy," I cut him off. "Seriously, it's cool." The last thing I wanted was to have some weird sappy moment with my bully in his hospital room. Or…ex-bully. But he kept going.

"The thing is…my parents aren't as rich as everyone thinks." He twisted some of the bed sheet in his lap into a tiny ball. "They can barely afford sending me to Hamilton."

I blinked at that. That was news to me. I had never thought Billy was up there with the Gibsons, but I had always assumed his family was at least as wealthy as everyone else. In my mind it was the Gibsons, everyone else, then me at the bottom. But then I remembered how his parents' couldn't afford his medical bills. Any other Hanilton family would have had better insurance to start with or would have been able to cough up that money easily. And it suddenly made sense.

"I guess I was just happy there was someone just as poor as me," Billy said. Then he winced again. "That came out wrong. I didn't mean it like that."

But I knew what he meant. He targeted me so that no one else would target him. It was still sick and twisted and didn't justify it. But I understood it.

"I guess what I'm trying to say is…" he went on. "I'm sorry."

I didn't say anything at first. I didn't know what to say. Was that a heartfelt apology from my bully?

"I got it!" Laura suddenly said as she spun to face us. "I know how we can prove they're behind this and catch them in the act." Then she glanced at me. "Fine wine."

I grinned and nodded.

Billy looked at me in confusion. "What does wine have to do—"

"But this has to be perfect," Laura interrupted. "Cuz we only get one shot at this."

Chapter fifty-three:
"Ready or Not"

The plan had three phases.

Phase 1: Laura stalked Mrs. Gibson and took undercover photos of her then printed as many copies as possible.

Phase 2: I kept taking on assignments from the Gibson Circle as if nothing had changed. Except this time, every time I completed a mission, I'd leave a Phantom of the Opera mask at the scene of the crime to let them know it was the Phantom. But the next day, I'd slip a picture of Mrs. Gibson into the victim's locker with a note on the back saying, "This is the Phantom. We take her down at the next Jefferson game. Your fellow savage."

Phase 3: Because Billy apparently had a LeBronian photographic memory when it came to every game that he'd ever played, he was able to give us the exact layout of the Jefferson campus, including all the places with the best hiding spots and the best lighting. Which brings us to…

Phase 4: I met with Kyle and the AV Club and talked them through preparing for their biggest project ever. During halftime of the next baseball game at Jefferson, I would convince Mrs. Gibson to meet me in the empty auditorium. There I would tell her that I knew she was an imposter and that I was done doing her dirty work. When she blackmailed me again and indirectly confessed to everything, I'd signal the A/V club and they'd pop out with their cameras and lights. We'd have the whole thing on video and be able to send it to Laura's uncle the FBI agent.

But a week later, when all the pieces were in place, I discovered something that flipped it all upside down.

Chapter fifty-four:
"Where is the Love?"

One Saturday I stopped by Bethanie with Fabi. As usual, there was a small crowd hanging out inside: Haitian uncles playing dominos, a family singing happy birthday to their daughter, some teens drinking soda and playing GameBoys, and Sister Mardi rocking a baby.

Fabi and I ordered a few patties(and paid for them this time) and waited as my father went into the back to get more. My mother came out from the back at the same time carrying a tray of *bon bon amidon* and the phone cradled between her ear and shoulder.

"But can you find it in your heart to give us some mercy?" she was saying. "Just a little more time. This has been really hard on us and it's about to be even harder."

She was probably talking to the investor. I guessed she was trying to get him to reconsider. I tried to eavesdrop as she walked back and forth behind the counter, but Sister Mardi interrupted me.

"Your parents are such angels," she said.

"Thanks," I replied with a smile. "I know."

"God made them with both His hands and took His time with them. You two are lucky to have them."

Fabi and I smiled at each other.

"Did you know she gave me patties for the funeral when my sister passed?"

Fabi and I nodded and tried not to laugh, remembering how annoyed Dad had been about that.

"And she decorated the church when I got married and did the catering and made it look like a royal wedding. And all for free."

Fabi actually laughed this time. "I believe it."

But I was craning my neck to hear what my mother was saying.

"But remember when I helped your son? I thought maybe…"

I couldn't make out what she said after. But if she had done something for this guy's son, he was probably Haitian. And that made me feel a blend of confusion and anger. On the one hand, I didn't know there were any Haitians in real estate. On the other hand, why was another Haitian willing to drive a fellow Haitian out of business? We should be looking out for each other, not ruining each other's lives.

"...and she catered my daughter's sweet sixteen," Sister Mardi was saying. "You remember that, right?"

"I do," Fabi nodded.

"I know it's not personal," I heard my mother say. "…okay…thank you. Have a nice day."

"Was that the investor?" I asked the second she hung up.

"Yes," she sighed. "I thought I could convince him to reconsider since we've known him for a few years." She shrugged and shook her head. "But I guess friendships don't mean much to Mr. Fairmount."

It felt like my whole world came to a screeching halt. If I had been holding something it would've shattered on the floor.

"What did you just say?" I forced the words out.

"Mr. Fairmount," she repeated, like it was nothing. "I told you that. Remember?"

"No, you didn't!" I almost screamed.

"Nicholas," my mother said. "Don't yell, there are customers here."

But I couldn't calm down. Because the investor wasn't Haitian. He was Lance's Dad.

Chapter fifty-five:
"Move"

The next day I went straight to Lance at his locker. I wasn't waiting for lunch. We were doing this right here. Right now.

"You're a liar," I spat at him.

He shut his locker and turned to me in surprise. "What are you talking about?"

"Fairmount Investments is the company trying to shut down my parents' bakery. Your Dad's company!"

Lance's face went red and he swallowed nervously, but shook his head to keep his composure. "I didn't lie, Nick."

"You knew!" I screamed at him. "This whole time you knew! I told you that my parents were getting bullied into selling their bakery and you sat there like you didn't know anything."

"It wasn't any of my business," Lance shrugged.

Was he being serious right now?

"You couldn't have given me a heads up?" I snapped. "'Hey, Nick. Sorry, but my Dad's the one trying to ruin your family's livelihood. So look out.'"

"That's what you wanted me to say?"

"I wanted you to say anything! I'm supposed to be your best friend."

"Your parents are better off selling to us anyway," Lance shrugged.

I couldn't believe what I was hearing. He wasn't even sorry. No apology. No sympathy. Just justifying his greedy, bully of a Dad.

"My Mom helped you when you were sick," I reminded him. "That *just* happened! And now you're letting your Dad tear down her business?"

"It's not personal," he said, swallowing and looking away.

"You knew why I was doing what I was doing," I said, lowering my voice. "And you still tried to make me feel guilty for it."

Gaslighting wasn't a popular term yet, but this would've been the perfect time to use it. He glanced at me then lowered his eyes.

"My parents came to this country with nothing," I went on. "And worked their butts off to make a life for us and built that bakery from the ground up—they worked for that. But your Dad—born into wealth and never satisfied—comes in and wants to take that dream away. And I'm doing what I do to keep that dream alive and you act like *I'm* the bad guy?"

"My Dad isn't doing anything wrong," Lance said. "But you are."

I wanted to punch him, but I slammed my fist against the locker instead. "I'm doing it because of him!"

"Two wrongs don't make a right," he said, but his voice was shaking.

"But one wrong does. As long as it's your rich white dad."

Lance made fists at his side and for a second I thought he was gonna throw a punch. I wished he would. I wished he would so I'd have an excuse to punch him right back and knock his head into the wall. But he didn't move. Then the bell rang and we turned and went our separate ways without another word.

***

That day in gym we were playing dodgeball. I was still fuming over my conversation with Lance and was hoping this would take my mind off it at least for the next twenty minutes. We'd been playing dodgeball for a couple weeks now and it had been pretty fun. Little did I know that today would be a different story. In case you didn't have the same dodgeball experience as I did, here's the basics.

We were playing in the gym and one team of fifteen boys was standing on one baseline while the other team was lined up on the opposite baseline. About twenty dodgeballs were lined up at half court and when Coach Williams blew the whistle, we'd all make a mad dash for them. If you got hit, you were out, but headshots meant the person who threw the ball was out. If your ball got caught, you were out. Pretty simple. But the most important thing was that if at any point in the game you managed to hit the rim on the opposing team's side, then everyone who was out on your team would be brought back.

I brushed the bottom of my sneakers as my team waited on the baselines.

"How do you feel?" Kyle asked next to me.

I shrugged as I glanced up and down the line. We had a few baseball players which was always good and one basketball player which could come in handy. I looked over at the other team and noticed that Lance had gathered everyone to huddle around him.

"What are they doing?" Kyle asked me.

I squinted at the other end until the huddle broke. Lance stared at me and titled his head to the side. This wasn't good. This wasn't good at all.

"Cover me," I said.

"What?" Kyle asked.

The whistle blew and everyone rushed to the line. Everyone but me. I stayed behind and watched as Lance's team beat mine to the balls. But instead of hitting my teammates that were closest to them, they all fired shots straight at me. But I was already on the run, sprinting across the court as balls blasted into the foam wall behind me. I ducked, rolled, and dove behind other teammates as the onslaught of balls came like neverending gunfire. The last ball that came almost hit me in my chest, but I barely caught it before dropping to the floor.

"What the heck was that?" Kyle asked, picking up a ball.

"Payback," I grunted, climbing to my feet. I found Lance standing at the three-point line, ran up a few steps, and pitched a fastball at him. It ripped through the air like a rocket and if Lance hadn't already known I was coming for him it would've been a direct headshot. But he ducked just in time and it hit a teammate behind him in the leg.

The game went on like this for a few more minutes: Lance's team saving their balls to rain Hell on me and me dodging like my life depended on it. I was rolling and sliding up and down the court so much I had scrapes and bruises on my arms and legs.

"How are you still alive, man?" Kyle asked as we met up in the corner. "You're moving like Mr. Fantastic out there!"

I bent over my knees to catch my breath. It did feel cool to dodge everything like that, but it didn't mean anything if I was too tired to keep it up. Plus, half our team was already eliminated and it was crazy that most of it was from stray shots aimed at me. Lance had really convinced his whole team to come after me. And for what? His Dad was the one ruining my life—I was the one who deserved to be mad. And he was taking it out on me?

"I got a plan," I said to Kyle. Then I called the three other teammates who were still in and we huddled real quick. "They're all coming after me. Which means we all know where the balls are coming. So the next time they blitz like that, everybody just follow me and catch the balls."

The guys nodded and we turned and threw shots at Lance and his team. Most of our throws missed and then, as predicted, they picked the balls up and aimed at me. I started off on side of the court and ran to the other like usual. But unlike before, the rest of my team followed closeby and dove at each throw. Some of them caught them, but there were still more balls than teammates. And when it was all said and done, I was still untouched on the other side, but every one of my teammates was out.

"You've gotta be kidding me," I said, watching my teammates walk off the court.

"It's just you, Nick!" Kyle cheered from the sideline.

I took a deep breath as I picked up a ball and faced Lance and his team. There were still five people left, including him. There was no way I'd last long against all of them by myself. I had to hit the rim and bring my team back. I walked up to half court to get a better shot and when I was a few feet away, I saw something move in my peripheral.

"He has a ball!" Kyle screamed.

I didn't even get a chance to turn when a ball came whizzing from the opposite baseline. Instinctively, I leaned back Matrix-style and it whistled over me, barely missing my shoulder. Before I could get back up another ball came from the other side straight at my legs. The next thing that happened was straight adrenaline. The instant my back hand touched the floor, I popped back up off one foot and spun into a front flip and the ball whizzed underneath me. I landed on both feet as my teammates went wild on the side. And straight ahead was Lance, his arm still stretched out after his throw. I winked at him then walked up to half court, tossed the ball, and watched as it hit the rim.

The gym shook from my teammates' screams as they flooded back onto the court and threw themselves onto me. Within a minute, they scooped up the remaining balls and took out Lance and the rest of his team. Kyle and a baseball player lifted me onto their shoulders and paraded me in a victory lap around the court. As surreal as this was, and as much as I wanted to drink think this in, I couldn't help but feel like all of this had just been practice for something bigger to come.

Chapter fifty-six:
"Prince Ali(Reprise)"

I had a bad feeling for the rest of the day that something bad was going to happen. I couldn't put my finger on it, but I didn't like it.

"I'd say you're just being paranoid," Laura said to me one class. "But, you know…it's not like you don't have a reason."

"Thanks," I scoffed. "That was really uplifting."

"That's what I'm here for," she winked at me.

But I couldn't shake it. Then, right before the final bell of last period, the intercom cackled and the entire class looked to the ceiling for the unexpected announcement. But instead of Principal Hanes, it was Lance's voice.

"Hamilton High," he said slowly. "This is Lance Fairmount. I have an announcement to make."

My blood went cold as I locked eyes with Laura.

"You don't think…?" she whispered to me.

I didn't answer. Because my brain couldn't even process what was about to happen.

"I hope you guys can forgive me for this," Lance went on. "I've held onto a secret for a while now. But I can't hold onto it anymore."

It felt like someone had sucked all the air out of the room as every single student shifted to the edge of their seats to listen. My heart pounded in my chest and my hands started shaking under my desk. I looked at Laura and she mouthed one word: "Run."

But I couldn't move. It was like I was frozen with panic.

"I know who the Phantom is," Lance said and the students started murmuring. "I didn't say anything because he's…well, he *used* to be my best friend. But I can't sit back anymore and watch him do all this to everyone."

I saw some students glance over at me. If I was gonna leave, I had to do it now. But I still couldn't bring myself to move.

"I'm sorry for not coming forward sooner," Lance said. "And for anyone who got hurt because of my silence. But the Phantom is none other than…Nicholas Toussaint."

It felt like someone dropped an anvil on my chest. And the silence that came crashing through the room was like the quiet before a firecracker exploded. Everyone slowly turned to me.

"Is it true?" one kid asked.

"I…" I started. "I can explain. "It's, uh…"

"Nicholas?" Mr. Hendricks said at the front. "Is this true?"

"Run," Laura was still mouthing to me.

"Uhhhhh," was all I could say.

And then came the accusations.

"You made my boyfriend break up with me!"

"My girlfriend cheated on me because of you!"

"You made me fail Calculus!"

And then the firecracker finally exploded.

"I'm gonna kill you!"

"Run, Nick!" Laura screamed.

I finally jumped out of my seat just in time to dodge one kid trying to grab me. I rushed to the door but three other students tried to cut me off. I slipped past one and Laura grabbed the other two by their collars, buying me just a second to slide out the door. But once I was outside, it was like that Kreyol phrase all over again. I'd run from the rain and jumped into a basin. Because kids were already waiting for me in the hall, pushing past each other to get a piece of me.

I turned and ran down the end with the least kids, but a few of them still tried to grab me—clawing at me, swinging at me, and even trying to tackle me. I ducked and dodged as best as I could, but barely made it to the double doors at the end, already bleeding from the scratches. I ran down the stairs, bent on making it to the bottom floor and sprinting out the front entrance, but I only made it down one flight before four guys were running up the steps towards me. One of them was Mike Taft and he was holding a baseball bat.

"You made Lisa break up with me?!" he wailed. Then he started swinging the bat wildly as he ran towards me.

I doubled back and rushed through the door I'd just passed and ran down the hall just to find more students waiting to pounce. They were all surprised to see me and in the second it took them to realize they wouldn't have to come looking for me, I jumped and did a wall run across the lockers to get past one group. Then I kicked off the other wall of lockers to pass another group. I was just about to spin around one student to duck into the stairwell, when someone tripped me and I crashed to the floor.

I scrambled to my feet and found myself backed into a corner as Dean and Gary approached me, a crowd growing behind them.

"You keyed my car," Dean snarled. He flicked his wrist and a pocketknife appeared in his hand. "Now I'm gonna key you."

He moved towards me, but there was a blur of blue and white as someone punched him in the face. Dean spun into a door and dropped his knife as Billy turned to me.

"Go!" Billy yelled.

I rammed through the door of the stairwell and luckily the stairs were empty. I made it to the first floor and a girl immediately tackled me to the floor the second I came out. She clawed at my arms and face like a feral cat and even bit my wrist. I finally managed to kick her off and saw that it was Angie Clarkson.

"You ruined my life!" she screeched at me.

"Nicholas Toussaint!" I heard a teacher shout.

But I got to my feet without looking to see who it was. The lobby was at the end of the hall, but I had to run past half a dozen classes, whose doors were now opening. If I didn't move now, the students would close in on me and block my only exit. Not to mention the ones already pouring down the stairs behind me.

"Nick, go!" Laura shouted as she burst out of the stairwell. I vaguely noticed she was holding a bottle of water.

I booked it down the hall just as students pushed out of their classes. Some of the doors smacked into me as they opened, flinging me like a ping pong ball between the walls. Then I heard screams and thuds and when I glanced over my shoulder I saw students slipping and sliding across the hallway tiles like they were on skates. They crashed into each other, fell into lockers, and landed in messy piles on their backs and faces. And there was Laura, pouring the water all over the floor.

I didn't wait for her to scream at me to go—I turned and kept running. I went straight out the front entrance and sprinted across the parking lot. But there were kids already out there so I cut back and ran around to the back of the building.

By now more kids had come out and were catching up and chasing me, screaming death threats and racial slurs for the whole town to hear. I had to get out of here somehow. But I didn't have time to stop and call Fabi. I just needed a few seconds to stop and think. And then I saw it—the weight room building was up ahead.

I risked a glance behind me and saw over twenty kids racing towards me like a stampede of angry rhinos and Dean was at the front, knife still in his hand. I pushed myself faster towards the building and when I was just a couple feet away, I jumped, ran three steps up the wall, and grabbed the edge of the roof. But just when I was about to pull myself over, Dean caught my ankle.

"'You're not going anywhere!" he screamed, trying to pull me down.

I was barely hanging onto the ledge and I could feel my fingers slipping. Then something sliced through my ankle and I shrieked in pain. He'd just slashed me with the knife! One hand slipped off and it felt like Dean's body weight was about to rip my legs off my waist. If I didn't do something, I was about to fall into the swarm of hungry students beneath us. Suddenly a car horn split the air and everyone turned to see who it was. Dean was distracted for a second and I kicked him in the face and he let go and dropped to the ground. I climbed onto the roof then rolled onto my back and collapsed, my breath coming out in heaves. My throat was dry, my lungs felt like they were about to explode, and my legs wouldn't stop shaking.

But I wasn't in the clear yet. Soon Dean would figure out a way to get up here and I'd be done for. I heard the car horn again, with a lot more urgency this time. But it was coming from the other side of the building. What was going on? I got up and ran to the opposite ledge and saw a black jeep behind the building. Billy was waving out of the driver's seat and Laura was next to him.

"Get in!" Billy screamed up at me.

I swung my legs over the ledge, dropped down with a roll at the bottom, then climbed into the back seat. Then Billy floored the gas and fishtailed out of the parking lot just as Dean and the students came sprinting around the building. I watched them as we drove off and had the sick feeling in my stomach that I was now a dead man.

Chapter fifty-seven:
"In the End"

"This is bad," Billy said as he pulled onto the highway.

"We know that, Billy," Laura said. "We need a plan."

I couldn't even bring myself to say anything yet. I was still gasping to catch my breath. My head was throbbing, my chest was heaving, and my shirt was sticking to my back from all my sweat. But Billy was right. This was bad. This was worse than bad. This was a nightmare. I felt like I was about to throw up.

"They're gonna come for you," Laura said, twisting in the front seat to look back at me. "We need to go somewhere they won't think of looking."

I sighed and took a few more seconds to catch my breath as I thought. Going home wasn't an option right now. I obviously couldn't go to Lance's house. I could go to Billy's or Laura's. But did I really want to drag them and their parents into this? I glanced out the window at the Sun in the distance. It was still early afternoon, which meant...

"Fabi," I looked at Laura. "My sister has class today. Billy, take us to Rutgers."

"New Brunswick?" Billy chuckled. "Road trip!"

"No," I shook my head. "Newark."

"Oh," he shrugged. "Even better. No one from Hamilton's gonna wanna follow us there. No offense."

"None taken."

It took us twenty minutes to make it to Rutgers. Fabi was in the middle of an exam and wouldn't be out for another half hour. So we slipped into the Dana Library and waited at a table near the back.

"Okay," Laura said, leaning across the table towards me. "Let's break this down. How bad is this exactly?"

I sighed. I didn't even want to think about it. My stomach was still in knots. Even though every other person in this building was a college student, I kept jumping at every sight of a backpack, thinking that some Hamilton student had found us.

"These college girls are pretty hot," Billy whispered as he scoped the room.

"Focus," Laura kicked him under the table. She looked at me again. "Your secret's out. So everyone at school–students and faculty—are gonna want your head."

I nodded. Wonderful. She was making me feel better already.

"Going back to school is not an option," she explained. "You're gonna be suspended at best or arrested at worst."

My heart sank at that. "Arrested?"

"I mean," Laura shrugged. "I'm just trying to be real here. You *did* vandalize some cars. And there's gotta be some law about stealing files from a school therapist's office."

I lowered my head. I could get arrested for that? Of course I could. I felt nauseous again and put my fist to my mouth to stop myself from throwing up. Laura's phone vibrated and she checked it as Billy checked out a girl that walked past.

"Don't worry, bud," Billy said once the girl was gone. "I'm sure it's not that bad. I mean, *we're* still in the clear. So if anything you could just crash at my place, right?" He smiled at me.

"No…" Laura said, staring at her phone. "Sarah just texted me. Apparently everyone thinks you and me are in on it too because we helped Nick escape."

Billy's smile froze on his face then he chuckled nervously. "Well…that's a plot twist."

"Yeah," Laura said, stuffing her phone back into her pocket. "We can't go back to school either."

I didn't know it was possible for me to feel any worse. Not only was I public enemy number one, but I'd dragged Billy and Laura into it too. I dropped my head onto the table and the thud made a few students look over at us. This couldn't be happening. They were gonna kill us. Suspend us. Arrest us. We'd be all over the news for this. My life was over. And then, like the universe wanted to make sure I knew how screwed I was, my phone vibrated. When I pulled it out, I saw one name and my blood went cold: MOM.

Frick.

I let it go to voicemail then put the phone back on the table.

"Your Mom?" Laura asked me.

I nodded and hugged my arms as I rocked back and forth. I wanted to throw up. I wanted to cry. I wanted to fall asleep and never wake up. I just wanted all of this to go away. This couldn't be happening.

"One thing's for sure," Laura said. "This is all the more reason we need to figure out a way to expose the Jefferson Moms. That's our only way out of this. If we can…" She went on saying other stuff, but I didn't hear any of it.

My body was cold, my legs were shaking, and my mind kept screaming one line over and over again: I should've never done this.

***

When Fabi finally met up with us, she brought us into an empty study room and locked the door.

"What happened?" she asked me.

And it was like a dam suddenly burst inside of me. I threw my arms around her and buried my head into her chest as I cried.

"I should've never done this!" I sobbed.

She wrapped her arms around me and rubbed my back as I washed her shirt with my tears.

Billy and Laura just stood there watching my breakdown. But it didn't matter. I was too scared to be embarrassed. Fabi let me cry it out for about half a minute before pulling me away and looking me dead in the eyes.

"Listen to me," she said firmly. "We're gonna get you through this."

"I'm gonna go to jail, Fabi," I said, my voice shaking.

"Hey, hey, hey," she said quickly, grabbing my face in both hands. "Nobody. Is going to jail. You hear me?"

"But I vandalized their cars," I said. "I stole someone's psych files. That's illegal right?"

"Probably," Fabi nodded. "Yes. Yes, it's illegal."

I started sobbing again.

"Hey!" she shook my shoulders. "Listen to me. You're not alone, okay? We're gonna get you through this. *I'm* gonna get you through this."

"Mom and Dad are gonna kill me," I said.

"Let me handle them."

"They're gonna kill me. They're gonna kill me. They're gonna kill me." I kept repeating.

"They won't kill you," Fabi said. "They'll probably send you to Haiti, though. Then Haiti will kill you."

I looked at her in horror for a second and she smirked at me.

"Listen," she added. "We're gonna get through this."

"Be honest," I said. "How bad is it?"

She dropped her hands and took a deep breath. "It's looking pretty bad, my friend. But we'll get through this, okay?"

"I keep telling him that we need to expose the Moms who are behind this," Laura spoke up.

Fabi looked at her, almost like she'd just realized her and Billy were still there. Then she snapped her fingers at her and grinned. "Exactly. They blackmailed you. On top of that, you're a minor. We can make a case just off of that."

I paused to think about it. I did feel slightly better when she put it that way. But not completely. "I still took the money, though."

"You did," Fabi nodded. "And it was a lot of money." She shrugged. "That does look bad, I'm not gonna lie, but…we can work this."

I sighed. "And what about Mom and Dad?"

"Let me talk to them," Fabi said. "It's not gonna be easy. But maybe I can get you off with a grounding and a butt-whooping."

I forced a laugh, but I was still weak. My mind was cartwheeling from everything that had happened and my emotions were spiraling out of control. Even if Fabi could pull off some miracle and appease my parents, even if she could somehow finesse some legal miracle and get me off the hook, I could never go back to Hamilton again. And this would follow me to any college I went to. No matter what I did, my life as I knew it was over.

Chapter fifty-eight:
"Apologize"

By the time we made it home that evening, my parents had already found out and were already waiting for us.

"Nicholas Emmanuel Toussaint!" my mother shouted when we walked in.

My legs turned to jelly at my full name and her and my father appeared in front of us.

"I'm sorry," I said immediately.

"Sorry?!" my mother shrieked.

"Mommy," Fabi stepped in between us. "Let me explain."

"Explain what?" my mother asked. "That our son is a criminal? The principal said you've been stealing from students, breaking into cars, getting into fights, and-and-and–" she couldn't even finish–she started stuttering whenever she got emotional.

Fabi furrowed her brow. "What? That's not what he was doing. They exaggerated that."

"So what was he doing, Fabiola?"

"He was…"

"So you knew about this?" my father stepped forward, his arms folded across his chest.

"No," I spoke up before Fabi could. "She didn't. I just told her everything today. Fabi had nothing to do with it."

Fabi looked back at me like she was about to protest, but I didn't have a chance to even decipher the look because my mother went on a rampage, pacing the living room and ranting at the top of her lungs.

"Is this what we sent you to school for?! To lie on students, to steal files, to-to-to…to sell drugs?!"

"That's not true," Fabi said. "He didn't really sell drugs. It was fake."

"It doesn't matter!" my mother shouted.

And in that moment I realized what was happening here.

"Nick got forced into doing this, Mommy," Fabi explained. "There's a group of Moms who paid him to do all those things and they said that if he didn't they would expose him to the whole school."

"Wait a minute," my father held his hand up. "How could they blackmail him if he didn't do anything wrong?"

"What do you mean?" Fabi asked and I could tell she was trying to think a mile a minute to anticipate where my father was going.

"So they were going to expose him for doing the things he had already agreed to do before the blackmailing?"

There was a short silence where the only sound was Fabi struggling to put a sentence together.

"Well…" she started. "…I, uh…that is a good point. Ummm…"

"They were paying me a lot of money," I cut in. "I lied to you guys. I don't have a job at school. These Moms have been paying me to do things to the students. A lot of money."

"Why would you do that, Nicholas?" my mother shook her head. "What got into you?"

"I did it for the family," I replied. "I knew you guys needed it. I didn't want you guys to have to sell the bakery."

My mother shook her head and all of a sudden tears started to fall. That hit me like a baseball bat to the chest. I rarely ever saw either of my parents cry. And now my mother was crying because of me.

"They're saying you could get arrested, Nicholas," my father explained. And hearing it from his mouth was like a truck hitting me head on. It was one thing to tell myself that or even to hear Laura say it. But my father wasn't prone to being dramatic and was a man of few words. So for him to let me know I could get jail time for this was the most devastating reality check.

"Do you know how embarrassing it was to have your principal call me?" my mother said softly. "And tell me that my son…that *my* son is a criminal?"

She sniffled and my father rubbed her back. "Do you know how this makes us look? What will people think?"

That's what was going on. In a weird twisted way, it didn't matter as much that I had actually done the things I did or that the rumors had been blown out of proportion. What mattered was that I'd ruined our image. The hard-working, law-abiding Haitian immigrant parents had raised a criminal. Mr. and Mrs. Toussaint–the parents of the *vagabon*. The one whose son had ruined Hamilton High. That was all that mattered. My mother buried her face in her hands and the sight of her crying broke something in me and soon I was crying too.

"Do you *want* to go to jail?" she said between sobs. "Is that it?"

"I'm sorry," I said. "I'm sorry. I just wanted to help the family. I was doing it for us."

"No amount of money is worth going to jail over," my father said.

I lowered my head as the tears kept coming. This wasn't going as planned. I expected the full brunt of their wrath to come next—for them to unleash the most brutal butt-whooping in the history of Haitian butt-whoopings. But what they gave me instead was worse.

"Nicholas," my father said and I slowly looked up at him. Then he stared me dead in my eyes and said, "We're disappointed in you."

I lowered my head and sobbed like a baby.

"I'm sorry," I tried to say again, but the words didn't come out. All I could see was my tears blurring the room and all I could hear was my mother's cries shredding my heart to pieces.

"Go to your room," my father said. "And don't come out until we know what to do with you."

I left and the last thing I heard was my mother wailing like she was giving birth.

***

I lay in my bed for about an hour without moving. Downstairs I could hear my parents arguing with each other and with Fabi. Eventually my father came in and explained the terms of my punishment.

"Here's the deal," he started with a deep breath. "Your principal said you're suspended until further notice while they investigate everything you did. They're also waiting to see if any of the students or their parents want to press charges."

I lowered my head. It was hard to imagine that no one would want to press charges. These were parents who would sue if their kid failed a class. My stomach sank so it felt like I'd swallowed a cannonball. Part of me hoped that my Dad would see how bad I felt and decide that this was punishment in itself. I mean wasn't the dread of going to jail bad enough? But he quickly dashed that hope to pieces.

"In the meantime, you're grounded," he said. "No phone. No video games. No computer. And no leaving the house."

I sighed. He held his hand out and I handed him my phone. Then he stood and unplugged the Playstation and the controllers. He carried them out of the room then came back a few minutes later and removed my desktop.

"How long?" I asked him, almost afraid of the answer.

He stopped at the door with his back to me. For a second I thought he hadn't heard me. Then he said, "Until we say so." and left the room.

Fabi came in a little while later to check on me. She handed me a brown paper bag and I felt myself smile for the first time all day. I opened it to find a beef patty and a bag of *bon bon amidon* inside. I had the best sister ever.

"Thanks," I said, pulling the pattie out first.

"How are you feeling?" she asked as she sat down next to me on the bed.

"Like a prisoner."

She frowned and watched me take a couple bites. "Thanks for covering for me."

I shrugged. "I dragged you into this. I don't want you getting in trouble because of me. Besides, you would've done the same thing."

She scoffed. "Don't be so sure of yourself." But she gave my shoulder a friendly jab.

She let a few moments of silence go by before shifting to face me. "Hey…we're gonna get through this, okay?"

I forced myself to nod, but I wasn't feeling it.

"We always have," she went on. "We always will. You and me."

I took another bite of the patty and my stomach twisted with a random pang of guilt. Even a Haitian patty couldn't make me feel better for long.

"Everything's gonna be alright," Fabi said.

But everything wasn't alright. Because a few days later, my parents accepted Mr. Fairmount's offer to sell the bakery. So in the end I ended up losing the very thing I had been trying to save by doing all this in the first place. On top of that, without that income flowing in we wouldn't be able to afford the house anymore. So we were gonna have to move into an apartment on the other side of town. We were moving in a week. So no. Everything was not alright. And it was all my fault.

Chapter fifty-nine:
"Where'd You Go?"

One afternoon I was sitting in my bed wallowing in my feelings. My parents and Fabi were gone so I had the house to myself. Which in a way made the feelings worse because it just reminded me of how alone I was. It had been a whole week without any contact from anyone at school. But who was I kidding? I didn't have anyone at school. I was just dumb sad that I hadn't been able to talk to Laura. My parents didn't know about my iPod so they hadn't confiscated it and I'd been secretly playing it to plunge myself deeper into my sorrow. And naturally, the song I had on repeat today was Fort Minor's "Where'd You Go?"

I sat there and let the lyrics pull at my heartstrings over and over again, remembering all the times Laura and I had met at lunch, all the times I'd destroyed her in NBA *Street* and the times she'd beaten me in chess. Round after round the song went until I was sniffling and sobbing like a baby realizing that I was gonna be alone for the rest of the year. Maybe the rest of my life. I'd messed everything up. My parents had lost their bakery. I'd lost my senior year. And now I'd lost the only girl I'd ever loved.

I heard a tap against my window and I glanced over at it. When I didn't see anything, I went back to drowning in my feelings and the tap came again. I pulled my headphones out then went to the window. When I opened it and looked down, my jaw dropped to see Billy and Laura standing in my backyard.

"'Sup, Tootsie?" Billy winked at me.

"What are you guys doing here?" I asked, my heart racing.

"We came to see you, stupid," Laura snickered. Then she turned to Billy and said, "C'mon, help me up."

I watched in amazement as Billy Richardson, my former bully, crouched down and gave Laura Wood, my crush, a lift on his hands. He launched her up like a cheerleader and she grabbed onto the windowsill then climbed into my room.

I wiped the tears from my face before she could see them and resisted the urge to throw my arms around her.

"Hey," she smiled at me and I felt the whole world melt away.

"Hey," I smiled back.

We heard a thud outside and looked to see Billy trying to claw his way through the window.

"A little help?" he said.

We both reached over and pulled him inside.

"Dang, Nick," he gasped, bent over his knees. "You make it look so easy." He grunted as he rubbed his ribs. "Still not a hundred percent yet."

Laura walked over to my bed and plopped down like she owned the place. "How's life being a fugitive?"

I sighed and dropped into my computer-less desk while Billy leaned against the wall.

"Sucks," I said. "Grounded. No T.V. No phone. No Playstation. No computer. Can't even leave the house. That's why I haven't reached out to you guys. It's straight radio silence over here."

"We figured," Laura shrugged. "Same deal here."

Billy scoffed. "Speak for yourself. My folks are cool. I'm livin' it up."

Laura shot him a look.

"And by livin' it up I mean, house arrest," he corrected.

"They suspended us too," Laura added. "We tried telling them about the Gibson Circle, but Principal Hanes wasn't having it. He thinks it's something you made up as a scapegoat. As far as Hamilton High's concerned, you, me, and Billy are the Phantom. It doesn't matter how stupid it sounds that I'd ruin my own GPA or that Billy would make Sarah break up with him. They just saw us helping you escape and that was that."

I lowered my head. I felt terrible. It was like I was ruining everyone's lives around me. The only thing left was for Fabi to get expelled from Rutgers for letting high schoolers into the Dana Library without ID. I didn't even know if that was a thing, but with my luck it probably would be.

"I'm so sorry, guys," I said. "I'm sorry that I did all this and that you got dragged into it."

Laura waved me off. "Yeah, what you did was wrong. But what they did was worse. And they need to pay for it."

"Oh-oh," Billy cut in. "Got a tow ten."

"Wrong time and wrong way," I corrected him.

"What was that?" Laura asked.

"He's trying to speak Kreyol," I waved it off.

"We can still expose them," Laura went on. "The plan's still the same, it's just the details are a little different. They can't get away with what they did,

Nick. And if we pull this off, it clears all of our names and we can get back to a normal life again."

"There's no normal anymore," I said softly.

"I know it looks bad, Nick, but—"

"I can't, Laura," I sighed as I buried my face in my hands for a second. Then I looked up and steadied my voice as I said, "My parents sold their bakery."

Laura's jaw dropped and Billy whistled.

"They sold it to Lance's Dad," I continued. "And without that income, we won't be able to afford to stay in this house too long. So we're moving in a few days. And I'm gonna finish out senior year at a public school."

Laura looked like she was about to say something, but kept swallowing her words like she was at a loss for them.

"It's over," I repeated. "Just forget about me."

She blinked several times then shook her head. "You can't leave. You…you can't. No. We can still do this."

"It's over, Laura. There's nothing I can do."

"No!" she shouted, jumping to her feet. "This isn't fair! I'm telling you, we can fight this. The faculty doesn't believe us because we don't have evidence, but if we can get that evidence, then we can expose these Moms and clear our names."

"Stop, Laura," I said softly. I'd spent a whole week burying myself in a grave of hopelessness. I couldn't bear the thought of her trying to dig me out just for me to get buried in something worse. I'd had enough of running from rain and falling into basins. I just wanted to move on with my life.

"Listen to me, Nick," she said, walking up to me. "I'm not giving up on you so you can't give up on yourself."

"No, Laura," I said, feeling the emotion threatening my voice. "Just leave it alone."

"But we can do this!"

"No we can't!" I jumped to my feet and she flinched in surprise. "I ruin everything that I touch! I ruined my parents' career, I ruined your senior year, I ruined Billy's, I ruin everyone close to me. So just leave me alone and forget about me."

Laura stared back at me silently and I could see the hurt in her eyes as she let my words sink in. For a second I wasn't sure if she was going to cry or hug me. But then something angry flickered behind her eyes.

"You put me through Hell, you know that?" she said and her voice broke for a second. "I've had the worst senior year of my life because of you."

"Technically, it's been the *only* senior year of your life," Billy cut in.

"Shut up, Billy!" she snapped at him then spun back on me. "When I failed that paper, I got depressed—more depressed than I've ever been. And then I met you. And I fell in love with you."

My chest melted with a sickening mix of joy and pain.

"But you didn't love me back," she went on. "But it was okay because we became best friends. And then I hated the Phantom. Then I found out you *were* the Phantom. And then I got suspended—all because of you! You put me through Hell, Nick. So you don't get to push me away just cuz you wanna give up."

I looked at the wall, wishing I could just will the guilt away that was twisting my insides in a vice.

"But if that's what you want, then I'll hop out that window and you'll never see me again. Just tell me to leave. Say the word."

I tried to look at her, but her eyes were blazing like flames in her face. I stared at my feet for several seconds as my guilt went on strangling me. Then I took a deep breath, looked at her, and said, "Just…leave."

And I watched the fire die in her eyes. Her face sank and her jaw dropped as a tear rolled down her cheek. It felt like someone had stabbed me in my heart. Then she smacked me across the face and stormed to the window. She was out and on the ground before I was done rubbing my cheek.

The silence in my room was deafening. But the pain in my heart was blistering.

Billy sighed as he walked up to the window.

"She's right, you know," he said over his shoulder. "These Moms can't get away with this."

"What am I supposed to do, Billy?" I asked, fighting back the tears. "I lost everything."

"Yeah," he shrugged. "You did. But the thing about losing everything is that now…you've got nothing to lose."

He let his words hang in the air as he lifted one foot onto the windowsill. Then he paused for a moment.

"You know, I don't care either way," he said. "My scholarship got ruined after the accident." He tapped his ribs. "But if you won't do this for you…"

He looked back at me again. "At least do it for her." Then he carefully climbed through the window and made his way down.

I shut my eyes as the guilt squeezed my heart tighter. I dropped to the floor and banged the back of my head against the wall as the tears came down like rivers. It was all over now. I'd just thrown away the last good thing in my life. But I had to. Why couldn't she see that there was no use trying to fight anymore? Why did she even want to keep doing this? I'd put her through Hell and she came back just for me to throw her back in the fire. And now she was gone. Once again, because of me.

I lowered my head and watched my tears drop like rain onto my knees.

Then her words came back to me.

And I fell in love with you.

That made the tears fall harder. I'd ruined everything and there was nothing I could do but sit here and cry my eyes out.

But then my Dad's words came crashing into my mind like a wrecking ball of conviction.

You're Haitian. And Haitians don't give up.

I stopped mid-sniffle and slowly lifted my head. He was right. What was I doing? My ancestors didn't take down three empires just for me to give up because of some suburban Mom. I jumped to my feet and ran to the window just as Billy was starting his car.

"Hey, guys!" I shouted as I climbed out. I made it to the ground and sprinted to the passenger side window where Laura was sitting. I stopped a couple feet away and sighed.

"You're right," I said. "Let's do this."

Chapter sixty:
"Bring Me to Life"

"Here's the plan," Laura said, wiping her hand across the pages of her spiral notebook. As usual, doodles, arrows, and words were scrawled all over it until it looked more like graffiti than notes. "Initially we were gonna expose the Gibson Circle at the Jefferson vs. Hamilton game, right? But I've got a better idea now."

"Let's hear it," I said.

We were in Billy's garage. It was date night so his parents were gone, but we didn't want to run the risk of them coming home early with us still in the living room.

"I was doing some digging," Laura went on. "And found out that Jefferson's prom is in two weeks at the Alexandria Hall in Union. And 'Mrs. Gibson' is a chaperon. We can expose her there."

I nodded. "That makes even more sense. Everyone's indoors. Better visuals. Better sound. And speaking of sound, how are we gonna broadcast this confession?"

"Old school," Laura replied. "You show up and say you need to talk to her. Get her comfortable and convince her to meet with you in private away from the crowd."

"But little does she know that we've already managed to wire her," I fill in.

"And how will we—or *you*—do that?" Billy chimed in. "Just curious."

"I'll take care of that," Laura said. "I slip a wire on her, Nick will have a wire on him, and when they're alone, we'll blast the confession through the speakers for the whole prom to hear."

I nodded, looking at Laura's doodles.

"I don't mean to be that guy," Billy said, examining his fingernails. "But there's so many things that could go wrong with this plan.'

"Please," Laura said. "Enlighten us, James Bond."

"Well for starters, how are you gonna get a 'wire' small enough that she doesn't notice? And even if you do, how are you gonna 'blast' this thing on the speakers if you guys aren't in the room anymore?"

"I get it," I said. "But it's not as farfetched as you think. My sister says this kinda stuff happens all the time by accident. Professors will forget to turn their mic off and go to the bathroom and the whole lecture hall hears them peeing in the urinal."

Billy's eyes went wide as he burst out laughing. "Are you serious?"

"I've heard that too," Laura nodded.

"See?" I said, feeling myself gaining momentum. "The idea is to make that happen on purpose. As long as the mic is on her, it doesn't matter if we're in the next room or the next floor, everyone in the room will hear the confession."

Billy pursed his lips like he was thinking it over. "And you guys are pretty confident in your A/V skills to pull that off? Cuz I don't know jack didly about mics."

"No," I shrugged. "But I know someone who does." I looked at Laura and we both said, "Kyle."

"So we've got the where," I said, counting off.

"Alexandria Hall," Laura answered.

"And the when…"

"Prom."

"And the what…"

"Record a confession."

"And the who…"

"You, me, Billy, and Kyle."

I paused and looked back and forth from her to Billy. "Not exactly."

They exchanged glances with each other then looked at me.

"There's something else," I said, looking at Laura. I narrowed my eyes as I thought my words over. "I wanna make a video."

"Now?" Billy asked, confused. "For what?"

"I wanna send a message to the school," I said, still looking at Laura.

Laura squinted at me. "And what are you staring at me for?"

"You told me that you think deep down everyone is actually good, right?" I asked her.

She nodded.

"Well…if that's true…then I wanna see if I can pull out some of that good." Then I turned to Billy. "You have a camera?"

Billy clicked his tongue. "Be back in a flash."

In a few minutes we had a setup ready with me standing in front of a blank wall and Billy's camcorder set up on a tripod in front of me.

"Whenever you're ready," he said behind the camera.

Now I was nervous. Like it was my turn to give my oral presentation–except this was a hundred times worse because I was giving a presentation to people who basically wanted me dead. I shut my eyes and took a deep breath. Then I looked straight into the lens and started speaking.

"Hamilton High, I have an announcement to make. I know I'm the last person you wanna hear from right now. And I get it. I've hurt a lot of you and I'm sorry for all those things that I did. You deserve to be mad at me. As a matter of fact, when all of this is over, I promise that you can do whatever you want to me–haze me, beat me up, sue me, press charges, whatever you think I deserve. But right now…" I paused and looked away from the camera for a second before bringing my eyes back. "I need your help. You know that I'm the Phantom, but what you don't know is that someone hired me to do what I did. A group of Moms from Jefferson High paid me to ruin your lives."

I looked briefly at Laura and Billy. Laura's eyes were fixed on me like she was watching the climax of a movie. Even Billy looked like he was practically leaning over the camera.

"I'm not justifying what I did. I was wrong. And I admit that. But you see me as your enemy and my whole time at this school I've seen most of you as my enemies. But this year I've learned that sometimes your enemies can turn into your friends." I looked at Billy and he raised an eyebrow then smirked. "And sometimes your friends can turn into…something more." I looked at Laura and saw her cheeks flush. I immediately regretted it. That was too much. That was too much. "All this time, the real enemy hasn't been me or you, it's been Jefferson. They want us to fight each other and we've been feeding right into it. But it ends now. If you wanna stop the cycle, then meet me at the Alexandria Hall at 7 p.m. on May 10th."

Laura smiled mischievously. Billy snickered then covered his mouth when he realized he was still recording.

"I may be the bullet that shot you guys," I went on. "But with your help, we can take down the people who pulled the trigger." I paused then took a deep breath before saying, "See you at prom."

Chapter sixty-one:
"Luxurious"

The next week felt like it crawled by the second. I was still suspended and still grounded. But I made good use of the time by running through the plan over and over and over again. Billy gave Kyle the video, who created a facebook group where he uploaded it and invited all the Hamilton seniors to join so they could watch it. Billy and Laura then scoped out the venue for the best ways to sneak in and they even brought Kyle to check out the sound system. I even memorized different variations of what I was going to say to Mrs. Gibson when it finally came to that moment. I was preparing for every single detail of this because it had to go right—or my life was over.

Then prom night finally came.

Fabi was treating our parents to a date night to keep them busy and I waited in my bed for them to leave. When I heard the car roll out the driveway, I counted to thirty for good measure then yanked my covers off. I was in an all-black tux and white button up and stepped into my black dress shoes.

This was the only tux I had, but it didn't look bad. I could've used some of my money to buy an even better one, but I figured it wasn't necessary. The only reason I was even dressing up in the first place was to not blow my cover. I didn't need to actually dress to the nines. I mean, I hadn't been planning on going to prom in the first place. But it was weird going now under these circumstances. I heard two honks outside and took a deep breath. It was showtime.

Billy's jeep was parked on the opposite side of the street and I hopped in the backseat behind Laura and next to Kyle. I couldn't tell in the dark what they were wearing, but I could smell that they were probably looking sharp. Billy had switched out his trademark overwhelming Axe body spray for an equally overwhelming woodsy cologne. Laura's usual strawberry scent had been replaced with an equally sweet smelling perfume. Kyle didn't smell like anything, but he was close enough that I could see his black suit and sky blue tie.

"I'm so pumped, man," he smiled at me.

Billy looked back at us with a mischievous smirk and said, "Let's go crash a prom."

Twenty minutes later we were parking outside of Alexandria Hall and my stomach was a nervous wreck. The lot was packed with Escalades, Hummers, and limousines of every color from black, white to pink. Dozens of students were making their way to the entrance and they were all dressed like they were going to the Met Gala—floor length gowns, sparkling dresses, skintight miniskirts. I suddenly felt underdressed. But it was nothing compared to what I felt when we got out of the car.

Billy was in a blood red tux with black flaps and black pants with a black bow tie. But it was Laura who made my heart stop. She was in a deep blue satin dress that hung over her black heels with a thigh high slit on the side. Her red hair was hanging over her shoulders in curls that bounced when she moved and her eyes that were normally hazel seemed like they'd morphed into a sapphire to match her dress. My jaw dropped and I found myself stuttering to say hi.

She caught my eye and flashed me a casual smile that made my knees buckle. Then she strutted up to me and looked me up and down.

"You clean up nice," she said.

"Thanks," I finally said. "You look…stunning."

She looked me up and down again, like she knew she had me wrapped around her finger, then said, "Thanks. It's a good thing you don't like me." Then she turned and walked towards the entrance.

Billy elbowed me in the ribs and chuckled into my ear. "You gonna hit that tonight?" He snickered and there was suddenly a condom between his two fingers.

"Stop," I waved him away and followed Laura towards the building.

There were about three other events happening in the Hall that night: a wedding reception, a quinceañera, and the Jefferson prom. There was a chance that they weren't checking people at the ballroom door for the prom and that it was like the wedding reception where people just grabbed their table setting cards to find their seats. But we didn't want to take that chance. Instead, once inside, we followed a group into the wedding reception, pretended to look at the seating cards, shrugged, then walked inside. Laura and Billy had discovered that this room was adjacent to the room the prom was in and that there was a hidden door in the partition. So while everyone was focused on making their way to their seats, we slipped through that door and entered the Jefferson prom, appearing in a dimly lit corner of the room.

The room was about the size of a gymnasium with about twenty round tables with bouquets of different colored roses as centerpieces and cream table cloths that kissed the carpet. There were some students eating at the tables, some boys around the punch table, and a few girls giggling on their way out—I assumed to go to the bathroom. But most of the students were on the dance floor, slow dancing to Gwen Stefani's "Luxurious".

This was it. I was so nervous, I had to grip my thigh to keep my leg from shaking. Just a few more minutes and this would be over. I just had to keep it together for a little while longer.

"Alright guys," I finally said. "Here it goes. Kyle, you know what to do."

"On it," Kyle nodded and left us.

Billy eyed a girl on the left in a little black dress and licked his lips. "I'll, uh…I'll be around." Then he sauntered over to her.

"Do you see Mrs. Gibson?" I asked Laura.

"Not yet," she replied, scanning the room. "C'mon. Let's get a better view."

I followed her through the tables and gave the area a visual sweep as I went, but didn't see Mrs. Gibson. I saw a bunch of adults standing on the fringes, but none of them looked remotely like Mrs. Gibson or any of the other Moms in the circle for that matter. Another thing I also didn't see were any Hamilton kids. My heart sank a little at that. I guess my message hadn't been enough to get through to them. I didn't blame them.

The next thing I knew I heard the tapping of heels against wood and when I looked up we were on the dance floor. My heart skipped several beats and as if she was reading my mind, Laura grabbed my arm and pulled me along to keep me from running away. Then she turned into me and put both my hands on her waist and rested her arms on my shoulders.

"Try to blend in," she said casually to me.

"Yeah," the word came choking out of my mouth. She swayed slightly side to side to the beat as she looked around the room. But all I could focus on was the fact that I was dancing with Laura Wood. There was no way this was happening. My whole body was on fire. How was I supposed to concentrate on some Mom that was hiding somewhere?

"You don't do this much, do you?" Laura eventually said to me.

I swallowed nervously. Was it that obvious? "Uh…no…not really."

"Just relax," she looked up at me.

"Easy for you to say," I replied and her smile made me melt for the hundredth time that night.

But on we went swaying back and forth to the song while scanning the room for Mrs. Gibson. But I wasn't seeing anything but more Jefferson students and Jefferson chaperones that didn't fit Mrs. Gibson's profile. Had she dressed up so well that she was unrecognizable? Had she changed her hair color? Or put on glasses? What if she wasn't even here? I shook my head. She had to be. Laura confirmed that she was a chaperone. So where was she?

"So how'd you do it?" Laura suddenly asked me.

"Do what?"

"Katie Mills," she replied. "The two Phantoms. It was Fabi wasn't it?"

I grinned. "Yeah."

She chuckled. "I figured. And the purses? Decoys?"

I nodded.

"Nice."

I didn't know if she was doing this to put me at ease, but it was working. "What about you? How'd you get my fingerprints?"

"Don't flatter yourself," she said without looking at me. "I got every senior guy's fingerprints. Not just yours."

"Well, excuse me," I laughed. Then a realization hit me. "My brush. Was that it? Was that why you took it?"

She smirked up at me. "A lady never tells."

I smiled back as she looked away.

We kept dancing and soon we were nearing the end of the song. So now that I felt a little more at ease, I decided to seize the opportunity to do something a little daring. If you know anything about "Luxurious", you know that it starts and ends with some guy speaking French lines over the music. So as it started winding down, I leaned in closer to Laura's ear, then just as the part was coming up, I whispered, *"T'es si jolie. C'est pa posible."*

She looked at me and I caught her cheeks flush for a moment. Then she pulled my neck down and said in my ear, *"Toutes les choses tu m'fait sentir…c'es parfait."*

I blinked several times and suddenly I couldn't remember if that was part of the song or if she'd just improvised. And now I was lost in the new blue tint of her hazel eyes. Then she squinted at something behind me and said, "She's here."

Chapter sixty-two:
"End of the Road"

As Laura made her way over to Mrs. Gibson, I found Billy drinking sparkling cider in the corner.

"What happened to your 'date'?" I asked him.

"Bathroom," he replied, taking a sip.

"Mrs. Gibson's here." I nodded in her direction and we both watched as Laura smiled and greeted herself. I looked on the opposite end of the room and Kyle was chatting it up with the DJ.

"Everything's going according to plan so far," I explained. "Just a few more minutes."

"You nervous?" Billy asked me.

I took a deep breath and didn't realize I'd been holding it this whole time. "Yes."

He slammed his hand on my back so hard I coughed. "You got this."

I looked over at Laura again and she was standing behind Mrs. Gibson. From this distance it looked like she was adjusting the back of Mrs. Gibson's dress. But we knew she was attaching the mic. Suddenly I was worrying about all the things that could go wrong. What if Mrs. Gibson felt the mic there? What if she realized Laura wasn't a student? What if Kyle connected the mic too early and there was feedback and Mrs. Gibson realized what was going on? But before I could calm my thoughts down, something else sent my anxiety through the roof.

"Holy frick," Billy muttered next to me.

"What?" I looked in the direction he was staring and saw Principal Hanes standing at the entrance of the room. Holy frick indeed. My heart raced and my first instinct was to run, but I forced myself to stay put. "What's he doing here?"

"He probably saw your video," Billy answered. "Oh-oh. Got a titty."

"Right time, wrong way," I corrected him. But he was right. This was ridiculous. Apparently none of the students saw it or at least cared about it, but the one person I didn't want to see it was the one who took it seriously. I wondered if he was the reason none of the Hamilton students had come in the first place. Had he seen it and threatened to expel any students who came? And now he was here looking for us—right when we were so close. This was a problem.

"Don't worry about it," Billy said, patting me on the back softer this time. "I'll distract him." At that moment, his 'date' came walking towards us and he met her, looped his arm into hers, and sauntered straight in Principal Hanes' direction.

It's gonna be alright. It's gonna be alright.

I smoothened out the flaps of my tuxedo to keep my hands from shaking. Laura appeared at my side and I nearly jumped from the nervous energy running through me.

"*C'est accompli,*" she said. It was done.

"We have a problem," I replied in French then nodded towards Principal Hanes who was partially blocked from view by Billy and his "date".

Laura let out a frustrated hiss.

"Billy's keeping him distracted," I went on.

"I see," Laura replied. "I'll watch in case he needs back up. She's ready for you. Move in." Then she touched my arm gently and said in English, "You can do this."

My stomach fluttered at that and I smiled back. Then she walked away.

This was it. No more time to waste. I checked my mic hidden underneath my collar, adjusted my flaps again, then made my way towards Mrs. Gibson at the edge of the dance floor. She was wearing a long black dress that came down to her knees and black heels. Her blonde hair that was usually tied up in a bun was cascading down her shoulders in waves. I had to admit she was attractive–not in a Stacy's Mom kind of way, but more of a Stepford Wife kind of way, just not as creepy. I could tell she was probably a heartbreaker when she was in high school, but that wasn't important right now.

I walked up to her and before she could turn to see me, I said, "Hello, Mrs. Gibson. May I have this dance?"

She whirled towards me and her eyes widened when she saw me. "Nicholas?" She scanned the room quickly then looked back at me, forcing a smile. "What are you doing here?"

"Asking you for a dance," I said, holding my arm out.

Her eyes went from my face to my arm then to my face again. Then the shock melted off her and a genuine smile appeared. But there was something different about her. "Sure."

She hooked her arm into mine and I led her to the dance floor as Boyz II Men's "End of the Road" played. I put my hands on her back and almost screamed as I bumped the mic. I froze for a second then quickly put my hands on her waist instead. Was it still in place? I casually looked down at the floor, but didn't see anything there. It had to still be in place. I had almost ruined the mission before we'd even started. I swallowed my nervousness as I looked at her, which I quickly found out was a mistake. Her eyes were like piercing emeralds drilling into my soul and it felt like staring at an angelic snake. But I held my gaze and said, "We need to talk."

"We're talking now," she said coolly. "What's on your mind?" And I realized what was different about her. She wasn't as oblivious as she usually seemed. That dumb blonde persona had apparently been an act and seeing the confident, collected woman underneath was jarring.

"I was expelled," I replied.

"I was wondering why you weren't answering my calls."

I looked away briefly and spotted Kyle still talking to the DJ. He caught my eye and gave me the slightest down nod. Then I looked at Mrs. Gibson again, whose eyes had never left my face. Had she seen that? Did she see Kyle nod at me? I forced myself to lock eyes with her and said, "Can we go somewhere private?"

She looked like she was calculating something or studying the details of my face. Either option made me uncomfortable, but she finally said, "Sure. Follow me."

Then she turned and led me off the dance floor. She grabbed her purse on the way and I made sure I was on the opposite side of her as we walked past Billy and Principal Hanes.

"What video?" Billy was saying. "Vikki here invited me…"

Mrs. Gibson and I were out of the room before I could hear him finish.

***

Mrs. Gibson brought me to an empty hall before turning to me. There was nothing here but a fancy ivory couch and a mirror on the wall. And because it was so quiet, I could still hear the faint hum of Boyz II Men from here.

"What's the problem?" she asked and it looked like there was genuine concern on her face, like she was a cool aunt that had found out I got suspended.

"I'm out," I said. "I don't wanna do this anymore."

She stared at me for a second then the cool aunt face slowly melted away. In its place was the look of an evil stepmother, dripping with condescension.

"Nichoas," she said. "What are you talking about?"

"You know what I'm talking about." I stared back at her. I needed her to actually say it for this to work. I listened carefully and noticed that I couldn't hear the music anymore, which meant that Kyle was the DJ now. So the entire ballroom was listening to this conversation. I had less than a minute to squeeze a confession out before Principal Hanes shut this down. "I'm done ruining my classmates' lives for you. I don't care how much you're paying me."

She raised an eyebrow at me and scoffed. Then she folded her arms across her chest and chuckled. "I'm glad you developed a conscience. But we've been through this before. You can't back out. If you do, then I'll…" Then she stepped forward and the unthinkable happened. The mic fell off and landed with a soft clatter on the floor. We both looked down at it at the same time and I stifled a scream as she bent to pick it up.

There was no way. I had loosened it when we were dancing! She examined it between her fingers like a detective inspecting a murder weapon. Then a cold look came across her face. She slowly bent back down and gently placed the mic on the floor. Then she stood back up and smashed it under her heel. Instantly, an ear-splitting feedback screeched from the ballroom into the hall.

"You think you're so clever," Mrs. Gibson said. She marched right up to me and snatched me by my tuxedo flaps. "Did you really think it would be that easy?"

"I-I-I," I stammered. This was bad. This was so bad. How had this happened? "I-I-I….I can still tell everyone what you've been doing."

"You mean what *you've* been doing," she clarified, still gripping me.

"You're the one who's been paying me to ruin everybody's life at Hamilton," I went on. "I can still rat on you."

She grinned and it was that pretty grin that says, "I may look nice, but I will eat you alive." Again, the evil stepmother.

"Rat on me?" she said. She shoved me back then smoothened the front of her dress. "And you think anyone's gonna believe you?"

"Yes," I said, but I didn't believe it myself. Without that mic, all of this was useless. We were in an empty hallway with no witnesses. But maybe I could keep her talking until someone came and found us. After all, there had to be some kind of scene in the ballroom by now.

Mrs. Gibson looked away for a second, but that sinister grin was still on her face. Then she brought her eyes back to me and sighed, almost endearingly. "Let me enlighten you on something, Nicholas. You are the child of Haitian immigrants—the only black kid in your entire school. You have very few friends, no extracurricular activities, you make no ripples in the social ecosystem of your school. If you tell anyone that I've been paying you to target your classmates, it would be your word against mine."

My breath caught in my throat at that. It had been one thing to see her transform from oblivious soccer mom to conniving evil stepmom. It was also one thing to watch her destroy literally the one thing I needed to beat her. But hearing that she had done her research on me was unsettling. I should have known, but the thought of her keeping tabs on me this entire time while I'd had no idea who she was had me frozen in my spot. If she had been watching me, then maybe this plan wouldn't have worked after all. I was a dead man and no one was going to save me. I had to get out of here.

But as if she was reading my mind, she suddenly reached into her purse and pulled out a gun.

"You're not going anywhere," she hissed.

And just like that everything changed. She had a gun? She had a freaking gun! What kind of Mom was she? I heard footsteps behind me and I looked back in relief, expecting to see Billy and Laura. But instead, it was two other Moms from the Gibson circle. They were ganging up on me.

"Holy frick," I said. "You have a gun." Then, remembering that my mic was still on and hoping everyone could still hear me, I shouted, "You have a gun!"

"Shut up!" Mrs. Gibson scolded me. Then, nodding behind me, "Ladies, help me get rid of him. He's threatening to ruin everything we've built. Just make—" She stopped when we heard someone cough around the corner.

All of us froze in our spots for two seconds. Then Mrs. Gibson dragged me by the arm to the corner where we saw Waldo the Weirdo standing there with his phone aimed at us.

He chuckled and said, "Gotcha."

Chapter sixty-three:
"One Jump"

I had never been so happy to see Waldo the Weirdo in my life. But that happiness instantly melted when Mrs. Gibson pointed her gun at him.

"Give me the phone," she said calmly.

Waldo looked back and forth from me to her then slowly shook his head.

"You have three seconds," Mrs. Gibson warned him with that same chilling calmness. "Three…"

Without warning, Waldo threw the phone down the other end of the hall. Mrs. Gibson moved to go after it, but I tackled her to the floor and her gun went sliding into the wall. I scrambled to my feet and sprinted to the phone. I snatched it up and ran through the nearest door just as I heard Mrs. Gibson shriek, "Get him!"

I stumbled through the door and ended up in the quinceañera, reggaeton shaking the walls. Latino families dressed to the nines filled the room, but only a few heads turned to me. But then two of the Gibson Moms burst in after and I slipped through the crowd.

"Stop him!" the Moms cried.

But before anyone could grab me, I was out the other end and running down another hall. I headed towards a set of double doors at the end and ran straight into them shoulder first. And they didn't budge. It felt like my arm was about to come out of my socket. I pushed again and got nothing. It was locked. I turned to see one of the Moms walking towards me, her gun pointed at my head. She had one too? Who were these women?

"Give me the phone," she ordered me.

I gripped Waldo's phone as I backed into the doors. The only way out was behind her, but I couldn't get past her if she had that gun. Was this it? She was about ten feet away when there was a clank and she dropped to the floor. I looked up and Vanessa Diamond was standing there holding a fire extinguisher.

"Ha!" I laughed. I was so relieved I didn't even know what to say.

"You owe me more than dinner for this, Nicholas," she said.

I laughed again. "I'll take you to Six Flags."

She shrugged. "Now hurry up. Get that phone to wherever it needs to go."

I went around her and the Mom groaning on the floor and ran through another hall. I didn't remember this place being such a maze. But maybe it was because having people chase me down with guns had a way of messing with my memory. Speaking of which, I didn't remember where I was even supposed to bring the phone to. The plan was to have the confession aired out to the ballroom audience. But now that that was ruined, where was I supposed to bring it? Principal Hanes? The police? Either way I just had to get as far away from these crazy Moms as possible.

I ran into a room where some servers were cleaning tables. There were other doors on the opposite walls and before I could pick one to run through, three other Moms ran through one.

"Everybody out!" one of them shouted at the servers.

When the servers didn't move, one of the Moms pulled out her gun and cocked it for effect. The servers stumbled over each other on their way out the farthest door. Then the Moms turned to me and I put my hands in the air. I took one step back, ready to spin and rush back out the way I came, but the Mom with the gun shook her head.

"Don't move a muscle, Nicholas," she growled. "Give us the phone or we take it over your dead body."

My heart was banging like a drum and my thoughts were racing too fast for me to think straight. But then there were simultaneous bangs as two of the doors on opposite sides of the room opened. Before I could fully turn to either of the doors, Laura, Billy, Sarah, and Lisa were running in and stood between me and the Moms.

"Get back!" the gun Mom ordered, waving the gun at them.

"If you want him, you gotta get through us," Laura said.

"You're not gonna shoot all of us, are you?" Billy asked.

I stood behind my friends, too shocked to say a word. I couldn't wrap my head around everything that was happening. Waldo had come. Vanessa had come. And now Sarah and Lisa were here with Billy and Laura risking their lives to help me escape. I didn't have time to stand around and get emotional about it. They had just bought me some time. So I spun and dashed out the room as the Moms screamed behind me.

I was gonna keep running into these Moms if I didn't find the exit soon and for some reason I was at a loss for where it was. And suddenly Mrs. Gibson was sprinting at me down the hall. I turned and went the opposite direction, shoving past women in gowns and knocking their purses down. And then a stupid idea hit me—so stupid that it just might work. I was pretty sure that I had seen a smaller building right next to this one when we were outside. If I could get to the roof, I could force Mrs. Gibson to follow me then jump to that other building and escape while she'd be wasting time getting all the way back down the stairs. Genius.

"Get back here!" Mrs. Gibson screamed behind me. I didn't know if she had her gun back, but I was banking on her not wanting to risk accidentally shooting someone else.

The fire alarm suddenly went off and more people poured out of the rooms, filling the halls quickly. I glanced behind me and caught a glimpse of Mrs. Gibson squeezing through two men as she tried to go against the flow of traffic. I had to make it to the roof.

I pushed and shoved my way through the growing crowd until I made it to a stairwell and went upstairs. There weren't many people in it yet so I seized the opportunity to put some distance and leapt up three steps at a time. As I was going, a tiny part of my brain told me, "You could just follow the crowd." And under normal circumstances I would've been smart enough to listen to that thought. But these weren't normal circumstances. So I kept going until I burst through a door at the top and rushed into the brisk night air of the roof. I sprinted to the edge and immediately realized how stupid I was.

Not only was there no other building, but Alexandria Hall was at least a hundred feet high. Even if I decided to risk it and jump anyway, there was no way I'd survive the fall. The limousines looked like queen size beds up this high. I turned to run back inside, but Mrs. Gibson was already there, aiming her gun at me, barely breathing heavy.

"You didn't really think this through, did you?" she said, her voice dripping with condescension. "Give me the phone."

I looked at her then down at the phone in my hand and pretended to think about it. Then I looked at her again and said, "No."

Immediately, a gunshot split the air like thunder and a searing pain sliced through my shoulder. I screamed and grabbed my arm to see that a piece of the sleeve had been ripped off.

"Next one goes in your chest," Mrs. Gibson said, both her hands still holding the gun steady. She hadn't even moved.

I took several deep breaths as I patted my shoulder in relief. She shot at me. She really shot at me. My ears were ringing from the gunshot and my heart was pounding so hard I felt like I was about to faint. This was it. I was on a roof with no way down and a psycho Mom had me at gunpoint. Everyone else who could help was already dealing with the other psycho Moms downstairs. I either gave her the phone or she killed me and took it from my dead hands.

So I took one more breath before getting ready to turn it over. But then I saw something that made me stop.

"Hold on," I said. "Why are you doing this?"

"If you think I'm gonna monologue, you're a lot stupider than I thought," Mrs. Gibson replied. "You have three seconds before I blow your brains out."

"Mrs. Gibson!" I said, feigning shock. "I'm a minor!"

"Three…"

I didn't move.

"Two…"

"One," another voice said and Mrs. Gibson whirled to see four men in vests with their guns pointed at her. "F.B.I. Hands in the air."

Mrs. Gibson hesitated for just a second before raising her hands and letting the gun dangle on her finger. The agents were on her like hounds and she was in handcuffs before I could even blink. Three of them escorted her to the stairwell and I released the breath I didn't realize I'd been holding. The last agent walked up to me and smiled.

"Special Agent Wood," he introduced himself. "Laura's uncle."

I forced out a laugh. No way.

"You did good, kid," he said, patting me on the back. "We've been trying to catch these women for years."

I blinked. I beg your pardon?

Chapter sixty-four:
"Welcome Back"

"Her name is Veronica Remington," Agent Wood said as the other agents left with her. "Her and her friends run a school named Zenith Academy. Ever head of it?"

I nodded. "They're the number three private school in Jersey behind us and Jefferson."

"Well, they used to be number one," Agent Wood explained. "That was twenty years ago before Mrs. Remington was charged with embezzlement."

"What?"

"But five years later, instead of using her wealth to make the school better she and her friends decided to make every other school worse. So for the past 15 years they've been infiltrating private schools across the state and tearing them apart from the inside out."

"Whoa," I breathed. My mind was doing backflips trying to keep up and connecting the dots. Fifteen years? They had been doing stuff like this for fifteen years? "Wait. So were they pretending to be other Moms too? Just like they did with Mrs. Gibson?"

"Sometimes. Their M.O. changed at every school. But their endgame was always the same: to make it so that no one would want to go to any school except for Zenith."

In a weird way that was morbidly impressive. Taking down the competition by sabotaging it from the inside to make yourself number one? I had to hand it to her. Mrs. Remington was good. Evil. But good.

"We have reason to believe that most of the major headlines involving private schools in the past decade," Agent Wood went on. "From vandalism, students attacking teachers, sexual assaults, and even some school shootings are because of the Remington Circle."

I pressed my fingers against my temple. I couldn't wrap my mind around this. I had been caught up in the middle of a statewide conspiracy?

"So if it's all the same to you," he held his hand out. "I'll take that phone."

"Oh yeah!" I had almost forgotten. I handed Waldo's phone to him and he patted me on the back then turned to walk away.

"But wait…" Something had just occurred to me. He stopped and looked over his shoulder. "How did you know we were here?"

He grinned a sly grin. "Facebook." Then he winked and walked into the stairwell.

I followed him, but by the time I made it back inside, he was lost in the crowd swarming for the exits. I eventually made it to the parking lot twenty minutes later and found a relatively empty area near one of the limos. None of our group was in sight so I just waited as I tried to process all of this.

The FBI had been tracking the Remington Circle down for over a decade and now they were going to jail. Because of me—and the others. But even though Mrs. Remington had been the brains of the operation, I was the hands and technically there was blood on these hands. Did that mean I was going to jail too? Or juvie? Either way, going back to school was going to be a nightmare because even though we had taken down the real villains, everyone still knew that I had been the Phantom. But before any of this crap hit the fan, I knew there was one thing I had to do.

There was still a massive crowd gathered in the parking lot with several police cars and a paramedics truck. Principal Hanes was busy talking to some of the FBI agents and there was even a news van with a reporter going live in front of a camera. How had they found out about this so fast? I felt a chill as I thought of my parents watching the news tonight. The whooping I was going to get would be one for the ages. But still, back to the task at hand.

I pushed my way through the crowd until I found Laura leaning against Billy's Jeep, holding her heels in her hand.

"We did it!" she cried as she ran up to me and threw her arms around my neck.

"Whoa!" I practically fell off my feet, but I hesitantly hugged her back.

"We did it," she repeated as she pulled away.

"Yeah," I nodded.

There was an awkward silence where she just smiled at me and I stared back.

"Listen…" I finally said. "I'm really sorry about everything that happened. I messed up your GPA and ruined your chances of being valedictorian. If you don't want me to talk to you ever again, I completely understand."

She squinted at me like she didn't know what I was talking about then snickered.

"I *was* upset at you," she said. "But honestly, this has been the most exciting thing that's ever happened to me." Then she paused and grinned. "And for the record…our friendship wasn't a lie. I really do like you. And I don't want you to ever stop talking to me."

I breathed a heavy sigh of relief.

"Besides," she went on. "Your birthday's coming up soon and I don't want you to celebrate that by yourself. And who's gonna beat you in chess?"

"And who's gonna beat you in *NBA Street*?" I countered.

We both laughed and she punched my arm and I punched her back.

There was another awkward silence and I stared at those eyes that made my insides melt. And all of a sudden, I felt something rising in my chest. Four years of pent up emotion was colliding with the Phantom pressure of the last couple months. The next thing I knew, the words were spilling out before I could stop them.

"I like you," I blurted.

She blinked several times.

"I like you, Laura!" I said again and it felt like I was coming up for air for the first time in my life. "Wow, that felt so good."

I could see the disbelief plain as day on her face.

"I've liked you for a really long time," I kept going. "Like, as long as I've known you. But I was too scared to tell you because I'm technically not allowed to date—or date anyone who's not Haitian—and then I became the Phantom and ruined your life and it's honestly all so embarrassing and I should probably stop talking. But I really, really like you."

She stared at me for a few more moments and for a second I thought she hadn't heard me. Had I somehow switched to Kreyol without knowing it?

"You're such an idiot," she finally said and I burst out laughing with relief.

"I know," I admitted. "It's been torture, Laura. Just a bunch of romantic tension that was going nowhere for the whole year. It was driving me crazy."

She smiled as she pulled her hair behind her ear and my knees buckled at how weak she made me feel.

"Well," she shrugged. "There's no more tension."

I shrugged back and grabbed her hands. "I like you, Laura Wood." Then I stepped in closer and she squeezed my hands in anticipation. We leaned into each other and our faces were inches away when her uncle came by and patted me on the shoulder. Billy came rushing at his side the next second.

"Way to go, kid," Agent Wood said and we pulled apart in a flash. "Laura told me everything you did."

"Really?" My eyes went wide, both from the whiplash of the interruption and from the revelation. Laura nodded next to me. But then something hit me. "She...she told you everything?"

Agent Wood nodded and my heart sank.

"So does that mean...?" I swallowed nervously. "Am I going to...jail? I mean...I technically hurt a lot of people."

Agent Wood made a face like he'd misheard me. "Jail?" He scoffed. "No way. Like I said, we've been looking for these women for years, kid. We wouldn't have found them if it wasn't for you." Then he glanced around casually before saying his next words. "We'll just tell everyone you were our informant. Wipe this whole thing under the rug."

Billy whistled. "The feds got your back. That's crazy, man."

My chest swelled. "You can...you can do that?"

He leaned in. "It'll be our little secret." Then he winked again.

I laughed as all the relief came out of me like another held breath.

Agent Wood stood up straight again. "I've gotta say, kid. I'm pretty impressed with you."

"Really?" I could feel my cheeks getting sore from how hard I was smiling. An FBI agent had just said he was impressed with me.

"What are you gonna study in college?"

"Biology," I replied. "My parents want me to be a doctor. You know, typical Haitian kid options: doctor, lawyer, engineer."

"Is that what *you* wanna do?" he stuffed his hands into his pockets.

"Not really," I shrugged. "But you know...culture."

He shrugged back. "Well, they could really use someone like you at the Agency."

My eyebrows shot up. "The Agency? You mean...the FBI?"

I looked at Laura and there was skepticism all over her face, but Billy looked impressed.

"No, no, no," Agent Wood waved me off. "You have to be at least 23 to work for the FBI."

"Oh," I said, disappointed. But that explained why Laura had looked so confused. Then what Agency was he talking about?

"But this is my friend Agent Russell," Agent Wood said. A black man in a black suit stepped to his side. He had a fresh cut with a nice fade and looked like he was in his thirties.

"Nice to meet you," he said, shaking my hand. "I work for the CIA. If you're interested, we might have a job for you."

I looked at Billy and Laura and said, "Oh-oh."

Then we turned back and said at the same time, "*Gad on tin tin!*"

Epilogue:
"Hang On"

"Are the patties ready?" my Mom called as she arranged a tray of *bon bon amidon* on the table.

"One more minute!" my Dad called from the back.

I carried a tray of warm bread to the counter and placed each loaf inside the glass case. With the smell wafting so smoothly into my nose, it took all my energy to resist taking a bite out of one. But apparently Billy didn't have that same self-control.

"Ahhhh!" he was crying, fanning his mouth as he walked past me. He had a case of Kola Lakaye under one arm and had just stuffed a plantain covered in *pikliz* in his mouth. "Why is this so spicy?"

"Why are you eating?" Laura demanded, snatching the soda from him and setting the case on another table. "We're about to open in two seconds."

"You're such a baby," Fabi scoffed at Billy. "Laura ate those like a champ."

"Laura probably…" Billy started then stopped to keep fanning his mouth. "…she probably has…whew! Why is it so spicy?"

We laughed.

"The patties!" my Mom shouted again from the front.

I looked over my shoulder at the back door where my Dad was still getting the patties ready then at the windows at the front door where a line of eager customers was standing outside and wrapped around the corner. Black people, white people, Asians, and some Hispanics were all waiting patiently for us to throw the doors open and finally let them in. And we would—as soon as the final tray of patties came out.

"Here we go!" my Dad said on cue, carrying a tray to the counter. Fabi and I ran over to him and we had the case stocked with the patties in less than a minute.

"Are we good to go, Mrs. Toussaint?" Billy called, pointing at the door.

"Get the ribbon!" my Mom told him and he and Laura grabbed a long white ribbon off one of the tables and a giant pair of pink scissors. Two minutes later, we were all standing outside in front of the customers while Billy and Laura held the ribbon taught between us and the crowd.

"Good morning, everyone, and welcome to our Grand Opening!" my Mom announced, beaming. "This has been such a journey, full of ups and downs and twists and turns. I want to thank you all first and foremost for coming out here—without our customers we would have no business, of course. I want to thank God for His faithfulness at every step of the way. I want to thank my husband Patrick for his endless support. I want to thank my children, Fabi and Nick, for doing everything they could to make their Mama happy and to make their father proud."

I glanced over at Fabi and we exchanged grins.

"Even when we didn't always agree with how they did it," my mother continued. "And last but not least, I want to thank Mr. Larry Richardson, our new landlord, for thinking of us when a vacancy in this building opened up. This was a Godsend."

I saw Billy's Dad raise a thumbs up from where he was standing in the crowd. Billy's mother was there too and if I wasn't mistaken, she had just wiped a tear from her eye. And if I wasn't careful, I was about to wipe a tear from mine. Mr. Richardson had been right—he really *was* a man of his word.

My Mom paused for a second then took a deep breath. "So without further adieu…" She lifted the scissors, cut the ribbon, and the crowd cheered. "Welcome to Bethanie."

Made in the USA
Middletown, DE
12 May 2023

30065933R00137